S0-CFW-183

A JACK CHRISTIE ADVENTURE

DAY
OF THE
ASSASSINS

JOHNNY O'BRIEN

templar books
an imprint of Candlewick Press

Text copyright © 2009 by Johnny O'Brien
Illustrations copyright © 2009 by Nick Hardcastle

Picture credits: p. 19: Archduke Franz Ferdinand: copyright © by the Mary Evans Picture Library; p. 21: Gavrilo Princip: copyright © by ullsteinbild/ Topfoto; p. 182: Archduke Franz Ferdinand and the duchess Sophie of Austria moments before their deaths: copyright © by the *Illustrated London News* Ltd./ Mary Evans Picture Library; p. 204: The five ringleaders of the assassination: copyright © by the *Daily Herald* Collection/Science & Society Picture Library

First U.S. paperback edition 2010

The Library of Congress has cataloged the hardcover edition as follows:

O'Brien, Johnny.
Day of the assassins : a Jack Christie novel / Johnny O'Brien ;
illustrated by Nick Hardcastle. —1st U.S. ed.
p.   cm.
Summary: Fifteen-year-old Jack is sent to 1914 Europe as a pawn in
the battle between his long-lost father, who has built a time machine,
and a secret network of scientists who want to prevent him from trying
to use it to change history for the better. Includes historical notes.
ISBN 978-0-7636-4595-3 (hardcover)
[1. Space and time—Fiction. 2. Adventure and adventurers—Fiction.
3. World War, 1914–1918—Causes—Fiction. 4. Franz Ferdinand,
Archduke of Austria, 1863–1914—Assassination—Fiction. 5. Europe—History—
1871–1918—Fiction. 6. Science fiction.]   I. Hardcastle, Nick, ill. II. Title.
PZ7.O1272Day 2009
[Fic]—dc22   2009023630

ISBN 978-0-7636-4995-1 (paperback)

10 11 12 13 14 15 LBM 10 9 8 7 6 5 4 3 2 1

Printed in Melrose Park, IL, U.S.A.

This book was typeset in Berkeley Book.

Maps and timeline designed by Leonard de Rolland

TEMPLAR BOOKS
An imprint of Candlewick Press
99 Dover Street
Somerville, Massachusetts 02144

www.candlewick.com

For Sally, Tom, Peter, and Anna

EUROPE
JUNE 1914

NORWAY

Christiania

NORTH SEA

DENMARK

Copenhagen

UNITED KINGDOM

IRELAND

Dublin

London

Portsmouth

Amsterdam

NETHERLANDS

Brussels

BELGIUM

LUX.

Paris

GERMAN EMPIRE

Be

ATLANTIC OCEAN

FRANCE

SWITZER-LAND

Milan

PORTUGAL

Lisbon

SPAIN

Madrid

CORSICA

Rome

SARDINIA

I

MEDITERRANEAN SEA

KEY

Triple Entente

Triple Alliance

Jack's route

* *The Western & Eastern Fronts came into being during the First World War.*

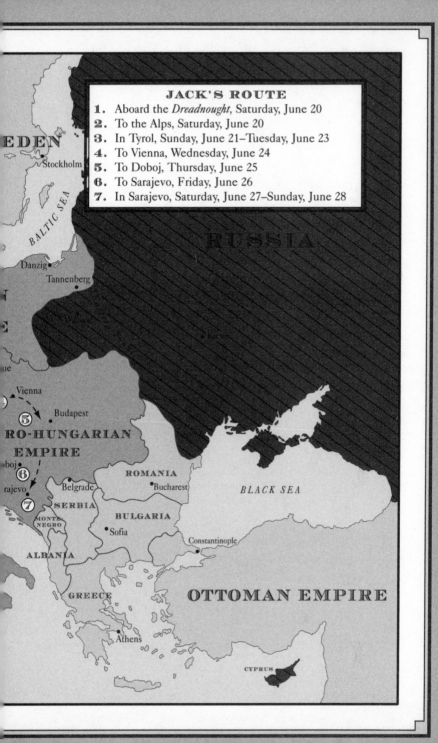

Contents

Front Line

The shock wave from an air burst lifted Jack up and threw him backward twenty feet, his body twisting in midair as he flew. Where there should have been churned-up mud to cushion his landing, there was nothing. Instead, he was falling into a huge empty space in the ground. With a crunching thud, his face, and then the rest of his body, hit the sloping inner wall of a large hole. As he slid down, mud filled his ears, nostrils, and mouth.

His helmet had already been blown free, as had everything else: webbing, gas mask, and, of course, his Lee-Enfield rifle. He continued his headlong slide down the sharply sloping wall, mud gathering around his collar and easing itself inside his uniform. He finally came to rest, headfirst, in a pool of putrid water that had settled at the bottom of the hole. He lifted his head from the pool, spitting and coughing, and peered upward at the lip of the crater from where he had just fallen. Just then, the noxious mix of smoke and gray mist above the crater lip flashed a dirty orange, and the concussion from another explosion ripped through the air. Instinctively, he dunked his head back into the water, seeking protection from the fury above. He waited a few seconds, until an icy chill started to seep through to his skin, then scrambled his way up so only his boots rested in the pool. He was breathing hard, but the explosions had stopped, although he could still hear the chatter of at least one machine gun in the distance.

Suddenly, on the other side of the mud puddle, he noticed two bright blue eyes staring straight back at him. They shone piercingly from a mud-freckled face and were locked onto him, trancelike. Like Jack, the figure opposite was prostrate and caked in mud. Across the thigh of one leg, Jack could make out a large dark patch. The soldier had kept his helmet, and Jack could see the familiar spike that indicated that his companion was a soldier of His Imperial Majesty's Grand Army of the German Second Reich. He quickly scanned the other details—the *feldgrau* uniform, the black boots. Jack studied the face peering back at him; his German friend could not even be sixteen years old. He was pale and trembling. It was then that Jack realized, with dismay, that within his white, fragile, boy fingers, the soldier held a large black pistol—and the pistol was trained on him.

The heavy lump of black metal was comically out of proportion with the rest of the boy's frame—like when you see a child wearing his father's boots. Jack felt a new wave of panic start to build, sickeningly, from the pit of his stomach. The boy looked to be as terrified as Jack was, but Jack could see a pendulous index finger slowly squeezing the trigger of the pistol. Jack pushed out a hand in a vain gesture of protection and started to scream, but it was too late. There was an orange flash as the chamber of the pistol emptied. Jack shut his eyes and braced himself, pushing back hard into the dirt, hoping it would somehow enfold him in its thick, sticky blanket and insulate him from the impact.

But the impact didn't come. He opened his eyes and looked at the boy, who was now shaking even more, a look of incredulity on his face. He held the pistol up again, this time with both index fingers wrapped around the trigger, and squeezed. . . . Jack braced himself again. But nothing happened. There was a click: the gun was empty. Jack felt a wave of euphoria wash over him. The boy fumbled furiously at his belt, but the dark patch on his leg had started to grow ominously, and his movements were labored. Jack had no weapon. Everything had been blown from him in the blast. Should he stay put or scramble free from the crater and run?

It wasn't his decision. At that moment a second figure loomed from behind the lip of the crater and peered in. Even at that distance, Jack could see that this new figure was stockier and heavier than the boy opposite. He moved with a confidence that came with the professional soldier's greatest accomplishment—survival. The soldier's helmet had the same distinctive spiked silhouette as the boy's. It signified one thing: Jack was about to die.

Despite his stocky build, the soldier descended the side of the crater with ease, assessed the situation, and made his decision. He muttered something gruffly in German to the boy and, without breaking step, marched directly through the puddle to where Jack lay with his back pressed into the damp earth. The soldier reached for something on his belt, which glistened in what remained of the daylight above. He fastened the object to the end of his rifle: a seven-inch serrated-steel bayonet.

The soldier raised the barrel of the Mauser Gewehr rifle and moved the bayonet slowly toward him. Jack caught the soldier's eyes, but they showed no excitement, no fear, no emotion. The humanity had been drained from him through years of attrition. The soldier pinned the bayonet under Jack's chin, resting it momentarily on his throat. Jack felt the prick on his skin and prayed for death to come quickly. The soldier looked down at him, steadied his boots in the mud, and, with a grunt, pushed the steel hard into Jack's neck.

Point-of-Departure

Jack groaned in frustration, turning to Angus. "I'm dead—again. This level's impossible."

"You're terrible." Angus put both hands behind his head and leaned back in the moth-eaten armchair, grinning smugly.

Jack rolled his eyes and tossed the controller to his friend. "So why don't you try?"

"Nah, this level's too much for me. I get this stuff all the time from Dad. . . . "

"Get what?"

Angus yawned. "Can't be bothered to tell you. . . . "

"Tell me what?"

"Great-Grandfather Ludwig . . . " Angus rolled his *r*'s mockingly.

"Who's he?"

"I'll tell you—but don't say I didn't warn you. My great- grandfather Ludwig, as we are all sick of hearing, was a German soldier—he fought in the war." Angus pointed at the screen, where Jack had paused Point-of-Departure. "That war—the First World War."

Jack was impressed. "You're joking?"

"No. And I know that 'cause he's still on the mantelpiece back home. In a jar."

"A what?"

"A jar. Not all of him, you idiot, just a bit of him. A piece of his left tibia . . . whatever that is."

"A bone in his leg."

"Whatever."

"Why would you have that on your mantelpiece? You guys are weird."

"Dad likes talking about it—Great-Grandfather Ludwig and Great-Grandma Dot." Angus looked across at Jack with a pained expression. "I'm going to have to tell you the whole story, aren't I?"

Jack nodded.

"Great-Grandfather Ludwig was a German infantryman." Angus nodded his head at the screen. "Like that guy who just owned you in the last level. Anyway, he fought in the war. He got medals and stuff. One day there was a big British offensive. Ludwig's trench was about to be overrun. Apparently, he refused to budge, even though everyone else was retreating. In fact, he did the opposite—he went over the top to search for German survivors in no-man's-land. Apparently, he saved at least one young soldier who would have died from his injuries otherwise."

"Amazing."

"Before he got back to his lines, the Brits attacked and he was captured, although he was wounded in the process—in his leg."

"The bone in the jar on your mantelpiece?"

"Right. They patched him up and he recovered. In fact, it seems he developed a bit of a soft spot for the British. There is some story about how he'd met some guys, some lost British soldiers or something, out there in no-man's-land when he was searching around. Apparently, they were going to kill him but decided to let him go. . . . I think so he could rescue his injured friend or something. I'm not sure . . . it's a little hazy."

"What happened to him?"

"He met Great-Grandma Dot. She was a nurse in the field hospital. She was Scottish. The war ended. They got married and he never went home. Moved to Scotland with Dot and took over the old sheep farm when Dot's old man died."

"What—your house up at Rachan?"

"Very same."

"So you're German, Angus?"

"I s'pose—eighth German or something. . . . My last name, Jud, is a German name, I think. It's pronounced *Yood*—but no one knows that, so everyone just says Jud. It's easier."

Jack smiled. "You never told me that before. It's a good story."

"Dad tells it all the time. I think he was close to his grandfather when he was a kid. I'll bring a photo in tomorrow, if I remember, but I'll leave the jar—" Angus suddenly looked at his watch. "I'm late!" He jumped to his feet and grabbed his coat, which had been discarded on the dusty basement floor. "Sorry, I'll have to leave it up to you. I've got Pendelshape first thing tomorrow—and I haven't even started my essay. You know what the Pendelino's like. . . . He'll go ape. I'm on his bad list anyway. He confiscated my iPod yesterday."

Angus was already disappearing back up the basement stairs to the kitchen.

Jack shrugged. "See you, then. . . . " He picked up the controller, still moist from his sweaty palms, and turned back to the game. The console's piercing light winked back at him, challenging him to try just one more time. Angus's story had somehow made the game much more real. He felt the adrenaline in his veins and, while holding the controller with one hand, instinctively fumbled in his pocket with the other for his inhaler. He felt a rush of comfort as his fingers located and then encircled its familiar plastic outline.

He muttered to himself, "Captain Jack Christie's ready—I hope you are."

Cairnfield

Jack stood by the imposing wrought iron gates as school dispersed. He turned the collar of his blazer up and stamped his feet to thwart a biting autumn wind that whistled past the Victorian buildings. His hands were turning pink with the cold.

"Where is he?" he wondered.

His head was still buzzing from history class, which had just ended. They were studying the First World War. Dr. Pendelshape, the history teacher, had become even more animated than usual. The man was obsessed. Even though it was a world away, Jack could not help being caught up in Pendelshape's story. Maybe it was because he had played Point-of-Departure so many times that he practically felt like a war veteran. . . . He could picture the opening screens of the game with its black-and-white pictures of the crusty, mustached generals of the great European imperial powers with their medals and uniforms—all the grandeur of empire.

Pendelshape had described the military hardware of that time: howitzers that could belch a shell Jack's size twenty miles, landing in a maelstrom of shrapnel and fire that would create a hole bigger than a house; new guns that could fire six hundred rounds per minute, dismembering anything in sight. Pendelshape had said, "It all lay amassed and untried in that beautiful European summer of 1914—poised, unknowingly, for the bloodiest war that mankind had ever unleashed." When he had said that, Jack had thought that Pendelshape was about to burst into tears.

Despite his interest, Jack hadn't hung around after school to chat like he sometimes did. He got along well with Pendelshape. But he figured today he should really be thinking about, well, about happier things. After all, today was his birthday.

He didn't want to wait any longer. He stamped his feet again, shivering. Suddenly he heard the pop and whine of a motorbike buzzing up the hill from the parking lot and saw the trailing plume of blue smoke from its 125cc two-stroke engine. Jack's heart sank. Angus had brought the bike to school again.

The blue-and-yellow Husqvarna WRE skidded to a halt, but Angus had misjudged the curb, and Jack jumped back to avoid being squashed.

"Idiot!"

Angus cut the engine and the air was suddenly still. He removed the full face helmet, revealing a mop of straight black hair. At sixteen, Angus was a year older than Jack, and at five foot eight, he was also six inches taller. With all the sports he did, plus helping his dad out on the farm, Angus was strong and broad shouldered. He had a wide face that always seemed to be flushed from physical exertion or from being outside. Jack, on the other hand, still had the slender frame of a boy. He had messy blond hair that could never decide whether it wanted to be curly or straight.

"Are you trying to kill me?"

"Keep your shirt on, Jackster."

"You're not supposed to be riding that thing. You don't have your license."

"Well, the test is only a few months away. Anyway, how else am I supposed to get to school?"

"The bus?"

Angus shrugged. "It was early this morning."

"You were late, you mean."

"Who cares? We're going to your place, aren't we? Let's stop farting around." Angus unclipped the spare helmet and tossed it to Jack. He grinned. "Climb aboard, big man."

Jack remembered the last time he'd been on Angus's bike. It was at his folks' sheep farm up the valley in Rachan. The family loved machines, and Angus had grown up with bikes. Trouble was, Jack hadn't. He'd tried it once but lost his balance, and the bike had spun off in one direction and Jack in another. He had ended up with a face full of mud. Angus had laughed so much he'd nearly fallen over.

Angus shrugged. "Well, you can walk if you like." He snapped down on the kick start, and the engine burst to life. Jack rolled his eyes, reluctantly donned the spare helmet, climbed behind Angus, and clenched his eyes firmly shut. Angus turned back the throttle, and the engine wailed; he dropped the clutch, and the bike jerked forward. The front wheel immediately lifted off the ground in a spectacular but completely unnecessary wheelie. Jack was taken by surprise and just avoided slipping right off the back. Once the bike had two wheels back on the road, it was too late for Jack to complain.

They soon reached the main bridge out of town. The river below was starting to swell from the extra rain in the hills. As they crossed it, Jack could feel the temperature drop. The river acted like the cold element of a freezer as it snaked through the fading light of the border hill country. In two minutes they would be turning into the long drive to Cairnfield. A journey that usually took him twenty-five minutes on foot had been completed in only five.

Jack and his mom had moved from Geneva back to Scotland to the home of Jack's grandparents—just before Mom and Dad had split up. Jack had been only six. Jack and his mom had lived at the Cairnfield estate with Jack's grandparents until they died. Then it was just him and Mom rattling around in the big old house together. Jack's mom didn't talk much about their life in Geneva or why they had left. Nor did she explain why she had split up from Jack's dad soon after they'd moved to Scotland. She had just said he was "too obsessed with work" or "there wasn't room for us and his work." Jack sometimes tried to find out more, but his mom would clam up or quickly change the subject.

Jack prodded Angus as they made their way down the drive.

"Stop!"

Angus pulled the bike to one side, and the engine puttered into neutral.

"Put it somewhere, and we'll walk from here. Mom'll go berserk if she sees me on the back of this thing."

"If you say so." Angus pulled the WRE behind the hedge and they left their helmets with it and headed up the drive.

Day of the Assassins

Jack's mom looked up as they came through the back door and into the kitchen. Carole Christie looked a lot like Jack. She had the same gray-blue eyes and blond hair. She was still slim, although her figure had thickened a little with her forty-three years.

"You're back early."

Jack looked at Angus nervously. Angus avoided the subject and attempted his most winning smile, displaying a mouthful of uneven teeth in the process. It was a sight that would have traumatized a small child.

"Hello, Mrs. C. My cake ready?"

Carole Christie looked at Angus with mock affront. "So it's *your* birthday now, is it?"

Angus started to move toward a large bowl of chocolate cake batter.

"Looks tasty." He brought a large, dirty-nailed index finger dangerously close to the sugary mixture. But Mrs. Christie was too quick. She whipped out a wooden spoon and landed a swift blow expertly on Angus's knuckles. He yelped.

Jack approved. "Nice one, Mom."

"You'll have to wait," she said. "Go do something for an hour."

"Mom—has it arrived?" Jack asked.

His mom's smile quickly vanished, and she gave him the look—a sort of grimace that passed over her face whenever the subject of his father came up.

"It's in your bedroom," she said. "But I don't think it's much to get excited about, love . . . definitely smaller than usual," she added.

He ignored the comment and rushed out of the kitchen.

There it was, sitting on his desk, just like on all his other birthdays: a package wrapped in brown paper and string. He flipped it over and instantly recognized the writing. His heart beat faster.

"Come on—open it," Angus said impatiently.

But his mom was right. Based on size, the package looked disappointing—compared to earlier birthdays, anyway. He inspected it from each side in turn. His mind flicked through the presents from previous years. The year before, there had been the remote-controlled airplane and before that, all the fly-fishing stuff. Every year the present had arrived like clockwork, and it had always exceeded his expectations. These birthday presents were his only connection with his father now.

Jack could no longer resist, and egged on by Angus, he tore open the wrapping paper. His jaw dropped in disappointment as the contents were revealed.

"It's a book." Angus was alarmed.

Jack picked it up and shook it. Maybe something would drop out—like a check for a thousand dollars or an airline ticket to some exotic vacation destination. But no. It was a book. And, worst of all, it was a textbook.

"It's a school book." Angus said. "It's called *The First World War,*" Angus added with growing horror. "Dull-o-rama."

"I can read."

This present definitely did not have the wow factor of those from previous years, but maybe it was better than nothing, Jack thought.

He scanned the front cover and then opened it to inspect the crisp, sharp-edged photographs arranged in three sections. They showed trenches, ships, barbed wire, "over the top" howitzers, airplanes, tanks, maps, women in factories, leaders, soldiers, medals, observation balloons, trains, and more. . . . Some photos were blurred and sepia, others were crystal clear, but together they gave Jack an instant insight into four years of brutal war.

Angus had already lost interest and busied himself with a wooden pyramid puzzle. Angus had failed to master it even after several months of trying, though it had taken Jack four minutes and twenty-eight seconds.

"Weird," Jack said.

"What?" asked Angus without raising his head from the puzzle.

"I get this history book from Dad, right? And Pendelshape was going on about the same stuff today in class."

"What stuff?"

"You know—the First World War—all that . . . "

Angus shrugged. "So?"

"Interesting—don't you think?"

"For a nerd like you. Doesn't do it for me."

He looked up at Jack with a piece of the puzzle in each hand. "How do you do this stupid thing, again?"

Jack took the pieces and manipulated them expertly. In under a minute the puzzle was done. Angus stared at it in awe.

"See? Easy."

"You're really annoying sometimes."

"Pendelshape was saying today that millions of people died in the war. Millions. And that if things had been slightly different, it might not even have happened."

Angus yawned. "If you say so. For me, it's all in the past. Gone, dead, finished."

"What about Point-of-Departure? That's based in the past. You like that, don't you?"

"That's different—it's a video game. It's real."

It's what Jack would have expected Angus to say. But something about the images and the clear black Antiqua text on each page of the book stirred a distant but strong emotion in Jack. He couldn't quite put his finger on it. He sometimes got a similar feeling when he played Point-of-Departure. A sort of flashback—a connection to somewhere else, somewhere different. He was transported back to a time—he was not quite sure exactly when, but he had been very young—maybe only four years old.

He remembered that they had been on a family vacation. He had been vaguely aware that his dad had not had a day off from the lab for months and had been working very late. This was to be his first break in a long time. They had gone to France or Belgium and had visited Cambrai or some such place—a monument to the First World War. He had been aware that his father was interested in history and, he supposed, this period of history in particular.

What had happened and in what sequence had remained a disconnected patchwork in his head—sometimes fragments came into greater focus when he thought back, but they would evaporate, ghost-like, as he struggled to make sense of it all. He remembered visiting graves—an endless sea of white crosses—and the grassy outline of old trench networks. He recalled a voice describing "how it was." Maybe it had been his father's voice, maybe a tour guide's, or maybe some audio-visual show. He had not understood the words, or if he had, he no longer remembered them, but the serious, gravelly voice conjured up a strong image of the war and the plight of its young victims.

There had also been one of those short but violent summer thunderstorms. Jack remembered it being very hot and then getting wet and running for shelter. He had heard thunder and seen lightning and remembered thinking the raindrops were huge—big pea-size globs that exploded on the pavement. He hadn't been frightened—more curious. The images of the thunder and lightning combined in his head with what his young mind imagined the soldiers must have endured. This had made it real to him—for a moment it was as if he had become one of them.

But the strongest memory of that time was waking up in the hotel. He'd had his own room, and the closeness of the night had woken him. He had opened the door to his parents' room and seen his mom and dad standing there. He remembered thinking that it was strange that they were not in bed and that the bedside light was on. He would never forget the pleading expression on his mom's face. Both his mom and dad had red eyes, and he felt uneasy when he realized that they were both crying. He had never seen an adult cry. Then his mom saw Jack there staring at them from the open door and whisked him back off to his bedroom.

He saw even less of his father when they returned home after that. He was hard at work at the lab—always working. Then the move back to Scotland had come, and suddenly one day his mom told him that his father had left and that "it would just be us now."

"Hey, what's this?" Angus had finally given up and tossed the pyramid puzzle onto the floor in disgust. The puzzle landed next to a piece of folded paper that must have dropped from the package when Jack had ripped it open. It was a letter.

Jack,

I am so sorry that once again I can't be with you on your birthday, just as I have been sorry to miss so many important events in your life. I hope that one day I will have a chance to redeem myself and that I can make it up to you. Fifteen already! I hope you enjoy your day. This year I have sent a gift of a more cerebral nature. I hope you're not too disappointed. In time, I think you will appreciate its significance. I know that you are a great student and are destined for a great future, so I think you will enjoy it.

Love,

Dad

Jack stared at the page blankly. Suddenly a wave of sadness welled up from deep within him. For a moment his eyes moistened. He bit his lip hard.

"What does he say?"

"It's just a letter," Jack said quietly.

Angus shrugged. "Whatever. At least your dad sends you presents. My dad only ever sends me to the farm—to work."

Jack looked at his friend and put all thoughts of his father out of his head. "Food. Let's go."

They sat around the kitchen table. There was a smear of chocolate on Angus's top lip. On the table were a few crumbs where the cake had been. It looked as though the kitchen had been visited by a swarm of locusts.

Mrs. Christie looked at Angus.

"Any more?"

"Sorry, Mrs. C, I couldn't eat another thing."

"But you've only had five slices. . . . " Her eyes twinkled.

"It was very good, thank you, Mrs. C." Angus groaned. "But I think I need to lie down."

Jack leaned over and poked Angus in the ribs. "Don't they feed you at home?"

Angus grunted.

"Off you go, Angus," said Mrs. Christie. "Jack, can you just help me clear the table?"

With some difficulty Angus rose from the table and waddled toward the basement.

Jack called after him, "Try the first level again. I'll be down in a second."

"So, come on then, what was the present?" His mom looked at him expectantly as they started to clear the table.

Jack shrugged. "Just some book." He squeezed out a smile. "I think you were right, Mom, Dad's presents are going downhill."

"Sorry about that—it happens when you get older."

Jack stared into the open dishwasher.

Suddenly he blurted out, "Mom, what happened to Dad? Where is he now"—he immediately regretted the question—"exactly?" The words hung uncomfortably in the air. His mom sat down, holding a plate, a sad look in her eyes.

"I don't know. We just kind of grew apart. That sort of thing just . . . happens."

"But why do we never see him? I mean, most people who are separated or whatever, well . . . they still see their kids, right?"

She shrugged. "Not necessarily. I don't think it's that easy for him."

"Why did he leave?"

"It was . . . complicated." She put a gentle hand on Jack's shoulder. "He was always working. He was kind of a machine, truth be told." She sighed. "Soon there was nothing left . . . for us, I suppose."

"But I thought that all ended when we left Geneva and came here."

His mom snorted. "What? It got worse! More work, more pressure, more stress. I loved him . . . and he loved me . . . and you, of course. But after a while, I figured"—her cheeks flushed—"he felt what he was doing was more important."

"And then he left—just like that. Where is he now?"

"I have no idea." She shrugged. "But whatever he's doing, he thinks it's important . . . and more important than us. And that's the problem—always was."

"But people always have problems. Couldn't you have made up? Shouldn't you have tried, I don't know . . . harder?"

This time she was defensive. "We did try. I tried, anyway. It's not easy to explain."

Jack knew he was about to reach the limit in this line of questioning. He didn't want a fight, but he pressed on, more boldly than before. "Well, I don't think you tried hard enough. I never hear from him. I get a present once a year—and that's it. Is that normal?"

"I know it's not a great explanation, Jack, but it's the only one I have. I'm sorry."

The Archduke and the Assassin

It's Europe 1914 and the continent is on a knife-edge. An alliance system of great powers has been created: Germany and Austria–Hungary on one side, Russia and France on the other. Britain has moved closer to the Russian and French camp. . . . "

Jack studied two images that had appeared on the screen: old photographs from before the First World War. In the left-hand photo stands a man who looks like royalty and has on the full dress uniform of a cavalry general—a dark tunic with a high gold-braided collar and cuffs, a golden sash, light trousers with a double stripe, and a hat adorned with ribbon and plumes. The subject of the other photo, on the right, was quite different. Dark shifty eyes peer toward the camera from an unshaven face with a defiant stare. The man looks like a peasant.

"On your left is Archduke Franz Ferdinand, the nephew of Franz Joseph I, emperor of the Austro-Hungarian Empire. Franz Ferdinand is the heir to the throne of a mighty sprawling empire that covers a quarter of Europe."

There was a pause before the narrator continued.

"To your right is Gavrilo Princip: student, freedom fighter, or terrorist, depending on your point of view. Princip is a Serbian who grew up in Bosnia in a very poor family."

Angus glanced at Jack. "Looks thin and pale—like you."

Jack ignored him.

The narrator went on, "Princip and his coconspirators of the Black Hand are planning to assassinate the man on the left, the archduke,

Day of the Assassins

in Sarajevo, a part of the Austro-Hungarian Empire. By shooting the archduke, Princip will set in motion a chain of events that will lead to the outbreak of the First World War. Eight million people will die in this war."

The boys both gripped their controllers tightly.

The narrator completed the introduction. "Your mission is to infiltrate the Bosnian Serb assassination cell, prevent the killing of the archduke, and thereby stop the countdown to war. In this way you will change the course of world history. Good luck."

They spent the next hour working their way through the level, taking turns. They traveled across 1914 Austria in a train to Vienna. From there, they journeyed by horse, cart, and even a motorbike to Belgrade. They dodged Austro-Hungarian imperial guards, secret police, and a range of other unsavory characters. On more than one occasion, their cover was blown and they were thrown back to the start of the level. Finally, they infiltrated the Black Hand in Belgrade. If they could stop Princip before he pulled the trigger of his pistol, history would be changed forever. Much more important, they would move on to the next level.

The great thing about Point-of-Departure was that depending on how you played the early levels, the subsequent levels would change—sometimes subtly, sometimes drastically. Sometimes the diplomatic intrigue would take a different course or the war, which was triggered by the assassination in Sarajevo, would be delayed or possibly even averted (although they hadn't figured out how to do that yet). In other scenarios, apparently, the war was successfully postponed only to turn into a much longer and even bloodier affair. It all depended on how you played the first levels and the choices you made.

Jack held the controller in two sweaty palms. In the game, he was standing on the Appel Quay in Sarajevo next to the Lateiner Bridge. He knew that Princip was near him in the crowd, but he couldn't see exactly where. Suddenly, a car passed in front of the crowd, then a second. There were a few muted cheers as a third car passed. He caught a fleeting glance of hat feathers and finery over the heads

Archduke Franz Ferdinand

in front of him . . . and then the Archduke Ferdinand and Sophie, his wife, and the rest of the motorcade were gone.

Suddenly, out of the corner of his eye, he saw the unmistakable figure of Princip furtively crossing the Appel Quay in front of him and then disappearing into Moritz Schiller's delicatessen. Beside him, Angus was on the edge of his seat, staring intently at the images on the screen.

"There he is!" he shouted. He jumped up and down in excitement as Jack expertly fingered the controller to maneuver himself toward Princip.

"Yes, I can see him," Jack said sarcastically.

"You've got to get him!"

"I know."

The tension mounted. Jack knew that in a few minutes the motorcade would be returning from the town hall and Princip would have his final chance to shoot the archduke—and strike a devastating blow for the Bosnian Serbs against their oppressor, the Austro-Hungarian Empire. Instinctively, he followed Princip and took up position next to the shop. History was about to happen before his eyes.

At that moment they saw the big headlights and fender of the Graf und Stift lumbering around the bend. The car was slowing down. He could see all the occupants, including the archduke, perched up high in the rear, and, to his left, Sophie. A man was leaning over to the driver to tell him something. Suddenly, only three yards away, Princip appeared. He had emerged from the delicatessen with a sandwich in one hand. He had a look of amazement on his face as the archduke's car ground to a halt, right in front of him. Princip dropped his sandwich and reached into his jacket pocket.

Angus was standing on the armchair. "There! Get him!"

But Jack kept his nerve. "Wait for it. . . . "

He reached into his own coat and pulled out the pistol that he had been given earlier in the game. He held it in both hands and leveled it directly at Princip, who was by now pointing his own gun into the large car.

Gavrilo Princip

Angus was apoplectic. "Shoot him!"

Jack pressed the button on his controller once. The pistol jerked in his hands on the screen and Princip collapsed.

"You got him! You got him!"

They had completed the level. They had foiled the assassination and thereby stopped the countdown to the First World War. They had changed history, but they would not know exactly how they had changed it until the next level. In his excitement, Angus leaped onto the armchair. The big old springs inside the chair absorbed his weight but then unexpectedly rebounded. Angus suddenly found himself flying over the back of the armchair and toward an old bookcase that stood against one wall of the basement. Jack turned away from the game just in time to see Angus's large frame crash headlong into the bookcase. There was an explosion of splintering wood and collapsing shelves as he made contact. Then, with a huge crash, the bookcase, its contents, and Angus landed in a heap of rubble, wood, and dust.

Missing Sim

As the air cleared, Jack peered into the gloom. The bookcase had fallen backward through a thin partition into . . . Jack was not quite sure what.

Angus groaned and pulled himself to his feet. "What happened?"

"I got him, like you said, but—"

Jack had put down his controller and had already stepped over Angus and the bookcase and into the opening in the wall.

Gingerly, Angus got to his feet, wiping the dust from his shirt and pants. As the air cleared, a mysterious annex became clearly visible. It looked like a . . . library. The hole in the basement wall had opened up onto a narrow balcony, which housed an upper section that swept completely around a small oval room. From this upper section you could reach the lower room by a spiral staircase. The lower floor had to be well below the level of the adjoining room where they had been playing Point-of-Departure only moments ago.

The upper level of the library was packed with books from floor to ceiling—although it looked like there were gaps where some books were missing. In the lower level of the library, papers and journals were stacked haphazardly. The walls were plastered with large panels of brown paper to which an extraordinary array of photographs, diagrams, and stapled notes was attached. In some places large arrows had been scrawled in black marker, connecting one section to another. Words and diagrams were scribbled and crossed out everywhere. In some cases different-colored string had been used to connect various items, and above each panel of paper there was a large label. These labels were the only things that seemed to exercise any kind of order on the messy array of items pinned on the wall charts. From right to left along the wall, the labels for each wall chart could be read in sequence: TIMELINE SIMULATION 0103, TIMELINE SIMULATION 0104, TIMELINE SIMULATION 0105, and so on, all the way up to TIMELINE SIMULATION 0109.

"What is this place?"

"Looks like a kind of control room. . . . " Jack replied.

"Or something out of *CSI*."

"Yeah—all those weird maps, pictures, photos, notes . . . kind of linked together. . . ."

"And what the hell is a timeline simulation?"

"No clue . . . " Jack looked along the wall at the various sheets. About halfway down the room he noticed that there seemed to be a whole wall chart missing—just a bare wall pockmarked by the Blu-tack remained.

"Funny," Jack said. "Simulation 0107 seems to be missing."

Angus shrugged. "Come on—let's take a closer look."

They stepped down the spiral staircase to the lower level. Soon they were in the midst of the lower room and it felt like they were drowning in a sea of paper, books, diagrams, pictures, and notes. It was as if they had entered the brain of some ghostly intellect and caught it in the midst of solving some mind-bendingly difficult puzzle.

Opposite the wall charts, there was a series of floor-to-ceiling shelves and glass cabinets.

"Look at all this stuff."

Each shelf and cabinet seemed to be stuffed with historical paraphernalia. Jack had done enough history with Pendelshape to realize that much of it was military in nature—possibly from the world wars. He spotted a trench telescope, some medals, old maps, at least five different types of shell casings, uniforms, plus an array of rusty-looking revolvers and other equipment.

"Amazing. Do you think any of it can still be used?" Angus asked hopefully.

Between two of the glass cabinets was a large easel to which was pinned a map. Jack recognized it immediately from one of Pendelshape's recent lessons—an old map of the Balkans. Just like the wall charts opposite, various notes, photographs, and diagrams were pinned to it. Some were connected to specific points by hand-drawn lines. The cities of Sarajevo and Belgrade were marked, but most of the other names he could neither recognize nor pronounce. The pictures pinned around the map included some sort of fortress in a town called Doboj near Sarajevo and a picture of a country church or monastery.

"What is that?" Angus was staring toward the far end of the library, his eyes bulging. There, in the shadows, was a low steel platform about waist high. It was about a foot and a half across and surrounded by eight curved pieces of metal that looped up from the floor, bulged out around the central platform, and then rejoined at the top. The whole thing was encased in a canopy of thick green glass. Around the platform was an intricate arrangement of metal pipework, cabling, and wires. There were two main work areas next to the platform, housing an array of oscilloscopes, tools, and old computer equipment.

"Look at this thing." Jack was peering at the steel platform within the glass canopy. He could make out a strange metal object lying on the platform. Jack leaned closer to try to make out what the object was. He put out a finger to touch the glass. Suddenly the glass casing opened away from the platform. He snatched back his hand.

"Help! It's moving!"

As the glass canopy rolled back, the boys had a clear view of the object before them. It was a piece of flat, shiny metal. One end was pointed. It looked incredibly sharp. The other end was clasped around a piece of cylindrical wood. Angus picked up the object. It was very much heavier than it looked.

"Kind of a spike?" Angus asked.

"Here, look, it's got an inscription. . . . " Jack said.

"What does it say?"

"No idea—the metal has a sort of brown stain on it, too."

"Lots of history stuff in here—maybe it's another antique?"

"We should take it to Pendelshape. He'll know." Jack placed the object in his pocket.

After a while, Angus said. "Maybe all this has to do with your father, don't you think? You said he was some sort of scientist, didn't you? And into history."

"Yes. But I don't know why it's all hidden away down here. . . . And such a mess." Then he added resentfully, "I don't know why Mom hasn't said anything about it before. I'll go and get her."

But he didn't have to. Having heard the commotion, Mrs. Christie had arrived on the scene and was on the balcony looking down at them.

"Looks like you've made a bit of a discovery."

"What is all this, Mom?" Jack looked up at her expectantly.

His mom shrugged. "It's your father's old workshop. When he left, he took some things with him, but he wanted the rest left alone and . . . well, we closed it off."

"But . . . "

There was a pause. "Sorry I didn't say anything." She sighed. "With your father's work, it was best not to get involved."

A Message

Dr. Neil Pendelshape slurped from a mug of tea as he inspected the artifact. Nobody quite knew how old the head of the history department was—but judging by the crow's feet around his deep-set eyes and the cropped gray hair, he had to be well into his fifties. He wore a tweed jacket, which struggled to cover a squat, portly frame. Pendelshape didn't go for the casual fashion of the younger teachers. Jack had never seen him without a tie. He marched around the history department as if it was his personal property—always in control. Jack had never heard him raise his voice, let alone lose his temper, yet discipline was never a problem.

Jack proudly presented the artifact to Pendelshape after school. He and Angus had spent quite a bit of time the previous evening exploring his father's extraordinary library and workshop. To Jack's dismay, his mom had continued to be coy about the discovery. She had said that she had been "meaning to clear it all out" for some time and that she "had always meant to tell him that it was there," but over time, and being so busy, had "kind of forgotten." Jack did not understand this at all. But as he and Angus had inspected the artifacts and the mysterious posters and all the strange equipment, he'd begun to feel a growing sense of pride that all of this had once belonged to his own dad.

Pendelshape listened to the boys' revelations with quiet interest. But as the story unfolded, his brow furrowed. He nodded thoughtfully and looked at the lump of steel more closely with a magnifying glass he pulled from his desk drawer. He studied the stem of splintered wood first and then carefully worked his way up to the arrow-shaped tip. He was staring intently, his nose nearly touching the object. His face flushed momentarily and a small bead of sweat formed on his forehead. They had expected Pendelshape to be excited. But instead he looked increasingly . . . worried.

"So, what is it, sir?" Angus asked.

"It's the tip of a lance."

Pendelshape thrust the magnifying glass over to Jack and pointed a finger at some lettering on one edge of the arrow-shaped lance head.

"I can see the letters, sir. But I don't know what they mean."

"Let me translate. It reads, BY GOD'S GRACE—F.J."

Jack stared blankly at Pendelshape. "F.J.?"

"Franz Joseph."

Jack remembered the name, but Angus shrugged, none the wiser.

Pendelshape rolled his eyes. "It means, boys, that we have here the ceremonial lance tip of one of the bodyguards of the emperor of Austria." His voice trailed off thoughtfully. "Or, to give him his proper title: emperor of Austria; king of Jerusalem; apostolic king of Hungary; king of Bohemia, Galicia, Lodomeria, Illyria, and Croatia; archduke of Austria; and duke, markgraf, prince, or count of some thirty other places in the Austro-Hungarian dual monarchy. . . . Indeed"—he smiled grimly and snorted—"they don't give them titles like that anymore!"

"Indeed," Angus said. Pendelshape narrowed his eyes and looked back at him sharply, trying to decide whether Angus was joking.

Jack pressed on. "Sorry, sir, I didn't think there were any empires left; I mean Austria isn't an empire. . . . Do they even have a king?"

Pendelshape was impressed. "Very good, Jack. You're absolutely right, but of course, this artifact is not modern. In fact it is at least ninety years old."

"And what's that funny brown staining on the metal, sir?" Angus asked.

Pendelshape delayed his response, rubbed the back of his neck, and then said matter-of-factly, "It's blood."

Jack's heart jumped, and he glanced at Angus.

Pendelshape stared out through the window, deep in thought. A sparkling autumn day had gradually been enveloped by clouds that had rolled down from the hills. Suddenly, Pendelshape seemed to come to a decision about something. "The Schönbrunn raid,"

Pendelshape finally muttered. "It might be . . . "

"Sorry, sir—what's that?" Jack asked.

"Little is known about it—some people think it didn't happen at all—that it's just a myth. Apparently, there was some sort of raid on the Palace of Schönbrunn in Vienna a few days before the assassination of Franz Ferdinand in 1914. The Austro-Hungarian government was very embarrassed about an attack at the very heart of the empire. They tried to erase any evidence that it took place. The story goes that Austrian lancers took on a group of Serbian rebels in the gardens of Schönbrunn itself. There were a number of casualties."

"You think this lance could somehow be linked to this . . . raid?"

Pendelshape shrugged. "Well, the design is distinctive and places it quite accurately at that time . . . and . . . "

"What?"

"It would certainly be an important historical find if we could trace the lance to that date. . . . It might even be evidence that the raid did indeed happen."

"Wonder how Dad came to have it in his workshop. . . . " Jack said.

"Yes, Jack," Pendelshape said thoughtfully. "I would be interested to know that too."

The room fell silent for a moment. Finally, Pendelshape announced, "Well, school's finished for today. I suggest you two stay around for an hour or so. Maybe do your homework in the library. I will go to the staff room and phone a few colleagues, make some inquiries. Let's see if we can find out exactly what the piece is and perhaps discover its value—maybe even test my theory. That might be interesting, don't you think?" He looked at his watch. "Why don't you come back at, say, five or so?"

Jack looked at Angus with an enthusiastic nod. Angus shrugged.

"Great. Thanks, sir. If you're sure." And with that they left Pendelshape as he picked up his magnifying glass and examined the lance head again.

As they left the classroom, Jack turned to Angus. "Pretty cool, eh? What do you want to do, then?"

"Not go to the library, for a start."

"Agreed. Gino's?"

"Nah. Boyle will be there—remember—four o'clock, Friday . . . and it's Friday the 13th—unlucky. I can't face that lot."

They walked slowly down the austere Victorian corridor past the old classrooms, wondering how to kill an hour.

"Watch out. Trouble ahead," Angus suddenly said, and nodded in the direction of the far corridor as two burly uniformed figures approached.

"The terrible twins. What have we done to deserve this?"

Sure enough, the two school janitors, Tony Smith and Gordon MacFarlane, approached as they checked each of the empty classrooms before locking up for the evening. Tony was tall, with a ramrod back and puffed-out chest and, as ever, was immaculately dressed. Gordon was shorter and stockier, but also strode around with the authority of an ex-army officer. Both men were feared and best avoided due to the pleasure they took in enforcing the pettiest of school rules and their habit of dispensing discipline with the maximum level of sarcasm. There was a rumor in the school that Tony and Gordon used to be in special forces—a notion that neither janitor made any effort to dispel. There was another rumor, too, that they were actually ex–traffic cops. This was the story that Jack and Angus thought more likely.

The boys looked for some way to avoid the two men. But it was too late. Soon the large figures were looming over them, Tony peering down at Jack over a carefully trimmed mustache, an eager twinkle in his eye.

"Well, now, what do we have here?" Tony asked.

"One waif and one stray," Gordon quipped.

"It's Mr. Christie and Mr. Jud, is it not?"

"Yes, Mr. Smith." Jack said.

Tony turned to Gordon and mockingly impersonated Jack's voice, "Yes, Mr. Smith . . . "

Gordon laughed, and repeated in a squeaky voice, "Yes, Mr. Smith." Tony said, "Remind me, Mr. MacFarlane, what is the penalty for loitering on school grounds twenty minutes after the final bell, outside designated zones?"

Gordon turned back to Tony, taking his time to consider the answer. "Mmm . . . I don't know, Mr. Smith. Outside the designated zones, I think the penalty might be a detention . . . but actually we could make up any penalty we wanted."

Tony looked back down at Jack. "Shall we do that, boys? Shall we make up a penalty?"

"But . . . we were going to the library. . . . "

Gordon exhaled skeptically, making a sort of drawn-out *psshht* sound as he did so. Thankfully, just at that moment, Pendelshape emerged from his classroom and marched down the corridor toward them.

"Good afternoon, gentlemen. Anything I can help you with?"

Tony and Gordon's manner changed instantly. It was as if the sergeant major had appeared and they had snapped to attention.

"Good afternoon, Dr. Pendelshape. I believe these are your pupils?" Tony said obsequiously.

"Yes, Tony, they're with me. They were just off to the library— weren't you?"

"No problem, sir—we were just closing down for the night. You know the rules, sir."

"Very good. You can leave my room open for a little longer. . . . I have the keys."

"Sir." And with that, Tony and Gordon slunk off in disappointment.

"Right, lads—along to the library—and I'll make those calls."

Five minutes after reaching the library, Angus was fidgeting with boredom.

"Stop it," Jack said, trying to focus on his math homework.

"I can't. I've got an idea."

"Great. Not another of your 'good' ideas. . . . "

"Yes," Angus said. "One of those." He lowered his voice and looked up and down the silent aisles of the old library furtively. "It's our big chance."

"What is?" Jack was getting worried.

"Well—Pendelshape is in the staff room, making calls. The terrible twins are out of the way . . . and . . . "

"And what?" Jack asked.

"And, well, we know that Pendelshape has left his door open."

Jack hissed at Angus across the table. "No way!"

The prim librarian, still sorting returns, briefly raised her eyes above her reading glasses.

"Angus—I'm not standing guard while you sneak in and rummage through Pendelshape's desk to get back all the stuff he's confiscated off you."

Angus looked hurt. "I only care about my iPod. . . . I can't do without that for a whole week. It's totally unacceptable."

Jack shook his head. "It's wrong and it's your own fault it got taken away, anyway. Pendelshape can be pretty severe. If he caught us, I don't know—maybe we could even get expelled." He considered this for a moment and then added, "Or something really bad."

Angus had an evil smile on his face. The kind he got when he knew he was about to get Jack to do something he really didn't want to.

"Come on . . . think about it."

"Think about what?" Jack asked.

"It'll be fun."

Angus grinned inanely. Jack stared across the table at his friend and shook his head. He looked over at the librarian, who was ignoring them. For some reason, he could feel his chest tightening. He felt for his inhaler in his pocket.

"You're a pain, Angus."

But Angus was already up, away, and heading out of the library.

Strangely, when they reentered the classroom, they spotted the lance head still lying on Pendelshape's desk. Jack had assumed that their teacher would have taken it with him to help in his inquiries, but it was still there. Without really thinking, he grabbed it and put it into his backpack to keep it safe.

A quick search for Angus's precious iPod in Pendelshape's large store cupboard proved fruitless. Angus was disappointed.

"Let's get out of here," Jack said. "Probably a good thing we can't find it."

But just as they were about to leave, Jack noticed that Pendelshape had left the computer in his classroom on. Jack could never resist computers, and as he made his way through the store cupboard door, he touched the keyboard absentmindedly. The screensaver had not kicked in yet. Without warning, a window popped up on the computer screen. It caught Jack's eye, because of its unusual design. It was some sort of an e-mail application, but compared to the slick user interfaces he was used to, it looked very basic: just simple black text on a white background.

"What's this?" Jack murmured. Then his brow furrowed. "What the . . . ?"

Angus turned back to look. They both stared at the screen. It was the title of the e-mail that grabbed them:

Subject: Lance artifact at Cairnfield

Then they looked at the recipient and sender fields:

From: Benefactor
To: Neil Pendelshape

"Who is Benefactor?" Angus asked.
"No idea—what's this . . . ?" They kept reading.

Do not concern yourself with the Cairnfield workshop. The lance is artifact from early experiments into the prewar period—a rare piece that helps confirm the Schönbrunn raid did occur. Anyway—it is irrelevant since things have now moved on. I have momentous news! Our own Taurus is complete! Yes! A functioning, full-scale system. We can now complete execution of Sim 0107 for real! We will activate Zadok. And very soon we will be in a position to defeat VIGIL. You must do something urgently, before we start. I fear that when they find out, they may take Orion. There is nothing we can do about Lynx now—she has gone over to the other side. But we must protect Orion. You need to enact the plan and then contact me as we discussed. We are about to change the world!

Good luck!

Your loyal friend, the Benefactor

They stared at the extraordinary message on the screen.

"What the—?" Jack started to speak, but stopped mid-sentence, dumbfounded.

"What's Taurus . . . ? VIGIL? Zadok?" Angus said. "What does it mean?"

Jack shook his head. "I don't know . . . but one thing's for sure."

"What?"

"Something's going on . . . and it's more interesting than whatever's on your iPod."

"But I don't—"

Angus didn't finish his sentence.

In the doorway stood Dr. Pendelshape.

The VIGIL Imperative

They hadn't even heard a footstep.

"Find anything interesting, boys?"

We're toast, Jack thought. Then, without a word, Dr. Pendelshape did something quite unexpected. He reached for his inside pocket and pulled out a thin piece of plastic that looked like a large pocket calculator. The sleek gadget seemed out of place among Pendelshape's dusty books and papers.

"Best encryption in the world . . . but it's no good if you forget to lock the screen."

Strangely, he did not seem angry. Instead he peered at the message from the Benefactor.

"It makes no difference now, anyway." He spoke urgently. "But I will explain all that later. Come, we haven't got long. I hope you two don't mind surprises. Step to the back, please." He ushered them to the rear of the small store cupboard.

Pendelshape pressed the calculator device in his hand, and, without warning, a slight aperture appeared in the floor. Angus gasped. Jack just stood, gaping. A very narrow, steep spiral staircase was dimly lit by a blue light, which produced an unearthly shimmer.

"You can't get out, so I'm afraid you will just have to follow me. But don't worry—you're perfectly safe. Please—on you go."

Jack and Angus didn't move.

With a little more firmness now, Pendelshape urged them forward. "Please—we have little time. Trust me."

Reluctantly they stepped onto the spiral staircase, quickly followed by Pendelshape. It was some sort of escalator, and the steps began to descend automatically. As they dropped beneath floor level, the opening above them automatically closed, and after a couple of minutes, they came to a gentle halt. Ahead of them was a door. Pendelshape pressed the device again, and the door opened to reveal a short metal-clad corridor illuminated by the same dim blue light. At the end of the corridor was a large circular door, like the entrance to a bank vault—it looked very heavy, maybe steel. It had five letters etched on it: **V I G I L.**

The door opened silently, and Jack noticed that it was at least three inches thick. Next, they found themselves in an oval-shaped room that felt like a sort of library. It was similar to his dad's workshop at Cairnfield, although there weren't quite as many books and there was no mess—in fact it was spotless. Toward one side of the library were two large leather sofas between which a glass-topped table was positioned.

Pendelshape waved them forward. "Please take a seat, gentlemen. I think I have some explaining to do." He looked at his watch and then waved vaguely in the direction of a modern fireplace, which suddenly erupted into a roaring log fire. Jack and Angus jumped.

"Don't worry—it's not real." Pendelshape snorted. "Just adds a bit of atmosphere. Otherwise it can be a bit grim all the way down here." He clapped his hands. "Now, first things first: would either of you like some tea?" But the two boys were still in shock. "I'm rather partial to cookies. We usually keep a few goodies here, you know, just in case. . . . " Pendelshape moved over to what appeared to be an anteroom to the library. He talked over his shoulder.

"I should explain where we are. This is a facility of VIGIL. They oversee everything."

Jack finally found his voice. "What's VIGIL?"

Dr. Pendelshape returned to the table with a pot of tea and a plate of cookies on a large tray.

"Ah, apologies. Of course, I will need to start at the beginning. One forgets how little is known. . . . "

"Sir, I'm sorry, we didn't mean to look at your computer,"

Jack blurted out. "We were just . . . waiting for you—"

"You're not in trouble," Pendelshape said firmly, and then added, "But I'm afraid you might be, if you don't listen very carefully to what I have to say."

"But, sir—"

Pendelshape put up a hand to silence Jack. "Please . . . just listen."

Pendelshape bit into an oatmeal cookie, then rocked backward and forward as if weighing something in his mind. "Indeed. I think you will find what I have to say quite surprising . . . shocking even." And with these words, their teacher launched into a story that was quite unlike anything either of them had ever heard from him in a history lesson.

"VIGIL is the governing body of an elite network of physicists, engineers, and computer scientists. However, VIGIL is not an institution that you will find listed in a library or on the Internet. It is secret."

Pendelshape picked up another cookie and waved it around in the air as he spoke. "We are beneath the radar." He coughed, took a sip of his Earl Grey, and swallowed. "Indeed. This is for the simple reason that VIGIL manages the most powerful technology ever invented."

Jack and Angus looked at each other—surely this was a joke.

"I am talking about the technology of time travel." He said it in a rather pedestrian way, as if it was something that he was quite familiar with and dealt with on a day-to-day basis—like switching on a light.

"The ideas have been around for many decades. I am sure you have heard of physicists such as Planck, Heisenberg, and Schrödinger . . . and the concepts of quantum mechanics, parallel universes, wormholes, and such. . . . " He looked at the boys expectantly, but all he got back were blank stares.

He waved dismissively. "Never mind. All you need to know is that the world of subatomic physics is an extremely mysterious one, not one where our normal experience of everyday life applies at all. It has baffled some of the greatest minds, including Einstein." Pendelshape frowned. "You have heard of Einstein, haven't you?" They nodded stupidly.

"That's a relief. More tea?" he asked matter-of-factly. But Jack and Angus hadn't touched any of the food. "Come on, eat up. You'll need to line your stomachs for what you're about to hear, I can tell you."

Jack steeled himself. "Time travel—that's just theory, isn't it? Mumbo jumbo. It can't actually be done"—his voice trembled—"can it?"

"Yes, Jack. It can. Let me show you something."

He pressed the device he was holding, and the room brightened. On the opposite wall, the shelves of books slowly moved apart, revealing a solid wall of thick green glass that extended from the floor to the ceiling. The glass had the same hue and texture as the casing around the small platform back at Cairnfield where they had discovered the lance head. Behind this glass screen was a flat metal platform surrounded by an array of scientific equipment—pipes, cables, and steel. The platform itself was bounded by a semi-closed arrangement of hefty black girders. Jack counted eight of them. They rose from the floor, bulged out to surround the platform, then rejoined at the top of the structure. All together it looked like a giant gyroscope. It was on a much larger scale and looked more complex than the device back at Cairnfield, but the basic structure was similar—with one exception. Between two of the large metal girders here, a ladder rose from the floor to the level of the platform. Through the thick glass they could make out some lettering. It spelled out one word: TAURUS.

Pendelshape gestured proudly toward the structure. "Gentlemen, here is where theory becomes reality. It's a far cry from H. G. Wells, I know, but Mr. Taurus there will take you back in time."

All Angus could say was, "Will it bring you back again?"

Pendelshape smiled. "Yes, it will." He paused. "Well, in general, it will." He shrugged. "Details, details."

Jack expected to wake up at any moment or, probably worse, for the host of some reality TV show to suddenly appear and reveal that the whole thing was a setup and they'd been humiliated on TV in front of millions of viewers. Neither happened.

All he could say, lamely, was, "How does it work?"

Preliminary notes on the Tourw

Armageddon scenario?
deep time limitation ?

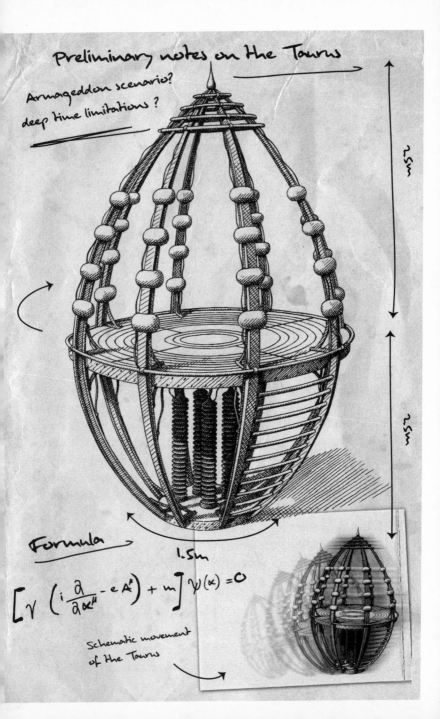

2.5m

2.5m

1.5m

Formula →

$$\left[\gamma \left(i \frac{\partial}{\partial x^{\mu}} - e A^{\mu} \right) + m \right] \psi(x) = 0$$

Schematic movement
of the Tourw

Pendelshape laughed. "I'm afraid that would take a little while to explain . . . and you would need a PhD in theoretical physics or computer science and maybe genetics." He frowned, looked down at his shoes, and paused. "In fact, probably all three . . . but, if you like, I can give you the ten-second version." He looked at the boys expectantly; there was no response.

"The ten-second version it is, then. You switch on the power. You might think that is just a question of pressing a big red button— but it is a little more complicated than that." He looked thoughtful. "The button is green, actually. Anyway, then you set the date and location you want to go to, you stand on that platform"—he pointed at the circular platform inside the Taurus structure—"and you click this—"

From his pocket he pulled something that looked like a cell phone—only a little fatter and longer. He flipped the device open and a very faint blue light came on. It was similar to the light in the stairwell and access passage. The boys could see a small screen and a number of small buttons.

"The Taurus itself, over there, stays put—it focuses the energy. But to move through time and space, you need to have physical contact with this little chap. It's a time phone. You need it to go . . . and to get back." He looked at them. "And that's about it. Oh, except that while back in time, the time phone is controlled and tracked by the Taurus and its console over there, using a set of codes—with a reasonable degree of accuracy. . . . " A look of doubt ghosted across his face. "Most of the time, anyway."

"What do you mean?"

"Well, it will only work when the Taurus is at the right energy state and also when there is a strong enough . . . signal."

"Signal? Like a real cell phone? Come on, sir, you're joking." Angus laughed.

But Pendelshape pressed on. "It's a bit more complicated, but you're more or less right. See that bar, there at the side?" He held up the device and pointed to one corner of the display. "It's grayed out at the moment, but when it turns yellow, you can exchange signals with the Taurus—text messages if you like. It means the Taurus here knows where you are . . . and it means you can time travel. When it's off you can't do any of those things."

"Wow!" Angus exclaimed.

"It's off at the moment?" Jack asked.

"Of course."

"But—"

"This is all completely irrelevant. I'm afraid that none of it can be used . . . great tragedy."

"Why not?" asked Jack.

"Not allowed. It's known as the VIGIL Imperative." Pendelshape sighed. "Rules, gentlemen, rules . . . which we must follow on pain of death. Literally."

Taurus Class

Pendelshape sat back and clasped his hands behind his head. "About fifteen years ago, a small group of physicists associated with the nuclear research facility at CERN, near Geneva, conducted the first practical experiments in time travel. At first, very simple nonorganic structures were transported backward and forward through space and time. Then we started to experiment with more complex structures. We moved on to the first organic material, then living creatures . . . and, finally, a human being. Up to this point the level of excitement among the group was incredible, as you can imagine. But then, one of the leaders of the group, Counselor Inchquin, started to think seriously about the power of what they had created. Here was a technology that had the potential to change the past, and thereby change the future. In the wrong hands, or even in the right hands, this could be catastrophic." He paused. "Think about it."

"You're right. You could go back and steal some money, and no one would know . . . " Angus said, intrigued.

"Of course. But I'm afraid that's the least of it. Think about the pivotal moments of history, some of which have been triggered by small, even chance, events that have had huge consequences. These are the 'what ifs' of our history." Pendelshape's eyes opened wide in enthusiasm. "Think about it: What if Hitler had been killed in the First World War and had not become the leader of Germany? What if Gavrilo Princip had not assassinated Archduke Ferdinand? The list is, of course, endless—and fascinating. The consequences for us and for future generations, however, are difficult to comprehend."

Jack spoke slowly, trying to understand what he was hearing.

"So you're saying that these scientists created this thing . . . the power to time travel . . . but decided not to use it?"

Pendelshape replied sadly, "It was debated. Despite the computer simulations we could create to model the consequences of any changes made in history, most felt that it was too risky and that no one should be given the chance to exercise such power. Counselor Inchquin felt this most strongly and led the group with this point of view."

"Who won the argument?" Angus asked, engrossed.

"Who do you think?" Pendelshape said. "In the end it was decided that, although it was not possible to 'un-invent' the technology, it was possible to control it. VIGIL was formed and everyone agreed to abide by a strict set of rules. A code of conduct, if you like. It came to be known as the VIGIL Imperative. All those in the know were forced to abide by it. The early Taurus experimental facility was closed down, and outside a select group, it was suggested that the project had been an abject failure."

Jack looked around. "What's this place, then?"

"It's a replica Taurus made using components from the original machine. Although you don't know it, yours is a special school—it secretly houses a working Taurus. All members of VIGIL have moved on to rather mundane jobs. I, for example, am now your history teacher. Rather appropriate, don't you think? And our rector, himself a brilliant scientist, finds himself here as head teacher—during term time at least. But in fact he has a much weightier responsibility: to keep this facility completely secret, yet in working order so that the technology is preserved."

"Why not just destroy it altogether?"

"That was certainly an option—but in the end the people who had worked so hard on it could not quite bring themselves to go that far. It was also anticipated that in the future, there might possibly be scenarios where it could be necessary to use Taurus. We might not even know now what these scenarios would be, but science moves very fast. It seemed sensible at least to retain the option to use it. But that's not all. . . . "

Day of the Assassins

"There's more?"

"Yes. There was also a small group with a different point of view from Inchquin and the others. They were led by the Benefactor, and they believed that the technology could and should be used as a force for good." Pendelshape paused for a moment and eyed Jack with an odd, inquiring look. He seemed to be thinking about something and to lose his concentration for a moment.

"Benefactor. That was the name in your e-mail," Jack said.

"Yes, Jack . . . and—" but before Pendelshape could continue, Angus butted in.

"OK, hold it right there, sir. . . . I'm not sure what this place is . . . but I have to tell you I'm finding it difficult to believe all this." He glanced at Jack. "Very difficult. It's a big joke—right?"

Pendelshape's eyes flashed in frustration. "Wrong. I know, Angus, it's a lot to take in. But I must ask you to try. It is quite important . . . for us all, as you are about to find out. However, I agree it is reasonable to ask for some proof. . . . " He looked around the room, then stood up and walked over to one of the shelves and started leafing through a thin folder.

"Here. Maybe this will do it."

Pendelshape produced a small photograph and handed it to them.

"So, Jack, remember our lessons on the First World War, the assassination in Sarajevo, the Black Hand, Gavrilo Princip, and all that . . . ?" He looked down at the photograph knowingly. "Well . . . ?"

Jack suddenly realized what he was looking at. His heart jolted. It couldn't be. But the image was unmistakable.

It was an old black-and-white photo of a group of four young men—grim faced and serious. One of them was the assassin from Sarajevo that Jack had seen in Point-of-Departure—Gavrilo Princip. But on the other side of the photograph, to the far left, was a fifth man. Jack narrowed his eyes to be certain. He looked a little younger, but there was no mistaking him. The man staring out from the photograph was Dr. Pendelshape.

Jack slowly raised his eyes to Pendelshape, who smiled knowingly at him.

"So you see, boys, this photo was taken in Belgrade, in the Balkans . . . in 1914. And no, it's not a fake or a digital enhancement. It's real. There's me on the left. On the right is Gavrilo Princip, the man who shot Archduke Franz Ferdinand in Sarajevo and triggered the First World War. To the left of Princip are two of the other assassins—Grabez and Cabrinovic."

"And what about him?" Angus pointed to a fourth man standing next to Pendelshape.

"Dani Matronovic. Lesser known—was killed before the assassination. History doesn't mention what happened to him. His sister took the photo." His eyes glazed over for a moment. "Pretty girl . . . Anna."

Pendelshape flipped over the photo. "Their names are on the back—look."

Sure enough, on the back of the photo, in Pendelshape's distinctive scrawl, were scribbled the words *Belgrade, Serbia, 1914,* followed by the names *Princip, Grabez, Cabrinovic, Matronovic.*

Angus just couldn't believe it. "So you've gone back in time using that . . . thing?" He looked over at the Taurus brooding silently behind the green glass screen.

"Yes, Angus. Even though the purpose of VIGIL is to preserve the technology—and not to use it—everything still had to be fully tested. No point in deciding to keep the technology unless you know it will work."

"But why did you go back, then, you know, to 1914?" Jack asked.

Pendelshape shrugged. "It was a pivotal point in history."

"Why you? Why did they choose you?"

"I'm the historian. Anyway, I thought it would be interesting. . . . " Pendelshape's eyes glazed over as he added dreamily, "and I was right. It was incredible; to see even a tiny piece of what you had learned from a textbook, to see it, to smell it. . . . " He smiled. "Keep the photo if you like."

Jack took it gingerly, as if handling a precious jewel. He stared at it silently for a moment longer, then stowed it carefully in his bag.

Pendelshape pressed on more quickly now, trying to bypass

interruptions from his bewildered pupils. He revealed more about VIGIL. He explained how the idea of hiding the Taurus in a school had worked well—the initial refurbishment of the school had been a good front for the early building work, holiday periods provided quiet time for research and maintenance, and, of course, it was easy to maintain a staff of teachers, who were, in reality, scientists from the original Taurus team. It had taken them some time to identify an appropriate home for the Taurus—until they had finally found this quiet and secluded hiding place. The local community had been grateful for the sudden injection of cash that the endowment had provided and for the creation of a new school on a rundown site. After a while an increasing number of local pupils began to attend, assisted by generous subsidies. Pupil numbers had been kept low, ostensibly to preserve academic standards but in reality to free up faculty time for more important matters.

As Pendelshape talked, Jack saw the expression on Angus's face gradually change. His mouth was morphing into that warped, toothy grin that meant only one thing. Trouble. Sure enough, as Pendelshape paused for breath, Angus seized his chance.

"So, sir . . . er, it all sounds great, but are you going to show us how it really works?"

To Jack's utter amazement, Pendelshape replied, "Yes, Angus. In fact I am."

Pendelshape looked at his watch nervously. "We've spent far too much time talking already. The truth is that unforeseen circumstances have arisen. This is why I have brought you here. I will explain more in a minute. I and, er, well, we have a kind of . . . mission to complete. But first, I would like you both to understand how it all works." He smiled. "You know, just in case . . . "

The three of them went to stand in front of the green glass barrier that stretched from one side of the library to the other, extending all the way up to the ceiling.

"This is the reinforced glass blast screen. Press this"—Pendelshape clicked the device in his hand—"and down it comes." Jack and Angus jumped back as, with alarming speed, the blast screen descended into a narrow gap in the floor and the whole Taurus structure was revealed to them in its full glory.

"Awesome," Angus whispered reverentially.

"Be careful. You don't want to be standing over that blast screen when it goes up again. It could give you a nasty bruise in your nether regions."

Pendelshape moved over to one of the control panels and began typing at a keyboard. Soon they heard a rising hum. Pendelshape explained the basics of how the machine was operated. It was surprisingly simple. He showed them how you synchronized the time phone with the Taurus console by placing it in a special recessed pod. He showed them how you entered the Taurus through the surrounding girders via the ladder and how you then positioned yourself on the steel platform by placing your feet between the etchings drawn into the metal. He reminded them of the limitations of the Taurus and its umbilical linkage to the time phone.

"As you said, Angus . . . it's like a cell phone—you can only use the time phone when you have a signal. Remember that bar?" He indicated the little grayed-out display on the time phone. "When it's yellow, you're good to go—you can communicate, we know where you are, and . . . the Taurus can send you back and forth through time. When there's no signal, you're stuck—although the phone's energy source will continue to tell you where and when you are."

"And if you lose the phone?" Angus asked.

Pendelshape looked back at Angus with steel in his eyes. "Lose that time phone, Mr. Jud, and you're not only *in* history . . . you *are* history. No way back."

Jack was engrossed. "Can you go anywhere?"

"There are constraints. The variability of the time signals through the space-time continuum is a major one. It's like shifting sands. Periods of time open up and then close. It's not as if all periods of time and all locations are accessible all the time. Then there's 'deep time.' "

"Deep time?"

"A specific constraint that exists along the lines I just mentioned. It seems that the Taurus is only effective at transportation from when you depart to more than about thirty years or so in the past. We call that deep time. Anything in the more recent past is a sort of no-go zone. This also means you can't travel from the past to just before you left."

Pendelshape's brow furrowed. "And there's one more thing. We call it the Armageddon Scenario." Pendelshape said the words quickly— as if he was hoping the boys might not even notice he had said them.

"Well, that sounds pretty harmless," Angus said.

Jack frowned. "What is it?"

Pendelshape shrugged nonchalantly. "Another part of time theory. It postulates that if you revisit the same point of space and time more than once, you dramatically increase the risk of a continuum meltdown. At worst, the possible destruction of the universe, but in reality probably not as bad at that—probably only the destruction of some piece of it. . . . "

"Oh—that's OK then. Presumably it's the piece we're in?" Angus said.

"Yes. Think of tissue paper. It's like putting holes in it with your finger. These are like visits to the past using Taurus. The tissue will hold together for a while, but too many holes and it will disintegrate. So best not to risk repeat trips in and around the same point. The precise parameters of this constraint are not known—and of course have not been tested."

Suddenly the pitch of the humming from the control room rose an octave. A number of lights around the console flashed on.

Pendelshape smiled in satisfaction. "We're in business! Right, gentlemen, before we go any further, I have to explain to you what we must do next and why we have decided to show you all this. It's not a step we have taken lightly. You're going to have to trust me one more time. I assure you it is in all of our interests."

The boys glanced at each other nervously.

Pendelshape marched over to a table and was eventually joined by Angus, who wandered backward slowly, still staring up, mesmerized by the Taurus and its cables and pipes. Jack remained by the quietly humming machine, still trying to absorb everything that Pendelshape had said. "Jack, please, if you would come back over here, quickly . . ." Pendelshape gestured impatiently for him to move away from the structure. He took a deep breath. "The Taurus is already set so that we can travel back in time to somewhere I know and where we will be safe, before being picked up. The truth is—"

But he did not finish his sentence.

Armed Response

The heavy door at the far end of the control room swung open and through it marched Tony and Gordon. Over their usual uniforms, each was wearing a ballistic vest. From his position next to the Taurus, Jack could just make out small silver lettering on each of the vests: VIGIL RESPONSE.

Behind Tony and Gordon were two other men—Mr. Belstaff and Mr. Johnstone, the gym teachers. They wore the same getup as the two janitors and moved with the same imposing power. But what alarmed Jack most was that, quite extraordinarily, all the men were . . . armed. If he had been an expert on military matters, he might have recognized the weapons that they carried to be Corner Shot APRs— one of the most advanced automatic weapons in the world. With their laser sights, video screens, and swiveling gun mounts, the machine guns also had a special feature—they could shoot around corners. What on earth they were doing in the hands of the school janitors and the gym teachers, Jack had no idea.

The four men were followed by a tall, slim figure with a bald head, poorly disguised with thinning wisps of silver hair. Jack recognized him immediately. With his trademark black gown flowing from a pair of hunched shoulders he looked like a raven. It was the school's head: the Rector.

He advanced toward Pendelshape and Angus, his face purple with rage.

Pendelshape jumped to his feet. He looked terrified. "John . . . I'm sorry . . . I—"

But the Rector shouted back, "Silence!"

Pendelshape sank to his knees; he seemed to be . . . begging.

"Please! I didn't mean—"

The Rector loomed over Pendelshape. "You idiot! Do you know— I always had a sneaking suspicion about you. Didn't you think we'd find out?"

Pendelshape really was begging now. "Please, please. John . . . I didn't—"

"I should have guessed you might betray us. You and the Benefactor. A bad combination of a hopeless romantic and a dangerous lunatic."

"I'm sorry. . . . "

"MacFarlane. Deal with him."

Jack couldn't believe what happened next. Gordon stepped forward. He had a sinister grin on his face—as if he was actually enjoying himself. He withdrew a large knife from a scabbard on his black belt. As he did so, he spun the six-inch serrated blade in one hand like a circus knife thrower. Suddenly Jack realized that Tony and Gordon were definitely not ex–traffic cops.

With one hand, Gordon reached down, pulled the whimpering Pendelshape to his feet, and smacked him hard against one of the wooden bookcases. Pendelshape moaned in pain. Again, with only one hand, Gordon lifted him off the ground. With the other hand he took the blade and plunged it into his neck. Jack felt the bile rise in his throat. He thought he was going to be sick. But then he realized that, expertly, Gordon had only nicked Pendelshape's neck, impaling him instead by both his shirt and jacket collar against the bookcase. Blood oozed from the wound, but Pendelshape was not dead. Yet. Instead, he was starting to choke as his weight pulled him down and his collar slowly tightened around his neck. His face was turning purple. The Rector nodded toward Angus, who, like Jack, was staring slack-jawed at the violent assault.

"Smith. Please deal with this young man."

Tony stepped forward, grabbed Angus by the scruff of the neck, and yanked him from the sofa with surprising ease. With no hesitation, Tony landed a punch to Angus's solar plexus. For Tony, it was a light, controlled blow. But there was no doubt, if Tony had chosen to, he could have killed Angus on the spot. But Tony had held back, and instead Angus doubled over, badly winded, and retched. The Rector now directed his attention to Jack, at the other end of the library, next to the Taurus.

"Bring Master Christie here. You know your orders—no damage."

Jack looked back across the library as Belstaff and Johnstone strode toward him. Pendelshape was slowly choking to death. Angus was on the floor clutching his stomach. It didn't look like Jack was going to get off any lighter. His heart was beating in overdrive. He needed time . . . time to think. But in five seconds the two men would be on him . . . and then what?

He snatched the controller that Pendelshape had left by the console and stabbed the button. Just as Belstaff was midstride, the glass blast screen accelerated upward from its housing under the floor. It caught him without warning clean between the legs. Belstaff screamed in pain and found himself powering upward, balanced precariously on the top edge of the thick glass. Two seconds later, with a dull thud and crunching bone, the rising panel crushed the unfortunate man right into the ceiling—like a finger caught in a car's electric window. The powerful motors beneath the floor continued to grind and push upward as the glass screen failed to slot itself into its upper housing, now blocked by Belstaff, suspended fifteen feet in the air. Johnstone, who had been behind his colleague, smashed into the side of the blast screen and reeled backward, clutching his head.

Cornered at one end of the library next to the Taurus and behind the blast screen, Jack knew he didn't have long. He didn't know why these people were after him, but he knew he had to escape. It was a long shot—but there was only one way out. Through the blast screen, he could just make out the Rector, Tony, and Gordon rushing around in alarm trying to find a way to lower the screen and get to him. Though safe for the moment, he now had a new fear. His breathing had intensified, and he was starting to wheeze. His chest had that awful hollow feeling that usually preceded an asthma attack. He reached for his inhaler and took a mighty suck. For a moment, it calmed him.

He leaned over the console that Pendelshape had shown them earlier. There, still nestling in its pod, was the time phone. Above it a small digital readout blinked invitingly: "Initiate synchronization procedure."

Jack looked back over his shoulder through the screen. In a few seconds they would have it lowered. There was no doubt about what he must do. He snatched the time phone from its pod and flipped it open. Immediately he saw the little bar to the side burning bright yellow. Just as Pendelshape had said it would. The readout on the console flashed:

`Synchronization initiated.`

Another message immediately flashed:

`Would you like preset space-time fix? Yes/No?`

"Come on . . . come on . . . " Jack, drenched in sweat, stared at the device. He stabbed a Y on the keypad. There was a pause.

`Thank you. Synchronization complete.`

The readout changed again:

`Board Taurus within thirty seconds.`

And then a final message popped up:

`Enjoy your time-travel experience.`

"This is not for real. . . ." Some propeller-head programmer had a warped sense of humor. He grabbed the time phone and then his bag and, shaking with fear, mounted the ladder onto the steel platform in the heart of the Taurus. From his new position, he looked out between the black girders, through the green blast screen into the library, where he could see Pendelshape still pinned to the bookcase and Angus bent over on the sofa. Seeing Angus there, helpless, Jack felt a stab of guilt—but what could he do? The Rector, Tony, and Gordon were fighting with a control panel to find some way to lower the blast screen. He suddenly spotted a small display that hung just outside the Taurus structure. His heart missed a beat when he realized what was happening. Taurus was counting down.

```
Preparing for transfer . . .
Transfer initiating
10 . . . 9 . . . 8 . . .
```

Suddenly the glass blast screen started to lower. Belstaff, no longer pinned to the ceiling, tumbled to the floor. He didn't move. Jack stared numbly at the body of his teacher and felt bile rise in his throat again as a terrifying thought suddenly occurred to him—Belstaff might be dead.

Jack saw Johnstone look down at his injured colleague and then up at him inside the Taurus. When he saw Johnstone's eyes, Jack knew that boarding the Taurus had been the right decision. All of those men had only had one thing on their mind as they rushed forward toward him.

```
3 . . . 2 . . . 1 . . .
```

Dreadnought

Jack looked down at the time phone in his hand. The readout had changed.

```
Date:       Saturday, June 20, 1914
Time:       7:00 a.m.
Location:   Portsmouth, England
```

The readout glinted back at him. Portsmouth? He was in Portsmouth? On England's south coast? He looked around. The Taurus and library had vanished; the people in the control room—also gone. He had escaped. But had he really moved? And had he moved in time?

He was standing in the open on a flat, concrete surface. There was a damp mist all around, but he could hear muffled voices. He was facing a giant wall—only about six feet away—extending upward and sideways as far as he could see, although the mist limited his view. It looked like he was on the outside of a large building, maybe a warehouse. The building was not made of bricks, but had a dark gray, smooth surface. He took a step forward to touch it, hoping to find an opening—and in so doing he nearly plummeted to his death. He jumped back, as if he had just touched an electric fence.

Fifteen feet below, there was a channel of icy, black water lapping between the side of the wall that he had tried to touch and the platform on which he stood. He'd nearly plunged straight into it. He craned his neck up again. The mist peeled slowly back from the wall and way above his head, to his left, he could make out some letters as they emerged from the mist:

T—H—G—U—O—N—D—A—E—R—D

What does that mean? The direction of the clearing mist had revealed the letters to him from right to left. But in the right order they spelled *DREADNOUGHT*. The wall he was looking at was made of steel. Jack was not staring at a warehouse, but a ship, and it was no ordinary ship. He could only see part of the stern, but even by the proportion of this, the ship was a monster. In fact, Jack realized, this was *the* ship—the one that Pendelshape had said revolutionized naval warfare. It had given Britain superiority at sea. *Dreadnought*. It was all the evidence Jack needed to prove he had indeed been transported through time.

He moved cautiously back from the ship. Nearby was a series of large pallets. Some were stacked with crates, others with large sacks. On one pallet was a gap between two large piles of sacks, and seeking temporary refuge, Jack managed to squeeze himself between them. He tried to control a growing sense of panic. Once again, he took out his inhaler, pressed the button, and inhaled deeply. The tightness in his lungs relaxed. He crouched down. A hundred and one questions flew through his head. What on earth had he witnessed back at the library? Why had the Rector been so angry? What had they done to Angus?

Having no answers, he tried to focus on an activity to distract himself. He checked what he had with him. First of all—the time phone. He still had it. So, in theory, he could go back . . . but to what? To a bunch of thugs who wanted to beat him up . . . or worse? He flipped the phone open, just as Pendelshape had shown him. The bright yellow bar was flickering and starting to gray out. He racked his brains. What was it that Pendelshape had said? They could only use it when the bar was yellow.

But he had been more specific than that, hadn't he?

You can only use it when you have a signal and when the host Taurus is in the right energy state. . . . When it turns yellow, you can exchange signals with the Taurus. . . . It means the Taurus knows where you are . . . and it means you can time travel.

That was it. Now the bar was completely gray, which meant that even if he wanted to get back, or communicate with someone, he couldn't. He would have to wait. But it also meant, Jack suddenly realized, that if he started to move away from here, where the Taurus had deposited him, he could not be tracked until the signal was restored. The Rector, and his henchmen, would only know his landing point from the Taurus's space-time fix, as Pendelshape had called it. If he moved away from this spot while the signal was off, it would be more difficult for them to follow him.

He also still had his backpack, for a start. He exchanged his blazer for his fleece jacket. It was warmer—and probably less conspicuous. Then there was the usual junk—tattered notebooks, candy wrappers, and a couple of textbooks. He could ditch those. Then he noticed that he still had the history book—the present from his father. The irony was not lost on him, and he briefly flipped through its pages. *Could be useful,* he thought, and stuffed it back into his backpack. As he did so, something else tumbled out. It was the lance head. He'd forgotten all about it, though this was what had gotten them talking to Pendelshape in the first place. He picked it up and checked the rest of his backpack. In a side pocket he discovered some crumbly remains of Mom's chocolate cake wrapped in plastic. He felt a lump forming in his throat.

Suddenly, the wooden pallet beneath his feet groaned. It was moving. Jack found himself rocking gently from side to side and had to steady himself with both hands. With horror, Jack realized what was happening. The pallet and its heavy load, including Jack, were being hoisted into the air. He looked up. He could make out some cables and the hook of a large crane. Then the crane stopped and he could feel the whole structure swaying gently. From his vantage point, Jack saw that both the ship and the wharf were throbbing with activity. Without warning, everything started to move again— sideways this time. *Dreadnought* was taking supplies on board—and the mighty battleship had an uninvited guest: Jack was about to be lowered into the hold.

Jack peered helplessly from his hiding place, scanning the edge of the ship and the wharf for some means of escape. Just as the massive crane started to lower its load into the ship, Jack spotted two figures not ten yards away. The Taurus must have somehow delivered a final spasm of energy after transferring Jack and before losing the signal completely. They were after him already: Tony and Gordon.

Jack had been lying in the dark hold for what seemed like ages. He tried to make himself comfortable. He was well hidden, and one thing was for sure: he wasn't going outside again, right into the hands of Tony and Gordon. After a little while, he detected a slight vibration as the ship's steam turbine engines gently pushed *Dreadnought* away from the wharf.

They were going to sea.

Jack tried to think logically through the events of the last few hours. Most worrying were Tony and Gordon. They must have been sent to get him. They must have their own time phones—also synched with the Taurus. He wondered if he had made a clean getaway—or whether they had guessed he had boarded the ship and had followed him aboard to hunt him down like a rat in a steel maze.

Jack thought back to the strange conversation that he and Angus had had with Pendelshape before the Rector had stormed in. Pendelshape had been about to tell them something. Something important—about the Benefactor—and this was linked to the strange e-mail they had discovered. He tried to remember what the message had said. It had been from the Benefactor, who had been replying to Pendelshape. So the two of them had been in contact— perhaps for some time. What had the e-mail said again? Jack racked his brains.

Do not concern yourself with the Cairnfield workshop. . . .

So the Benefactor knew about his father's workshop at Cairnfield. And he had also written, *Our own Taurus is complete! Yes! A functioning, full-scale system.*

But . . . could that mean the Benefactor had somehow developed another time machine? Maybe there were two Tauruses? The one at the school and a separate one—belonging to the Benefactor. That would be incredible. But already Jack felt he had seen enough incredible things to last several lifetimes. It would have been strictly against the rules of VIGIL that Pendelshape had talked about. But on the other hand,

the Benefactor was a key member of the original Taurus team. . . .
So perhaps he had the brains to pull it off. It sounded like Pendelshape
must have known about it . . . known what the Benefactor was up to.
Maybe that's why the Rector was so angry with Pendelshape.

Jack tried to remember what else the e-mail had said:

*I fear that when they find out, they may take Orion. . . . We must
protect Orion.*

Who was Orion? And the e-mail had mentioned someone else
too—a "she"—"Lynx." A man and a woman who could not be
named. More mystery.

Then, just before the Rector had stormed in on them, Pendelshape
had said that he had set the Taurus "so that we can travel back in time
to somewhere I know and where we will be safe, before being picked
up." So Pendelshape was concerned about something. Concerned
enough to have already planned to use the Taurus—against VIGIL
rules—to carry out some sort of escape. He must have set it to send
them to the Portsmouth naval shipyards—where Jack had been
transported. Maybe that made sense. Pendelshape knew all about
1914—he had proved from the photo taken in Belgrade that he had
traveled back to this time before. So he would be in familiar territory.

But Jack was still no closer to understanding why any of this had
happened. Why was the Rector angry with Pendelshape? Why had
Pendelshape wanted them to escape to 1914, and why did Orion need
to be protected? Somehow, Jack and Angus, whether they liked it or
not, had become embroiled in something big—and something they
did not understand. Now Jack was alone and he was scared. It wasn't
like being on the back of Angus's bike—then you knew it would be
over quickly, one way or another. This was different. The fear Jack felt
was an all-enveloping fear that seemed to suck away at him from
the inside.

But Jack had always been good at thinking things through,
at solving problems. And he knew that part of the trick was to try not
to let emotion get to you. But he simply did not have enough
information yet to solve the confusing list of questions, so he would
put them to one side until he did. But there was one question he did

need to answer: What was he going to do now? He fumbled around for the time phone, flipped it open, and read its telltale message:

Date: Saturday, June 20, 1914
Time: 11:00 a.m.
Location: English Channel

He remembered now that Pendelshape had also said that the phone had its own energy source, so it would continue to indicate where and when he was. The screen had a kind of GPS with a map. Jack noticed that both the time and location had changed since his last reading. It confirmed they were sailing up the channel. At least he would know where he was. That might be handy. The yellow bar was still grayed out. Until it went on again, there was nothing he could do, and the Taurus and the people who controlled it—the Rector for one—would not be able to locate him. So he should be safe. In fact, he thought ruefully, perhaps the best thing to do would be just to waltz out and . . . give himself up. Say he had gotten lost or something. . . . And then the crew would have to look after him until they could drop him at a port. It was a risk, but if Tony and Gordon had managed to spot him and then follow him aboard *Dreadnought,* he knew he would be a lot safer in the hands of the Royal Navy. Wasn't that their job, anyway? To protect people?

Suddenly, the door of the hold banged open and light streamed in. Jack crouched down as far as he could, but it was in vain. A moment later a large pink face loomed down at him.

"Sir—you ain't going to believe this. . . . "

"What is it now?" A gruff voice answered. The first face was joined by a second, equally surprised.

"I've seen it all now. A stowaway!"

"What's your name, son? How did you get in there?"

Jack stared back at the two faces and calculated that politeness was the best policy.

"Sorry, sir. I mean, I was with the loading gang, er, kind of fell asleep. . . . "

The two men looked at each other and then guffawed loudly.

"Someone's going to pay for this! Come out of there, for a start. What did you say your name was?"

"Jack Christie."

"Well, Christie, we will have to report you; it's lucky for you that we're just on exercises. Better get you tidied up. And then I'm sure we can make use of you." Jack thought the man looked like a cook. He laughed again, nodding at the sacks around him. "There's this to sort out for a start."

And with that, Jack was marched from the hold and soon found himself seated at a small table outside the galley.

"You stay there." The cook went off, but the sailor with the pink face looked at him sympathetically. "Don't worry, lad. Navy has a fine tradition of young men at sea. Nelson himself. We'll get a signal home to let them know you're safe. You look famished. Tell you what—one of the boys will get you something. . . . "

The sailor hurried off but reappeared a few minutes later with a large plate of stew and potatoes.

After a while the cook reappeared.

"Your lucky day, my lad! Seems that you have an audience in the chart house. Captain wants to know your story, exactly. Security breach and all that. Jones will take you up. And then"—he pointed back up the corridor—"we'll get you to work."

The sailor led Jack through a maze of metal corridors and up and down a series of ladders.

"We'll take a shortcut through the admiral's lobby," he said.

As they moved on, Jack saw two figures ascending a ladder ahead of them. They were dressed in sailor's garb but had packs on their backs. Jack's worst fears had come true—Tony and Gordon had followed him aboard *Dreadnought*.

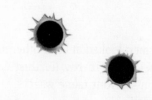

Cannon Fodder

We've been asked by the bridge to take him from here," Tony said with authority to the young sailor.

Jack turned to run, but in an instant Gordon had his arm in a viselike grip. "Not so fast, Master Christie. You need to come with us."

The sailor looked bemused but shrugged and wheeled around, leaving Jack alone to his fate.

Jack smelled Tony's stale breath as he whispered sneeringly into his ear, "Any noise, any tricks, and you are dead meat. You've caused us a lot of trouble."

Gordon parroted, "A lot of trouble . . . "

"Right, then," Tony said. "We are hoping to have a Taurus signal in the next few hours. But you never can tell. In the meantime, we've got to find somewhere to hide on this floating dung crate until we can return to civilization."

"Somewhere we won't draw any attention," Gordon added.

"That's right, Mr. MacFarlane: attention is bad. Tell the boy why attention is bad, Mr. MacFarlane," Tony said.

Gordon looked at Jack sardonically. "Attention is bad because it can lead to interaction with the 'istorical environment."

"And why is interaction bad, Mr. MacFarlane?" Tony asked.

"Because, Mr. Smith, interaction can cause stuff to happen."

"That's right, Mr. MacFarlane. What stuff might that be?"

"Consequences, Mr. Smith, in the space-time continuum."

"Continuum, Christie. Do you hear that?"

"You don't want to mess around with the continuum," Gordon said.

"Or, to be more precise, a small change now might have significant repercussions for the future," Tony added. "And that's where we come in. . . . We're here to help VIGIL sort out problems—like this one. Sort of tidy up any unfortunate mess."

"Time traveling janitors if you like . . . " Gordon gave a little shrug.

Tony gave his colleague a sidelong glance, not sure whether he approved of this particular description of their role.

He turned to Jack. "Do you understand, my friend?"

Jack didn't. He was very scared. "But . . . I . . . "

Tony interrupted him. "So, to be sure we have no more interaction than we possibly need, we are going to ask you to help us. Mr. MacFarlane?"

Gordon let go of Jack and unzipped his backpack. Jack could see that it was stuffed with all sorts of equipment . . . not least the carefully packed APR. Gordon opened a small plastic case. It contained an array of medical equipment, and Gordon removed a rather large syringe together with a small bottle of fluid. Carefully, he placed the needle into the top of the bottle and sucked up a small quantity of the liquid.

Jack suddenly realized what they were going to do.

"Sleepy time . . . " Tony said mockingly.

Jack tried to struggle free.

"Now, now. . . . Let's all behave, shall we? Mr. Smith—may I ask you to restrain the young man while I attend to the business at hand?"

Gordon momentarily relaxed his grip, expecting Tony to take hold of Jack so that the injection could be administered.

Jack had his chance. Without thinking, he lashed out with his forearm. It was more out of self-defense than intent to harm, but his arm cracked straight into the bridge of Gordon's nose. At first, Gordon was surprised rather than hurt. But then he wobbled—like a large building just after the demolition charge has gone off. To steady himself, he instinctively reached out with his hand. But he only managed to grab a handful of Jack's hair. It was not sufficient to prevent Gordon from losing his balance, and with one hand still clutching a shock of Jack's hair, he tumbled to the ground, taking Jack with him.

Day of the Assassins

Jack was breathing hard, and he knew that with his weak lungs he might not last long. Out of the corner of his eye, he saw Tony leering down at them, a look of mild amusement on his face as Gordon struggled to get Jack under control.

Jack pawed his pocket instinctively for his inhaler. His fingers scrabbled desperately as Gordon twisted him this way and that, looking for a way to insert the syringe. But then Jack's fingers encircled something else in his pocket—the lance head! In one movement, Jack pulled it from his pocket. It flashed briefly in the dull light as it cut through the air and into the black leather of Gordon's boot. Gordon screamed with pain and clutched his ankle with both hands as blood spurted from his boot. Jack picked up the syringe that Gordon had dropped. Tony's look of amusement had turned to alarm. He moved forward, but Jack was too quick—he stabbed the syringe into Tony's thigh and pressed home the plunger. Tony fell to one knee, groping his leg. Then he reeled backward, his eyes flickering as he tried to fight the anesthetic.

Jack stood up shakily, wheezing and coughing in equal measure. He felt a brief moment of triumph as he surveyed his two assailants groaning on the floor. . . . Then he ran. The door from the admiral's lobby exited straight onto the starboard upper deck, just below the forecastle. He had to find help, or at least a hiding place—but where? He looked around and spotted the squat gray steel outline of a turret positioned a third of the way down the ship's starboard side. Its giant twin fifty-eight-ton gun barrels loomed only a couple of feet above his head. Between where the twin gun barrels protruded from the turret was a short ladder that led onto the turret roof for access to the two smaller twelve-pounder guns. Without thinking, Jack clambered up the ladder.

Then Jack did something that he would later reflect on as both inspired and completely crazy. He lowered himself gently from the lip of the turret roof onto the left-side gun barrel. The gun seemed to stretch endlessly toward the bow. He started to shimmy his way along the top of the gun toward its tapering end.

In a minute he was there. He looked down over the end of the barrel. It angled slightly upward, and he could even make out the rifling in the aperture. A few feet below, the starboard deck yawed as the ship moved through the water. Jack turned around on the gun so that his back was facing away from the turret and toward the bow. Balancing dangerously, he inserted first one foot and then the other into the barrel and pushed his body carefully into the end of the gun. It was a tight squeeze, but he was small for his age and he just made it. As long as he kept his blond head down, nobody would ever know he was there.

But he did not have much time to enjoy his new hiding place. Suddenly he felt a slight vibrating sensation around him, coupled with a low, grinding sound. Imperceptibly at first, the giant gun barrel in which he was encased slowly started to move. The massive gun swung from its position parallel with the starboard deck out to point out toward the sea. As it moved laterally, it also rose upward into the air. Below, in the gun turret itself, Jack began to hear muffled voices and the commotion of men preparing . . . for what? Jack, whose head had been flush with the end of the barrel, pushed himself up a couple of inches and sneaked a look. He was shocked at what he saw. His gun was now pointing well out over the starboard side of the ship. All he could see was the gray water of the sea churning to white thirty feet below as *Dreadnought* drove through it at a mind-spinning twenty knots.

Emerging from a light mist on the distant horizon, he spotted first one, then two, and then three ghostly shapes. They didn't look to be ships—they seemed to be stationary, although it was difficult to tell. He remembered what the sailor had said: *Exercises.* Were they on some naval drill? The gun rose a little farther into the air, and he realized with sickening fear that *Dreadnought* was about to open fire.

For some reason, Jack remembered very specifically what Pendelshape had explained about the awesome firepower of the *Dreadnought*. The shell from the twelve-inch naval gun weighed about eight hundred and fifty pounds—combined steel and explosive. When the gun was fired, the shell would leave the muzzle at about eighteen hundred miles an hour. In a few seconds, Jack would too.

Day of the Assassins

The angle of the gun was nearing maximum elevation. Before he could take any further action, Jack started to lose his grip. Slowly at first, he began to slip down the inside of the dark barrel. The sixty rifling grooves etched on the inside of the gun, designed to spin the shell to achieve greater stability in flight, started to act on him—in reverse. His whole body twisted around and around inside the barrel like he was on some crazy ride at the fair. The circle of daylight from the end of the gun rapidly contracted—it was like looking out from the rear of a train after it had entered a tunnel. Then, almost as soon as the uncomfortable ride had started, with a rather painful *bang*, he came to rest. There was a mechanical whirring sound and suddenly, as the breech of the massive gun was opened, he tumbled out, landing inside the turret.

The operators stood like statues, their faces blank with amazement. Unhurt, Jack clambered up from the breech loader and, not knowing what on earth else to say, announced, "Clean—ready for use—carry on," marched purposefully to the side entrance of the turret, and left.

There was no sign of Tony and Gordon. Jack suspected that Tony was sleeping like a baby, given the anesthetic that he had pumped into him. Presumably Gordon was playing nursemaid, as well as tending his own wound. Regardless, he needed to try to put as much distance as possible between himself and any potential pursuit, then find somewhere more sensible to hide . . . and think. He sneaked toward the stern and the port side of the ship. Tethered to the port side was a vast observation balloon. As he got closer, Jack realized that it did not look like the observation balloons he had seen in books. The kite balloons they had used on the Western Front for artillery spotting had a ventral fin underneath and lateral fins for stability. This one looked like a more modern design—it even had its own gas burner. Jack could make out the large passenger basket, which was just touching the aft deck area on a small raised platform, ready for flight. A single cable was holding the balloon precariously to the ship, and four crew members manhandled long hooked poles to control the basket, which wobbled in the wind. Jack could make out a man's head peeking over the side of the basket. He was agitated, rushing from one side of the basket to the other, shouting orders at the crew on the deck.

Jack crept slowly toward the platform. He turned to look back up toward the bow of the ship. Still no sign of any pursuit. What should he do? As he considered his options, he spotted a strange red dot on his white sneaker. At first he thought it might be some blood from Gordon's wound, and he leaned down to wipe it off. Then he noticed it was moving around, even with his foot still. Suddenly it dawned on him what it was. He glanced back along the side of the ship. Poking surreptitiously from a porthole was a stubby black barrel attached to what looked like a large zoom lens. Clearly someone was using the unique characteristics of the Corner Shot APR, and he had Jack nicely in the crosshairs of its laser sight. Jack wasn't going to hang around to find out what would happen next.

He raced toward the balloon crew, who was still struggling to control the huge gas bag that rocked back and forth in *Dreadnought*'s draft. Jack heard a muffled *crack*. With a hop, skip, and jump, Jack leaped from the deck of *Dreadnought* and grabbed the rope ladder attached to the side of the balloon basket. He knew he couldn't hold on for long. The basket was swirling dizzily just off the deck, and it felt even more unsteady than it appeared. Over the side of the balloon basket, a man's head appeared. He stared down at Jack with a mixture of amusement and confusion. He was wearing a strange leather skullcap from which wispy strands of yellow hair escaped and blew around in the breeze. He was also wearing aviator goggles over small round spectacles. He looked ridiculous.

Suddenly, there was a second loud *crack*. The basket, with the rope ladder attached, shot upward. Jack could only just hang on. A bullet had split the mooring cable, and the balloon had broken free. One of the crew still had his tether pole hooked to the basket, and as he clung to it, he was lifted right off the deck of *Dreadnought* and carried out over the sea. He held on for a few seconds, then let go and plunged into the churning wake below. His head bobbed up a few seconds later—but he was already way behind *Dreadnought's* stern. Jack screamed to the man just above him in the basket. "Please . . . help!"

The man stretched down, leaning out dangerously as he did so, but Jack was still too far down on the rope ladder. Paralyzed by fear, he was unable to move farther up the rope ladder, so he wrapped his limbs around its rungs as the balloon powered upward.

"One step at a time, young man!" the man shouted. "Don't look down!"

Only with a supreme effort was Jack able to cage his fear sufficiently to take a single unsteady step from one rung to the next, then unclench one hand and slide it up to the rung above.

"Very good!" the man shouted encouragingly. "You can do it!"

Jack gritted his teeth and repeated the maneuver. Finally, the man was in reach and able to grab the shoulder straps of Jack's backpack.

"One more step, my friend!" he called.

Jack swallowed hard and pushed up once more. Using this momentum, the man leaned down precariously and, placing a hand under each armpit, gave Jack an almighty heave that landed him on the floor of the basket.

"Well done, my friend!" the man said, giving him a hearty slap on the back.

Jack stood up but had to quickly grab the side of the basket as it swayed in the air. He peered down nervously. He couldn't believe how far up they had already traveled. Maybe sixty yards, and the wind had already taken them way aft of *Dreadnought*—which now looked like a toy ship. He could make out the specks of the crew and all the features of the ship—the guns still pointing starboard—and the wide, white wake. The unfortunate seaman who had fallen from his tether pole was bobbing around in the water like a champagne cork. He had been tossed a life vest—but would have a job to swim to it.

Jack slumped back down onto the floor of the basket and, panting, reached into his pocket for his inhaler. He glanced up at the man standing over him. He wore a full-length, weather-beaten, brown leather coat with a high collar. His neck was wrapped in a bright red scarf. The leather skullcap was placed on his head at a slight angle.

He pushed his aviator goggles onto his forehead and peered curiously at Jack with piercing blue eyes, as if examining some sort of botanical specimen.

Then he smiled warmly, thrust out his hand, and in a surprisingly high, somewhat accented voice, said, "Professor August Pinckard-Schnell. Delighted to meet you."

The Professor

Jack said the first thing that came into his head.

"Are we going to die?"

"Well, we may die or we may not. But one thing is for sure, there is nothing that either of us can do about it." The professor paused. "So we might as well enjoy the ride."

"Great," Jack said sarcastically.

"I wouldn't worry. We will soon be over land, and hopefully we will be able to come down safely. Of course, if I am wrong, we may plummet like stones and our bodies will disintegrate as we hit the earth at terminal velocity. Our guts will be spread around Germany or Holland like cow manure." He paused again, thinking. "Or alternatively, we may hit woodland, in which case, assuming a good wind, we will be ripped from the basket and dismembered limb from limb as we crash through the canopy. . . . " He shrugged. "Or maybe we will hit a town and be slammed into the side of a tall church just as a family wedding is taking place below. Or—"

"Stop!" Jack pleaded.

The professor paused, apparently still contemplating the limitless scenarios by which they might meet their demise. "Indeed, that is what makes it so very interesting, all these possibilities."

"Fantastic . . . "

He stared back at Jack for a moment and then guffawed loudly. It was a high-pitched, intermittent wheezing—quite unlike any laugh Jack had heard before.

"Very good. Very good. I never tire of the English sense of humor. Most excellent . . . " But his voice trailed off self-consciously as he realized that, judging from Jack's pale face and trembling hands, he did not share his own nonchalance about their predicament.

"I apologize, my friend. One forgets that it can be quite frightening the first time. . . . But I assure you: we are reasonably safe. I speak from experience. Please . . . allow me to show you." And with that the professor confidently stepped over to Jack's corner of the basket and placed his hand sympathetically on Jack's arm.

"It takes a little bit of getting used to, and it's no good if you are afraid of heights. But tell me, where on earth would you get a view like that . . . ?"

The professor opened both arms, preacher like, out into the sky. Jack rose gingerly to his feet and, gripping the side of the basket tightly, reluctantly peered into the void.

"Look. We are over the North Sea and there ahead is the Dutch coast."

The view was breathtaking. Below, the English Channel merged into the broad blue-gray of a calm North Sea twinkling in the strong afternoon sun. There was no roar in his ears—they were traveling with the wind. In fact, it was very peaceful.

The professor smiled at the look of wonder on Jack's face.

"Beautiful, don't you think?"

"Bit scary."

The professor grinned broadly and slapped him on the back. "Well, let's see if we can't find something to make you feel better."

He moved over to his bags. He seemed very well equipped and soon had Jack wrapped up in a thick woolen blanket in one corner of the basket. Next he produced a large flask of steaming coffee and then some hard, bitter chocolate that crumbled dryly in Jack's mouth.

"Main course later . . . we might need to ration ourselves a little." The professor's English was perfect, but he had a strong accent. Jack began to warm up, and he felt a little more confident.

"Are you English?" he asked.

The professor looked back at him from his own corner of the basket as he cupped a tin mug brimming with coffee. He pretended to be offended. "Certainly not. I'm German. Well, by nationality anyway. I'm a scientist. Or more an inventor, really."

"How does a German get to be aboard a British battleship? Particularly when war is about to break out."

The professor looked puzzled. "War? I don't think so." He frowned. "The European powers certainly have their differences, but war— I doubt it. . . . Our diplomacy is too good. Many crises have been averted over the last few years—Agadir, the Balkans. Surely nobody wants war—certainly not between Germany and England."

"Even so, how does a German get to be aboard a British battleship?"

The professor shrugged. "As I said, I'm a scientist. This"—he gestured proudly to the huge balloon above their heads—"is my invention. The navy is interested in using it for spotting at sea. We were about to conduct a test, but something went wrong with the winding gear."

"You can say that again."

"It's very exciting."

"What is?"

"Well . . . obviously the navy is paying me for my new design, but I had planned that, once perfected, I might use the balloon to set a world record. Your navy and I are helping each other, if you like."

This was getting better and better, Jack thought. "A world record for what?"

"Distance traveled by air—of course."

Jack's heart sank. "Oh no. And now you think you might have a chance."

"I admit not quite in the circumstances I expected. . . . " The professor peered out over the basket. "But, I must say, the conditions look most favorable."

"Why would the British employ a German scientist on one of their most important battleships?"

"Well, of course *Dreadnought* is not as state of the art as she once was . . . and I have helped the navy out on various bits and pieces. Anyway, they know my politics."

"Politics?"

"I have none. Well . . . I'm a pacifist. Don't approve of politics." He shrugged. "But if you need your research funded or your balloon tested, there are limited options." He gave another apologetic shrug, and there was a pause before he looked across at Jack curiously. "Well, I have given you my story," he said. "Perhaps you should tell me how you come to be here." Jack started to feel nervous as the professor's eyes drilled into him. "You seem maybe a bit young to be a regular sailor in the king's navy. And the escapade back down there might suggest that you are maybe, shall we say . . . in trouble?"

Jack said the first thing that came into his head.

"Oh, that's easy. I'm Jack Christie. I'm a time traveler from the future—and I'm being chased by time police who want to kill me."

For a moment there was silence as the balloon cut through the sky. Then the professor shook as he let out a second wheezy, high-pitched laugh. "Excellent, excellent!" he cried. "Jack Christie—you and I are going to get along very well. Very well indeed. . . . " He then scrabbled inside his bags again, chortling to himself, long after Jack's remark ceased to be remotely funny.

"More chocolate?"

Professor August Pinckard-Schnell might be as mad as a March hare—but at least he was making Jack feel better.

"Thanks, Professor."

Shortly the professor became distracted. He rose once more from his position, sniffed the air, and then moved around the basket from one corner to the next. "Now, we need to make sure we prepare ourselves properly. . . . It is all about optimizing our chances." He checked the burner, which had not yet been used, and ensured that all the gas cylinders were properly secured. He looked toward the gas bag above, which completely overshadowed them, inspecting it carefully. He glanced several times at the afternoon sun, narrowing his eyes, and then scribbled in a battered notebook. This went on for a full ten minutes while Jack hunkered down in his corner of the basket.

When the professor finished, he announced, "We seem to be maintaining our height. Still going east, or more southeast, really. Fast, we are traveling fast. Maybe fifty miles an hour. Although it does not feel that fast." He pondered what all this might mean. "If we keep going at this rate, well"—he grinned—"a world record! Easily. A world record for manned flight!"

"I'm very happy for you."

"We should maybe try to increase our height a little. What do you say, Jack? Would you like to try the burner?"

Jack was not quite sure what he meant, but then the professor pointed at the large metal burner in the middle of the basket.

"It's easy, quite safe," the professor said. "You just do this." He pulled a lever, and there was an ear-splitting whoosh as a large flame licked up toward the aperture underneath the balloon, way above their heads. The professor smiled reassuringly and gestured for Jack to try. Jack put his hand on the lever and repeated the procedure. Again there was a roar as the flame from the burner shot skyward. He jumped back and watched as the flame receded, soon replaced by the silent sky as they sailed on. Reassured that the procedure had not resulted in the balloon going up in a ball of flames, Jack gained a little more confidence and took a second opportunity to inspect the breathtaking view from their vantage point. Soon his remaining fear melted away—replaced by a surging exhilaration. The air was like crystal, and you could see for miles in every direction.

"Funny," Jack remarked. "No vapor trails."

The professor looked at him oddly. "No *what*?"

"You know, vapor trails. I was just thinking, Professor, it's funny that you can't see any vapor trails from all the jets. There're usually lots"—Jack suddenly realized what he had said, and his voice trailed off self-consciously—"even where I live. . . . "

The professor looked puzzled. "*Jet, vapor trail*—these are English expressions I have not heard before."

Jack grimaced. "Sorry, Professor. Doesn't matter—it's just where I come from . . . we have some funny words for stuff. There's a bunch more I probably need to teach you as well, like *Google, iPod,* and *global warming.* That kind of thing." He shrugged. "But you won't need to worry about any of them."

The professor frowned. "I see. Oh well, you must, er, tell me what they mean . . . sometime." He put his notebook back in his bag and began to busy himself with retrieving some more provisions. Soon he had laid out quite a feast. Sausages were produced, along with bread and some cheese.

As they ate, the professor probed again.

"So, come, Jack—the truth now. What were you really doing aboard the ship? Had you stowed away? Trouble with your family—at home? Maybe I can help."

Jack considered his options. It was going to be difficult to hide the truth. His earlier blunder about there being no jets in the sky could easily be repeated, and more important, he knew he was still in danger—he had escaped Tony and Gordon once, but with all the technology they seemed to have at their disposal, they could definitely turn up again. Maybe the bizarre Professor August Pinckard-Schnell was right and he could help in some way. He seemed kind, if eccentric. Honesty, however unbelievable, was probably the best policy. He glanced at the professor, toying with a piece of cheese, took a deep breath, and launched into the incredible events of the last few hours. As he did so, the professor studied him with a look of amused skepticism.

After Jack had finished speaking, the professor put his hand over his mouth to hide a doubting smile. "Well, it's an impressive story, Jack, but I'm not sure it is quite believable." He clearly thought that this strange boy he had inadvertently rescued either had an overactive imagination or had escaped from the local lunatic asylum. To be fair, Jack could see his point.

Then he had an idea. He felt inside his jacket pocket. It was still there: the history book. In triumph, he tossed it over to the professor, and it landed at his crossed feet on the other side of the basket. It blew open, and the crisp white pages ruffled provocatively in the breeze.

"Well—if you don't believe me—take a look at that."

The professor took the tome gingerly in his hands and leafed slowly through the pages. As he did so, the expression on his face changed.

Jack looked at him smugly. "It might be difficult for me to make all that up. Published in the year 2006, for a start . . . a few years from now, I think you'll find. It would be hard for me to create the detail in there—the whole history of the war . . . all the horror . . . the pictures . . . "

The professor's amused skepticism had evaporated, and after a while, he raised his head and looked at Jack with ashen-faced incredulity. He tried to say something, making a couple of false starts in the process. "But . . . how did . . . ?" and finally he muttered, "So this war of yours, this Great War, it really happens?"

"Oh yes, Professor, it happens all right."

"It's incredible. It cannot be true."

"Incredible. And true. Either that, or I've fallen asleep in Pendelshape's class and it's a complete nightmare."

The professor was concentrating intensely, his brow deeply furrowed as he thumbed the book with increasing fervor. He began to speak to himself in a rapid-fire stream. "Well, I suppose, the new physics; of course I am familiar with this. Einstein, Planck—relativity, quantum mechanics. The new physics has incredible conceptual leaps. Few understand it, and probably none can comprehend the implications. But nothing like this, surely . . . surely not . . . "

The professor shook his head in awe as the enormity of it all started to sink in.

"The consequences of this are . . . profound. And this war—you say it kills how many?"

"I'm not sure. I think around eight million. Over sixty million are mobilized." Jack reached over and located a table at the back of the book that he remembered seeing. He showed it to the professor—statistics of the dead by country. The professor gaped at the numbers.

"In fact, I believe your own country, Germany, suffers greatly. Nearly two million dead. And Germany loses the war *and* takes the blame for starting it."

A shadow crossed the professor's face.

Jack shrugged. "But if it's any comfort, my history teacher says that people are still arguing about the causes of the war." He continued gloomily. "But that's not all. That book tells you all about the war . . .

but what I haven't told you is that this war leads to another, even more horrific war. The Second World War, twenty years later."

The professor shook his head. "Sorry, Jack . . . this . . . book, your . . . story. It is so incredible. I find it hard to believe."

Jack fished around in his pocket again. He'd started now, so he might as well go whole hog. He produced the time phone and presented it to the professor.

"Here. The time phone I told you about. It links to the Taurus, which sends people backward and forward through time—when it decides to work, that is. It's a bit tricky. Look . . . " He flipped open the device and showed the professor the mysterious blue light, screen, GPS, and buttons. "You're a scientist, Professor, but I bet you've never seen technology like this."

The professor studied the time phone with a look of wonder. Jack imagined that he must have had the same expression on his face upon first hearing Pendelshape's revelations back at the Taurus control room.

All the professor could say was "Incredible . . . incredible . . . " He repeated the words to himself, trancelike, over and over again— as if it were the mantra of a Tibetan monk.

As they stared into the time phone, Jack noticed that the gray bar on the screen was starting to flicker. Gradually the gray was replaced by a yellow light, which was soon burning brightly. Jack's heart leaped.

"A signal! Professor! We have a signal!"

He grabbed the phone. Suddenly a message appeared on the display.

"Someone's communicating with us!"

Jack could scarcely contain his excitement.

"Look! Look!"

You have one message from Taurus:

Jack—you are in great danger. Your trip through time threatens us all. You must give yourself up to VIGIL's agents—Tony Smith and

Gordon MacFarlane—as soon as possible. They are trying to locate you and bring you back. I love you. —Mom

Jack was flabbergasted. *Mom? A message from Mom . . . on the time phone?* He couldn't understand it. How could his mom possibly be involved?

"What does it mean?" the professor asked.

"I don't get it. The yellow light is on. . . . That means we are now being tracked, and that's why we can receive messages from the Taurus. I also think it means that we could travel back to the Taurus."

"Astonishing. But this message, it's from your mother?"

Jack grimaced. It wasn't making any sense. "Yes . . . it seems so. Or maybe Tony and Gordon or the Rector are playing a trick."

"Maybe she is with them," the professor added.

Jack was dumbfounded. "It can't be . . . can't."

He tried to think back through the recent course of events. How was Mom involved in all of this? And why hadn't she told him? He felt a sudden twinge of anger—it was as if she was always keeping things from him.

He had an idea. "I know!" he said triumphantly. "I could send a message back! Pendelshape explained how to do that. I can ask them!"

He scrutinized the time phone once more, trying to recall how to create and send a message. But as he stared into the device, the bright yellow light flickered.

He groaned. "No! Please, not again! I think we're losing it. . . . "

The yellow light went dead; the gray bar took its place.

"Stupid thing!"

He shook the device in disgust and then sank back into the corner of the basket, dejected. The professor moved over to him and pulled the blanket over his shoulders. He gave Jack a reassuring pat on the back.

"Don't worry, my friend. I don't understand either . . . but I'm sure we can work it out."

Jack looked up at the professor and tried to squeeze out a smile. It wasn't easy.

After a while, he fell asleep—the nervous energy from a tumultuous day had finally taken its toll. In silence, in the opposite corner of the balloon, the professor studied Jack's history book. As he worked his way through the pages, his natural cheerfulness evaporated and his expression became grim. Occasionally he glanced across at Jack, shook his head, and murmured something to himself. Once or twice he stood and gave a blast on the burner and then gazed from the balloon as it moved steadily southward, pushed on by a relentless tailwind.

The sky was finally beginning to darken in the east as the early summer sun set. Way below, the European canvas spread out from the English Channel to the Russian steppes. Far away, the professor spotted an irregular, jagged outline on the horizon silhouetted against a faint, pink glow.

He mumbled something—half to himself, half to Jack, who slept soundly on in the opposite corner.

"The Alps."

Revelations

Wake up!" The professor shook him hard. Jack woke shivering. He raised his head above the woolen blanket and unfolded himself from his fetal position, curled in the corner of the balloon's basket. Every bone ached and the temperature had dropped dramatically overnight. He peered gingerly over the edge of the basket and was staggered by what he saw. Mountains. Everywhere. The balloon was scarcely clearing the peaks—vast rock outcrops, many snow tipped, interspersed with verdant pine-clad valleys. Wedged into the north-facing bowls, snowfields and glaciers still stubbornly resisted the early summer warmth.

The professor seemed to be very excited.

"The Alps! Mountains! Isn't it beautiful? Austria. Incredible!"

"Are we going to land?"

"No doubt about it . . . out of gas. . . . We're going down. Fast! We may even crash. Isn't it marvelous!"

Jack wasn't so sure. Wasn't there supposed to be some procedure for this kind of event?

"Don't we need to fasten seat belts, stop serving hot drinks . . . that sort of thing?"

The professor wasn't listening. He was now staring out from the basket, concentrating hard on the mountainous terrain. "I think you should wrap yourself up in the blankets . . . and hold on tight. We are descending quickly. Let's hope we get lucky . . . some of those peaks look, well, they look high."

"Why didn't you put us down safely before we ran out of gas?"

"What's that, my boy?" the professor shouted back over his shoulder.

"I said, why wait until now to land?"

"In the dark? Suicide! We reached the mountains faster than I anticipated. The wind speed was even greater than I expected. I have been looking for a safe spot since first light. No luck. We'll have to take our chances."

The professor had scarcely finished his sentence when there was a loud grating as the underside of the basket made contact with a craggy peak and scraped along it for a full twenty yards. Then the mountain dropped sharply away and they were again suspended half a mile above the floor of a green U-shaped valley.

The balloon swooped up the side of the next mountain as it caught a favorable updraft from the valley. It cleared the next ridge, but the basket suspended beneath was less fortunate. They hit a snow-covered arête hard and were both slammed face-first into the inside of the basket. The professor groaned, and blood started to stream from his nose. Then a great slab of snow fell onto them as the cornice on the opposite side of the arête collapsed onto the basket.

Breaking free from the cornice, they found themselves swinging high above the next valley. The weight of the snow in the basket forced the balloon to descend rapidly. With only their bare hands, Jack and the professor desperately shoveled snow from the balloon to reduce weight. Ahead, they could see that they were heading for a large glacier resting below the next ridge. They made contact—hard. The basket bounced once, and the snow exploded into a sparkling cloud of icy vapor. But their journey wasn't finished. The balloon continued to drag them across the rising plateau of the glacier. The basket was now lying on its side, and Jack and the professor were pressed into the wicker floor by the snow that was rapidly accumulating inside. They were helpless. But finally the angle of the glacier pitched upward and the balloon decelerated. The momentum of the balloon slowed, and they came to a gentle rest.

Jack was encased in snow. He couldn't believe the weight of the stuff—he could hardly move. It was in his ears, his eyes, his mouth. He pressed his legs into the bottom of the basket and with a momentous heave managed to wrench himself free. He tumbled out onto the glacier and lay on his back, panting heavily. A moment later the professor managed to do the same, and they both lay—prostrate and exhausted—staring up at an azure Alpine sky. They looked back at the tangled mess of the balloon and the trail of detritus their landing had sprayed onto the pristine ice shelf. The professor managed to lift his head a little farther to inspect the damage.

"I hope the Royal Navy doesn't want its balloon back," he said, and promptly dropped his head back onto the snow. Jack was too bruised and drained to respond, but just for a second, he smiled.

Way above them on the same mountain, two men watched the spectacle of the balloon's crash landing and its occupants' fortunate escape. The men were well equipped and wore skis. Quietly, they slid from the shoulder of the mountain and started to carve regular turns in the graduating slope of deep snow. The steep slopes at the top of the glacier made for outstanding powder skiing even at this time of year. They put in neat regular turns to control their descent, bouncing knee-deep in the light powder, which sprayed up behind them in a mist of twinkling ice crystals.

Toward the bottom of the initial descent, the slope leveled out and gave way to the main glacier field. The men went straight down to where the balloon and its contents were strewn over the glacier. In minutes they arrived where Jack and the professor still lay. The glare of the morning sun was intense, so Jack was only able to open his eyes into a thin slit. But the two figures who now appeared in his narrow field of vision were unmistakable—Tony and Gordon.

Tony and Gordon stared down at them both, surrounded by the wreckage of the accident.

"Well, you've made a bit of a mess, haven't you, son?" The moisture on Tony's breath instantly condensed to vapor in the freezing air.

"Bit of a mess . . . " Gordon parroted.

Jack could only stare back at them defiantly.

"Aren't you going to introduce us to your friend?" Tony asked.

The professor got to his feet shakily but still managed a smile. "Professor Pinckard-Schnell—delighted to meet you."

He thrust out a hand. "Are you here to rescue us? You've been very quick."

Tony and Gordon looked at each other and laughed.

"You could say that, Professor, you could say that," Gordon replied.

Tony turned to Jack, who still lay prostrate on the snow. He leaned down and Jack flinched.

Tony put up his palms defensively and said, "Whoa, lad—let me help you now." For a moment, Jack was taken aback—his tone was almost . . . kind. He helped Jack into a sitting position, dusted off the snow, and then started to examine him—looking into his eyes for symptoms of concussion and checking for other signs of injury.

Soon he pronounced himself satisfied. "A little battered and bruised—but you'll live." He turned to the professor. "What about you, my friend? Looks like you could do with something for that nose."

The professor was holding his hand under both nostrils. His nose was still bleeding profusely. "Thank you."

Gordon took some cotton balls from his pack and started to wipe the blood from the professor's face. "Not broken, anyway. A lucky escape."

Tony shook his head. "Yep—it looked like quite a heavy landing from up there. You had us worried for a moment."

He turned his attention back to Jack, who was regaining some composure. "Now, son, first things first. We're under strict orders from VIGIL to take you back to base—safely. No harm is to come to you."

"That's disappointing, because my foot still hurts from where you impaled it," Gordon added.

"Never mind that. Anyway, rules, as they say, is rules. So we'd better get going." Tony looked up at the sky. "At least the weather looks good."

Jack didn't understand why, having tried to assault him back at the library and aboard *Dreadnought,* Tony and Gordon were now attempting to be nice. He frowned suspiciously. "So you're not going to harm us? No more injections? What's happened?"

"You're safe, son. That's all you need worry about. The Rector will explain everything."

A million questions rushed into Jack's head. "The Rector, but—? How did you get here, anyway? And where are we going?"

Tony tapped his breast pocket knowingly. "With time travel you can go anywhere . . . any time."

"When it decides to work," Gordon added grumpily.

Tony ignored him. "Save your energy, lad. You'll need it." He half-turned and gestured down toward the snout of the glacier and the wilderness beyond.

"Let's just concentrate on getting off this mountain first." Then he shook his head and said, "Oh, I nearly forgot. I'm afraid that you will need to hand it over."

"Hand what over?"

"The time phone, of course. Can't have you gallivanting around space and time. There'd be no end to the trouble you could cause. Have already caused. Once you're debriefed, we'll get you back home"—he added with a rueful smile—"safely. Don't you worry about that." He put out his hand. "If you please."

Jack rummaged in his pocket and fished out his time phone. He clutched onto it for a moment, then reluctantly dropped it into Tony's vast leathery hand.

"Thank you, lad. We will put that one safely away with ours."

Tony and Gordon roped Jack and the professor together, and they made their way down the edge of the glacier. Eventually, it gave way to steep moraine fields. They picked their way through until they reached the tree line. A gentle breeze hissed through the fir canopy as they followed an old trapping trail. Later on, the forest opened onto a large expanse of high pasture, an *Almen,* and for the first time the group was rewarded with breathtaking views of the valley far below. It was a pristine wilderness of dark green firs interspersed with pastureland, guarded by towering granite walls. Along the valley sides they could see the shimmering silver threads of at least three plunging waterfalls.

Jack had been in the mountains before. Last year his mom had let him go on the school skiing trip. But that had been nothing like this. It had been busy—lots of people, the mechanical whirring of lifts, waiting in lines, the slopes dotted with people in ant trails all competing to find the best way down. Even there, on a sunny day, a gray band of smog from cars and factories would hang stubbornly midway between the valley and the high mountain. But here, there was nobody, and the air was champagne clear. The greens were somehow greener and the sky bluer—beyond empty and beyond silent.

They had been going for five hours, and even with regular breaks and provisions from Tony and Gordon, Jack was exhausted. At last, they emerged onto the broad valley floor. Ahead of them was a river that wound its way lazily through the fields. It looked like it could be deep in places, even though the spring thaw was well past. About two miles away they could see a small town, with the rounded spire of a chapel peeking above the tiled rooftops. Slightly beyond this, a craggy outcrop jutted from the side of the valley, rising to perhaps eight hundred feet, maybe more. A castle had been built high upon the exposed lump of black rock. It had narrow windows like slits and at least three turrets with conical roofs projecting from high stone sides. It dominated the valley.

As Jack wearily craned his head up at the castle, it dawned on him that he could not see any possible way to approach it. Perhaps there was a route from above, where the rocky outcrop joined the main cliff face. Or perhaps there was a winding track that approached the building from the rear—currently hidden from their view. Then he spotted it. Rising silently from the village ahead of them, a red box magically appeared and rose at a steep angle upward toward the castle. A cable car. And sure enough he could just make out the gossamer-thin wire that looped gracefully from the village right up to the castle. The village was strangely deserted when they finally reached it. They entered the small cable car station. After a short wait they boarded the return cable car, which transported them smoothly upward and gently delivered them onto the precipitous landing high up in the castle wall.

Day of the Assassins

Tony and Gordon led Jack and the professor from the landing, down a stone staircase honed from the rock, and into the small courtyard of the castle. Jack followed, zombie-like, fatigue overwhelming him. Out of the corner of his eye, he spotted an occasional dark figure high up on the battlements, peering down at them. The place was eerily quiet. It had been a clear day, but the high, dark walls shielded the sun and the courtyard was left in gloomy shadow. On reaching the opposite side of the courtyard, they entered the main keep and were led into a hall. Contrasting with the austere exterior of the castle, the inside of the hall was magnificent. Tapestries and paintings adorned oak-paneled walls, and chandeliers hung from a high-vaulted ceiling. At one end, a large open fire crackled away. They were invited to sit on one of several sofas and armchairs that surrounded the log fire. In front of them refreshments were already laid out on a low table. Jack barely made it to a chair before his legs gave way and he collapsed into it. His eyelids drooped as the physical exertions of the day and the gentle warmth of the fire took their toll. In a moment he was fast asleep. Two minutes later, the professor was also snoring loudly.

Jack didn't know how long they had been asleep when they were awoken by the creak of a door opening. A man with two burly guards on either side marched in. The tall, stooping frame and the wisps of silver hair adorning the balding head were unmistakable. Just the gown was missing. It was the Rector. The last time Jack had seen him was in the library, directing Tony and Gordon to attack Angus and Pendelshape. Now here he was with them—in an Austrian castle in 1914. The Rector marched forward, and the two guards took up positions elsewhere in the hall. Then he did something that took Jack completely by surprise. He opened his arms warmly and said, "Welcome!" He gestured for them to stay in their seats. "Please, please, stay where you are. I know. You have had a very tiring and traumatic day. Mr. Smith has already briefed me. You've certainly given us a run for our money!" He turned and called back toward the hall entrance. "More food! Our guests are hungry!"

The Rector's friendliness was unsettling.

"Time travel—it creates a bit of an appetite, don't you think?"

Jack was confused. He couldn't work out why the Rector was being friendly. Unable to control himself, he blurted out, "What's going on? Where are we? What have you done with Angus and Dr. Pendelshape?"

The Rector tried to soothe him. "Please, Jack—calm yourself. You are quite safe. And we owe you an explanation. You are one of the school's better pupils, after all." The Rector smiled at the professor. "He really is, you know." The Rector nodded. "Yes—we have much to discuss and much to explain. But first, some proper introductions." The Rector thrust out his hand to the professor. "John Blanding—rector at Jack's school, back at, er, home. Pleased to meet you, Professor. My men have told me all about your miraculous escape in the mountains."

The professor half rose from his seat. "Pinckard-Schnell, at your service. I must thank you for arranging our rescue so quickly. . . . And thank you for allowing us to be guests"—he looked around, unsure of himself—"in your, er, house."

"A pleasure. I understand from Mr. Smith that you were taking an unexpected opportunity to set a new world record, Professor?"

"Yes."

"Well, as you are no doubt aware, you have landed in the southern Tyrol. Since you departed from HMS *Dreadnought* somewhere in the North Sea, I think you will have more than achieved your objective. Congratulations are in order."

The professor blushed self-consciously, then his expression turned to one of puzzlement. "You seem to know a surprising amount, sir. How exactly . . . ?"

Jack piped up, his voice a little unsteady. "Professor—I don't think you quite understand—this is the Rector from my school, the headmaster, the one I told you about." He turned to the Rector. "I told him what happened, sir. I had to, really, although I'm not sure he quite believes me."

The Rector smiled. "Yes, of course. I understand. Well, now we are all here safe and sound, and I think you deserve to understand the full picture." He turned to the professor. "Both of you."

Day of the Assassins

" . . . You can see, I'm sure, how the technology we are dealing with—time travel technology—is extremely powerful. Those who use it can potentially change the past and therefore change the future. The people who are in charge of it have a huge responsibility. Sometimes we have to make difficult decisions—and we have to make them quickly."

Jack and the professor were sitting back in their chairs while the Rector paced back and forth in front of the log fire. The professor was engrossed in what the Rector had to say. Jack, however, refreshed after his short nap and the food, was impatient for answers.

"Have you killed Dr. Pendelshape?" he asked.

For the first time, the Rector's warmth evaporated. "Pendelshape! That idiot! Jack—do you have any idea how dangerous Pendelshape's actions could have been?"

Jack shook his head sheepishly.

The Rector took a deep breath. "For your information, no, we have not killed him. Not our style, although he has been severely reprimanded. I don't think he will make the same mistake twice." The Rector, calming himself, explained Pendelshape's sins in more detail. "Pendelshape was collaborating secretly with the Benefactor in his quest to build a separate Taurus. We had no idea. Not only is this quest exceptionally dangerous, but it is against VIGIL rules—the VIGIL Imperative that he signed. And what's more, it's a personal betrayal of all his colleagues—including myself."

He stooped down to place another log on the fire. "The scientific team that developed the time travel technology decided that using it would be too dangerous—making interventions back in time might have unforeseen consequences for the present. We had developed very good computer-modeling techniques to predict how changes in the past would alter the future course of history. But despite this, we believed it was just too risky. We decided instead to mothball the technology, and we founded the school as a cover for what we were doing. VIGIL was set up, and we agreed to be bound by its rules. In the end there was really only one dissenting voice—the Benefactor. He could not agree that we should never use the technology—he honestly believed that it could be used as a power for good. The argument became very heated. Eventually, we agreed to part company with the Benefactor. It was very sad in a way. He was one of our most brilliant scientists and one of the architects of the Taurus. But he left the Taurus team seven years ago, and we had heard nothing from him until yesterday."

"Until you intercepted the e-mails between him and Pendelshape."

"That's right, Jack. We were doing a routine check, as we do on all the team members from time to time. We have to. What we found was extremely alarming."

"The Benefactor had built a separate Taurus."

"Exactly—we were staggered by this. We could not believe that he could have done it on his own." The Rector stared into the flickering orange-and-yellow flames. He shook his head and added grudgingly, "You have to admire him. Now there are two working time machines. The Benefactor has the ability to time travel and, potentially, to make his own changes in history—just as he always wanted."

"And you can't do anything about it?"

The Rector turned back to Jack. "Well, of course we can, as we also have our original Taurus at the school. If the Benefactor made a change in time, we could go back and try to reverse that change. In fact, one of the reasons we kept the Taurus intact and even tested it was in case somehow, someone developed similar technology in the future. We had considered that scenario but believed it to be highly unlikely. But science moves quickly. . . . "

"Two time machines? Sounds like things could get really messed up. Dr. Pendelshape said something about an Armageddon Scenario."

"Yes—a theoretical possibility. Once you got into a series of interventions and reversals in history, anything could happen. It's unpredictable and very dangerous."

The professor removed his round glasses and started to polish them energetically on a napkin.

"A kind of time war," he said, with more enthusiasm than he probably intended.

"If you like, Professor, but we don't even want to contemplate that. We must stop the Benefactor from doing anything at all."

"But you can't do that—you don't know where he is. He has his own Taurus—he can do whatever he wants . . . whenever he wants."

The Rector stared down at Jack. His expression had changed—he now had a sympathetic, even sad, look in his eye. "Of course, you would be right, except for one thing."

Jack cocked his head, not sure what the Rector meant.

"Sorry—I keep calling him the Benefactor—old names, old habits, I'm afraid. You, of course, know by now who the Benefactor is?"

"Some nutcase—sounds like." Jack glanced over to the professor and smiled nervously.

"He's your father, Jack."

A Gilded Cage

Jack heard the words, but they made no sense. For a second, he just stared blankly at the Rector.

"What?"

"The Benefactor—he's your father."

"But . . . how . . . ?"

"Jack, I know this is hard."

Slowly it started to become clear. "The library at Cairnfield . . . "

"Yes—your father's workshop."

It all made sense. All the First World War memorabilia they had found there. Then there was the present of a history book and his strange flashbacks of the trip to the First World War battlefields and cemeteries—no doubt driven by his father's interest in history and maybe his desire for Jack to share the same interest. And then there was his early childhood near Geneva—where his father had worked with the rest of the Taurus team. And his father always working— never home—which wasn't surprising given the importance of what he was doing. And, of course, the separation from Jack's mom. It was obvious now why that had happened. The stress must have been unbearable. Jack couldn't believe that he hadn't realized it before.

"But why wasn't I told? Why didn't Mom say?"

"To protect you. Knowledge of the Taurus, and the people involved with it, is strictly controlled. Carole, your mother, is aware—she has to be—but she is on our side. Your father pleaded with her desperately for you both to join him when he left. But Carole was determined that she should try to give you a normal life . . . not caught up in all . . . this. And anyway . . . "

"Anyway what?"

The Rector turned away again, rubbing his hands by the fire. "Sorry, Jack. Your father could be . . . difficult."

"So, this explains the message we received from Jack's mother on the time phone in the balloon," the professor said.

"We managed to send a temporary signal from our Taurus to your time phone. We told Carole immediately what had happened, and we sent the message from her to try to warn you that we would be bringing you in. Not to resist. We thought you would trust her. We would have tried to get you back right then—but there wasn't enough of a signal."

"So you sent a couple of thugs instead?" Jack said crossly.

"MacFarlane and Smith?" The Rector raised his eyebrows. "This is not a game, Jack. The fight you witnessed at the school was . . . unfortunate. But we were desperate—we had to act very, very fast."

"But on the *Dreadnought* . . . they were going to inject me with some stuff, then Gordon shot at me before I managed to get on the balloon."

"No. It might have appeared like that to you. You were under intense stress. They had strict orders to sedate you if necessary, but to bring you home safely as soon as we had a signal. I understand that Mr. MacFarlane's shot to the balloon was an attempt to free it from its moorings before you boarded it. It was the shot of a marksman. He was certainly not aiming for you. Those two are utterly trustworthy." He added under his breath, "Although sometimes they become a little over-enthusiastic."

"But you still have not explained why this young man is so important to you—why he needs to be mixed up in all of this," the professor said, glancing across at Jack sympathetically. "Surely it's Jack's father you want, not Jack?"

The Rector sighed. "Don't you see? I'm afraid, Jack, in a way, you are a kind of hostage. If we have you, then the Benefactor, your father, has his hands tied. . . . You are the only person in the world that he cares about. He even thinks Carole has betrayed him now. The only way we can stop him from using the Taurus is by threatening to harm you if he does."

Jack suddenly realized the terrible logic of his predicament and thought back to the e-mail from his father that he and Angus had read in Pendelshape's office.

I fear that when they find out, they may take Orion. . . . We must protect Orion.

Orion. At last he knew who that was. Orion was himself. His father had wanted Pendelshape to make sure that Jack was safe, so that he would be free to use his own Taurus, without the Rector and VIGIL stopping him by threatening to harm his son. It explained, too, why Pendelshape had taken them into his confidence so suddenly and taken such a risk in showing them the Taurus and its control room. Pendelshape had been working secretly with his father all along. Before the Rector had arrived with Tony and Gordon in the library, Pendelshape was about to take Jack somewhere so that the Rector could never find them. In fact, as he had guessed, Pendelshape had been planning to use the Taurus to hide Jack in time. In 1914. Then his father could use his second Taurus to locate them and rescue them—so they would be permanently free from the clutches of the Rector and VIGIL. But the Rector had arrived too soon and had upset the plan. Ironically, Jack had been so frightened by the sudden arrival of the Rector and the VIGIL guards that he had panicked and used the Taurus to escape anyway.

But the e-mail had also mentioned someone else: *Lynx.*

There is nothing we can do about Lynx now—she has gone over to the other side.

Jack looked at the Rector. "So, if I am Orion, who is Lynx?"

"Carole—your mother."

Of course. "So, what you're saying is that I'm a kind of pawn in a battle between you and my dad?"

"I'm afraid so, Jack."

"And while you have me, you can threaten my dad that you might kill me . . . or . . . or torture me. . . . Then you know he won't do anything—anything silly—with the second Taurus to change things in the past. To change the course of history."

"Yes. But you are more than a pawn. You are much, much more

important than that. In fact, I would say, right now, until we can track down your father and bring him under control, you are possibly the most important person in the world. It's only the threat to harm you that prevents your father from acting. We are all involved in a deadly high-wire balancing act. It's not how we want it to be. But it's the way it is."

Jack felt confused at first. . . . Then he started to feel angry. Angry that these men, with their intellects and ambitions, had created a technology so powerful and so potentially lethal that it could scarcely be discussed, let alone used. Angry that, for some reason, it was in him that the precarious balance of power between these two enemies was maintained. Angry that his mom had not found it possible to explain any of this to him before. Angry that it was the battle to control this great power that had torn his own family apart.

Later, with the night upon them, they were led through a series of spiral staircases and passageways to their rooms. Separate rooms. Jack's seemed to have been hewn straight from the massive stonework of the castle walls. The door closed behind him, and he heard a key turn in its lock and a dull clunk as two bolts on the outside were slid into place. It was like being in an underground bunker. The air was completely still and there was no sound. Although it was small, some attempt had been made to make the place comfortable. On the floor, a thick rug covered the gray flagstones. There was some simple dark oak furniture and a pair of maroon curtains. There was a made-up bed with pillows, sheets, blankets, and a richly embroidered gold-and-red bedspread. It looked like it must have taken months to hand sew. It was nothing like his blue-and-white striped duvet at home that had probably spun off a textile machine in China in five seconds.

Jack peered through the small window. It was getting late, and the ragged outline of the mountains was darkening against an indigo sky. The window was set solidly into the four-foot-thick castle wall and could not be opened. For the time being he was caged. Of course he now knew why. He was being held hostage.

He remembered the awe he had felt when he discovered that the extraordinary workshop beneath Cairnfield actually belonged to his own father. He had been proud to be associated with somebody so brilliant—his own flesh and blood. Now he realized just how powerful his father, the Benefactor, was, and therefore how important he himself was, and his feelings were agonizingly mixed. There was pride in feeling special, but at the same time he was scared and confused. He didn't know whom to trust—the Rector, VIGIL, and his mom, or Pendelshape and his dad. He didn't know who was really right and who was really wrong, and he didn't want to have to choose.

Rescue

It was still dark outside. Jack had been dreaming again of the visit to the Western Front graves—the endless sea of white crosses, the grassed-over outline of old trench networks, then running for shelter from the storm and opening the door and seeing his mom and dad . . . crying. . . . And then Mom whisking him back to his bedroom. He was relieved when gradually the curtains lightened with the arrival of a bright mountain dawn.

Breakfast was set out on a white-clothed buffet table at the end of the hall where they had met the Rector the night before. A fire had already been started and was crackling away merrily. The professor had been up early and sat alone at the long breakfast table nursing a cup of coffee. His head was still buried in Jack's history book. Occasionally a figure would scurry silently into the hall from an anteroom to clear a plate or bring fresh coffee. As Jack entered, the professor raised his head in acknowledgment and waved absentmindedly at the food. Having helped himself, Jack settled down opposite the professor, unfurled a napkin, and was about to dive in to two large poached eggs and several strips of bacon when he noticed a rather strained expression on the professor's face.

"OK, Professor?"

The professor looked to the left and to the right as if to make sure that they were alone and whispered across to Jack conspiratorially.

"It's not right."

"What do you mean?" Jack asked loudly.

The professor winced. "Keep your voice down!"

Jack looked around him and shrugged as if to say *why?*

The professor maneuvered a prune around his bowl with his fork. "Were you locked in your bedroom last night?"

"Yes. But the Rector explained, they can't take any chances, can they? They have to protect me. But they don't want to harm us. It's just the threat of being able to harm me that gives them power over Dad. I don't like it either."

The large oak doors swung open, and the Rector strode purposefully toward them.

"Good morning, gentlemen! I see you are making yourselves at home . . . excellent! I trust you both had a good night's sleep?"

The professor continued to prod the prune, which had already made several weary circumnavigations of his bowl. The Rector inspected the fare on offer at the buffet.

"Not bad at all, considering the short time we've had to set this place up." He started to load his plate and was soon sitting with them at the table.

"Is there a plan, sir?" Jack asked. "Will we be going home soon?"

"Well, your priority should be to have a good breakfast. You've had a traumatic time." He filled a large cup from the coffee pot. "And then for the rest of today, you will stay in the castle. We have taken over this place because it affords us a number of obvious advantages— isolation, security . . . But I think you will find the main courtyard a pleasant place to while away a few hours." He glanced over at the high-arched windows that dominated the far end of the hall. "Looks like it'll be a nice day."

"And then what?"

The Rector thought for a moment. "Well . . . as soon as we finally achieve a reliable signal connection, we shall send you back to the twenty-first century. Simple as that, really, Jack. The small VIGIL team we have here will follow, using our time phones, once we have, er, done some tidying up. Closed this place down in an orderly manner, for a start. This might be today. It might be tomorrow. It's a little difficult to tell. But our plan is that you should arrive back just after the point that you made the original trip from the Taurus." His face tightened. "It will be hard, Jack, but at that point you will need to continue your life as if nothing has happened. We will be there to guide you. As I explained yesterday, our aim will be to ensure that you lead a normal life. Of course, we will need to keep you protected . . . "

"From Dad?"

"Yes. I'm afraid if ever he gets a hold of you, then, well, we will have very little control over him. There will be nothing to stop him."

"Is there no way of finding out where he is? Dad, I mean. Negotiating or something?"

"We have no idea where your father is or where the second Taurus is, but of course it is something we are working on. As for negotiation—I'm afraid we're well past that stage."

The Rector took a slurp of coffee and then turned his attention to the professor. "As for you, Professor, you will be free to go, with your world record for the most distance traveled by balloon intact. But we must ask you not to speak of the events you have experienced. I am sure you understand."

The professor looked up from his prune and nodded half-heartedly. Something was obviously bothering him.

Later, they sat in the small courtyard of the castle, sipping lemonade at a table while awaiting instructions from the Rector. The castle was very quiet, although occasionally a VIGIL guard could be seen moving along the crenelated outline of the upper walls. The afternoon sun cast a sharp, diagonal shadow midway across the courtyard.

The professor continued to be engrossed in Jack's book. Occasionally, he would raise his head and contemplate the bright reflection of the sunlight on the cobblestones or ask Jack some question about the war or the future. Nearby, water from a stone fountain gurgled into a flat earthenware basin. Presumably this place still existed in the future. Jack vaguely thought about surreptitiously scratching his name or something on one of the walls, to see if it would still be there nearly a hundred years in the future. He sighed. He'd only been away a couple of days, but he missed home. It would be good to talk to his mom about everything that had happened. Properly this time. No more awkward silences or changing the subject. He could speak to her as an equal: this time they would both know the truth about his father.

"You've been reading that thing for hours."

"It almost didn't happen," the professor replied.

"What?"

"The war."

"Sorry?"

"There have been several Balkan crises before now. . . . In fact, the Balkans are always in a crisis of some sort. Do you know what I'm talking about, Jack?"

Jack tried to tune in to what the professor was saying. "Yes, Professor, I think so. Pendelshape was always going on about it. When the Ottoman Empire's power declined in the Balkans, it kind of left no one in control."

"Yes. Well, it's not just the Ottoman Empire; the Austro-Hungarian Empire has also struggled to impose itself over all the different nationalities within its borders. There have been many crises and wars there. The point is, though, they have mostly been successfully sorted out by the diplomats. In fact Europe has been at peace since 1871. Problems in the Balkans have happened before and have been successfully worked out. . . . Or at least have not led to a wider war like the one in here"—he held up the book and tapped its spine vigorously with his index finger—"a world war."

"So?" Jack said.

"But 1914, now, this time, my time, is somehow different. This time the great European powers—Germany, France, Russia, Britain, Austria-Hungary—don't work it out. But they could have!" he said triumphantly. "And then things would have continued as normal! In fact it was all just a silly mistake. . . . There was no need for war at all! And this silly mistake is responsible for the deaths of millions of people! People just like you and me."

The professor stared at Jack through his round spectacles with his intense blue eyes. He looked around the courtyard furtively and whispered, "Jack, to be honest, I think your father might be right about all this—if I understand correctly what he is trying to do. Maybe it is right to use this amazing time machine of his to go back and try to change things so that they are better. Maybe even . . . maybe we have a responsibility to . . . stop it. Stop this war . . . and maybe, I, as a German, living now, maybe I have a special responsibility to stop it."

Jack didn't like where this was going. "Professor, I'm not sure—"

The professor spoke with an intensity that Jack had not heard before. "I am not like you. I am of this time. For you this is the past. For me this is the present. I have a responsibility."

Jack shook his head slowly. "I'm not sure that's how it's supposed to work. You heard what the Rector said."

"But think!" the professor pleaded. "We have the power to stop many deaths. Why wouldn't you do that . . . if you could? If you had that power."

Put like that, Jack could see his point. But he had also heard what the Rector had said—about the unknown consequences of fiddling with time, with things in the past. Anyway, he didn't want to get involved in this conversation. He just wanted to go home.

"But if we try to change things, it might make them worse. We don't know . . . " He strained to order his thoughts. "Maybe the war is supposed to happen; maybe it will happen no matter what we do."

The professor was unconvinced. "Many lives will be lost, Jack. With your father's help, maybe we could find a way to save them . . . to save them all."

The suggestion hung provocatively in the air. When the Rector had explained everything to him, it seemed that VIGIL and its leaders were right. He had even started to believe the Rector when he'd said that his father was a dangerous fugitive. But, with the professor's unexpected plea, suddenly he was not so sure. Maybe his father was right.

Their troubling conversation was interrupted by the sound of heavy footsteps coming down the stone stairs in the tower behind them. Tony and Gordon entered the courtyard, closely followed by two other VIGIL guards and the Rector. They marched over to where Jack and the professor sat.

"Gentlemen, I am so sorry to disturb you, but we have rather worrying news," the Rector said. He stroked back wisps of his silver hair nervously. He was sweating.

"It appears that Dr. Pendelshape's collaboration with your father was closer than we first thought—and their plans well advanced."

"What do you mean?" Jack asked.

"I am not sure we explained to you that all time phones, including the one that you used, are linked to our Taurus back at the school. We had not previously considered a situation where there are in fact two time machines. Two Tauruses." The Rector's brow furrowed. "It appears that Dr. Pendelshape may have passed the identification code for your time phone to your father."

Jack and the professor looked at him blankly. The Rector sighed impatiently. "This means that, assuming a reliable signal, your time phone can be tracked by your father's Taurus, as well as our own."

"So if the yellow bar is showing on my time phone, Dad knows where I am?"

"He knows *when* you are as well."

"So, he could—"

"Yes. He could try to mount some sort of kidnap attempt."

Jack suddenly had an idea. "Hold on! If he's got the codes for my time phone . . . then can't we use my time phone to find out where he is?"

The Rector smiled. "Good thinking, Jack. You're a bright lad. But in that case, we'd need the codes for his Taurus—"

"Which you obviously haven't got," the professor added.

"No. And we have now destroyed your time phone so it can't be tracked. But that's not the only thing. We are now receiving a good signal from our Taurus."

"But that means—"

"Yes. We have an opportunity to get you home before we lose the signal again. However, there is a real possibility that your father managed to get a space-time fix of this location before we destroyed your time phone, in which case—"

"He could time travel back . . . to the castle—right here."

"Exactly. We must act quickly."

The Rector, with Tony and Gordon close by, ushered Jack and the professor from the courtyard.

But they were not quick enough.

In the shadows of one corner of the courtyard there was a sudden disturbance. It was as if the air had gone strangely liquid. There was a flash of white light. In an instant the shimmering of the air stopped. Where previously there had been nothing, now there was a figure— just standing there. He had a thin face, and his straight black hair flopped below his ears. Jack couldn't believe it. Angus. But it was not the Angus that Jack knew from school. He was dressed like a member of the special forces. On top of that, to Jack's amazement, he was carrying a weapon so large that he was struggling to hold it level.

Angus screamed over to them, "Hit the deck!"

Free Fall

Jack dropped flat to the cobblestones as the whole courtyard erupted into a maelstrom of ricocheting machine-gun bullets. Taken by complete surprise, the Rector, Tony, Gordon, and the other guards dived back into the main block. Angus's weapon dispatched heavy caliber rounds and, as he was unable to control it properly, he was soon spraying bullets everywhere and, in the process, dislodging great lumps of stone and mortar from around the courtyard. In ten seconds it was over. The fountain had been leveled and the table vaporized.

Angus dashed over to Jack and helped him to his feet.

"Come on, we've got to get out of here."

"What? What about him?"

"Who?"

"The professor—there!" Jack pointed at the professor, who was still on the ground next to him. "Professor, are you OK?" Jack asked, trying to pull him to his feet.

"Come on, there's no time—just leave him," Angus said.

"I can't!"

The professor rose shakily to his feet, ashen faced.

"Right—he's fine. So let's get on with it." Angus said.

"Why?" Jack asked.

"What do you mean, *why?*" Angus said desperately. "There's no time to explain. You are in great danger. We all are. I've been sent to rescue you."

They heard the Rector shouting.

"Put down your weapon. There is no escape. We will not harm you. Give yourself up."

Angus screamed back. "Everyone stay where you are!" And as if to make the point, he opened fire again, spraying the stone wall of the castle accommodation tower with bullets and smashing a number of windows in the process. As the gun fired, Angus reeled backward with the force, and the nose of the barrel veered upward, dispatching rounds in a random pattern up the side of the old building.

"Put that thing down before you kill someone," Jack said desperately.

Angus ignored him. He lowered the gun and looked at the time phone that hung around his neck.

"No! The signal's going! I was told this might happen. It's over."

"What do you mean?"

"We can't time travel out. We'll have to run for it! Come on!" And to make his point, he unceremoniously poked the smoking barrel of his gun at Jack.

"Hey! Watch where you're pointing that thing."

Angus pleaded with his friend, "I'm telling you, stay here and we're finished. Trust me. There's a lot you don't know."

In the background, they heard the Rector's voice again, booming orders.

"The others should be here by now to help me. But something must have happened. We've got to get out of here." Angus was starting to panic. He appeared to know something that Jack didn't. If they could escape, maybe there would be some time to think.

"How?" Jack said.

"You're the brains. You tell me. I've never been here before."

"There's only one way down. And that's on the cable car," the professor said.

"Well, let's move."

Luckily, Jack knew the layout of the castle and they were soon racing up the other side of the courtyard to the cable-car landing. Angus waited briefly at the bottom of the stairs and fired some final rounds randomly into the courtyard to deter any immediate pursuit. The red cable car was waiting snugly in its arrival gantry. Jack opened the door to the small control room directly behind the landing. There was an array of switches, gears, and dials labeled in German. The boys turned to the professor.

"Well, Professor?"

"I am a scientist, not a cable-car operator," the professor said pompously. Then he surveyed the control room and smiled mischievously back at the boys. "Which means, for me, it won't be that difficult." He maneuvered himself in front of the main control panel. "I have always found that, in the case of technical difficulty, the best thing to do is to press the biggest button you can find." The professor poked a pendulous index finger at a large green button and then, reading a few of the other labels, made a number of further adjustments. A bell rang above them, and he pressed another button. The machinery sprang to life.

The professor jumped up in excitement. "Let's go!"

They moved across to where the cable car waited. The professor slid open the door, and they piled in. He inspected the control panel inside the cable car.

"Here goes!" Suddenly, the car moved and began its descent into the valley below. The castle was soon receding into the distance.

"What happens when we get to the bottom?" Angus said.

"They'll telephone down . . . someone will be waiting for us there."

"Unless we can find some way out," the professor said.

Angus laughed. "Be serious. We're suspended hundreds of feet in the air."

The professor moved over to the large metal bench at one end of the cabin. It had a small hatch in the side. He slid open the retaining cover.

"Just as I thought. Nothing overlooked."

They peered into the chest that the professor had pulled from the storage space. There was a medical kit, a tool bag, some harnesses, and an array of other equipment. But there was also rope. Lots of rope.

Angus said, "Well, that's not a lot of help. What are we supposed to do—suspend it from the bottom of the cable car and rappel down?"

Jack and the professor looked at each other, and then Jack said quietly, "Angus, I think that's exactly what the professor has in mind."

Angus turned white. "No way. There is no way that I am climbing out of this sardine can and dangling myself on the end of a bit of thread six-hundred feet in the air. I've already risked my life to time travel back a hundred years to rescue you."

Jack smiled at him slyly. "Not scared, are you?"

The professor was already unloading the rope from the chest.

"Is it going to be long enough?"

"Should be. Otherwise someone made a stupid mistake."

"How do we get down it?"

"Here." The professor handed Jack a small metal object. "It's a friction device. One end attaches to you. The other to the rope." The professor was busy securing an end of the rope to the anchor point inside the cabin. He leaned over and slid free the bolts on the trapdoor, which was built flush into the floor of the cabin.

"Stand to the side and hold on!" the professor said. And with that he released the trapdoor and flipped it over on its hinges so it landed with a crash on the inside of the cabin. Cold mountain air blasted through the large square hole in the bottom of the cable car. Jack stole a glance through the hole—far below, a landscape of firs, rock, and alpine grass flitted silently past as the cable car floated downward.

Angus was staring out of the front window. "I think you'd better hurry, Professor."

They looked up and spotted the cause of Angus's concern. Soon they would be at the midpoint of their journey. Still quite far below, but approaching fast, was the return cable car—making its way up the other cable as their car descended. Even at a distance, they could make out a number of figures eyeing them from the oncoming car.

"What do we do now?"

"We keep going. What can they do?"

"They can shoot us, for a start," Angus said.

The professor dropped the rope through the trapdoor. It rapidly uncoiled and trailed freely from the car until it started to drag along the ground far below.

The professor looked toward the oncoming cable car. He was working something out in his head.

"Let's get ready," he said.

They attached the friction devices to the rope.

"Angus, you go first." He pointed at the gun. "And you'll need to leave that thing."

"Great. Just as I was beginning to enjoy myself."

The professor showed them how the friction devices worked. They seemed straightforward. The problem was going to be launching into the abyss in the first place.

Angus's face was white. Jack didn't look much better.

"Fun, isn't it?" said the professor enthusiastically.

Angus nodded in the direction of the professor. "Where did you get him from, Jack?"

The professor ignored him. "When I apply the brakes, you go. Then it's my turn. Then Jack, you wait a little, and then you go." The other cable car was closing on them fast. They waited, poised above the open trapdoor, the air still rushing in and the earth racing by far below. They gripped their friction devices anxiously. The professor held his hand over the red emergency stop lever. And waited.

"OK?"

Jack and Angus nodded. They were getting so close to the approaching car now that they could see the whites of the guards' eyes. The professor pulled the lever. The cable above their heads decelerated. As it did so, the cable driving the other car also slowed. Their forward momentum caused their whole car to arc upward alarmingly, the centrifugal force pinning them to the floor. The car swung back on its pivot point. Out of the window, they could see that the men in the up car had all fallen over—unbalanced by the surprise halt.

"Go!" The professor shouted.

Angus froze. Unable to move, he just stared blankly into the abyss.

"Go!" the professor shouted again.

But he still couldn't move. The professor gave him a sharp kick on the backside. One moment he was there; the next he was gone. He had just enough presence of mind to apply the friction device to control his descent.

"Sorry about that," the professor called after him. "My turn!"

He leaped through the hatch with what Jack thought was an unnatural degree of enthusiasm and slid down the rope, just as Angus had done seconds before. The cable car continued to sway as it slowed, and it was all Jack could do to remain on his feet. Both cars were nearly side by side. Peering down, he could just see the white smudge of Angus's face as it craned upward.

Suddenly, Jack noticed that the roof hatch in the opposite cabin had been flipped open. A VIGIL guard was crawling up onto the roof with a grappling iron. In a moment, he had tossed the device over to Jack's car. With the rope between the two cable cars secure, he crawled, monkey-like, across the precipitous divide that separated them. There was a loud scraping on the roof hatch of Jack's cabin as the guard started to pry it open.

Jack wasn't about to find out what would happen next. Swallowing hard, he plunged out through the floor hatch, just as the others had done moments before. Initially, he closed the friction device too hard, so he barely moved on the rope. By gradually loosening it, he gained speed. He glanced downward. The professor and Angus had made it to the ground and both seemed to be safe.

Suddenly the speed of the rope through the friction device accelerated. Instinctively Jack locked the device and waited, swaying in the light wind, suspended from the rope, the Austrian Alps all around. And then, slowly, he felt himself being pulled . . . up. There was no doubt about it. He was being pulled back toward the cable car. He felt a wave of panic as he realized what was happening. The guard above had started to yank the rope up . . . with Jack suspended on the end.

He had to make a decision. Angus and the professor were on the upper bank of the river that meandered through the valley, but as the cable car had continued to move before finally coming to rest, Jack was now suspended directly over the river. It was wide but there were also rocks, and he had no idea how deep the water was. He felt another violent tug on the rope as he was dragged inexorably upward. The adrenaline gave him a moment of clarity. It was all he needed. As the rope was tugged up once more, he took a deep breath and flicked open the friction device.

Fishing for Answers

Jack closed his eyes—tight. If he was about to be splattered onto some piece of unholy granite, he didn't want to see it coming. Three seconds later, he hit the river, feet first, and the freezing water exploded around him in a plume of spray. His speed forced him down until finally his feet hit the bottom. It felt like it took an eternity for him to rise, but then he broke the surface with nearly the same speed as he had entered. He gulped down air. He'd made it. But then the cold from the river hit him like the left hook of a heavyweight boxer and took his breath away again. He started to swim, desperately, to the bank. Soon his breast stroke disintegrated into a flailing dog paddle. Exhausted, he pulled himself up onto the grassy bank and collapsed in a soggy heap.

From the other side of the riverbank he heard the voices of Angus and the professor. The professor was waving and jumping up and down excitedly, a broad grin on his face.

"Bravo! Bravo!" he shouted. The professor had clearly been impressed by Jack's decision to jump. Jack pulled himself onto his feet, still breathing heavily. Then it dawned on him. As he gulped down air, his lungs were . . . working. He felt no wheezy emptiness, no panic that he was about to suffocate, no familiar craving for his inhaler. It was bizarre. He took deep breaths and it felt—completely normal. He began to feel stronger and stronger, and soon this feeling grew into a tingling elation.

He glanced back over at his companions and noticed that to their left, on the far riverbank, was a small cabin built right on the edge of the water. It was dilapidated and overgrown—well camouflaged, unless you were actually viewing it from the river itself. He waved, pointing out the cabin to Angus and the professor. They followed Jack's line of sight. When the professor spotted the small wooden building, he became even more excited.

From the opposite bank, Jack saw Angus and the professor clamber up to the rear of the cabin, where they disappeared from view. They had been gone for a few minutes when two wooden doors at water level gradually opened out onto the river. It was a boathouse. Soon, Angus and the professor emerged triumphantly with a rather disheveled-looking skiff. They pushed it free, and with the professor at the twin oars, the boat glided across the river toward Jack. It looked like they might have an escape route. Soon the boat had nosed onto the bank where Jack stood shivering. Angus beamed smugly from the bow.

"All aboard! All aboard!" he shouted. "Next stop, er, down there somewhere!" He thumbed in a general downriver direction. Jack jumped into the boat. The professor reversed and then pointed the craft downstream.

They were off.

The professor gingerly maneuvered the craft back into the center of the river, where they soon caught the best of the downstream current. The boat was larger than a standard rowboat, and in the back it had a low metal frame attached to each side. It looked as if you could assemble a canvas sheet on the frame and maybe even sleep in it.

The professor concentrated on rowing, but it took some getting used to and initially they zigzagged uneasily.

"Any sign of them?" asked the professor. Nervously, they scanned each riverbank. There was no movement, and all they could hear was the lapping of the water and the late afternoon birdsong rising from the dense woodland. Way above, they could still see the gossamer-thin threads of the cables—but both cars had vanished.

"Seems quiet. But it won't take them long to catch up."

The river narrowed and they could feel the current speed up beneath them. Up ahead, perhaps a half mile away, they saw that the banks heightened dramatically as the river passed through a deep mountain gorge.

"We may have a chance. The river will be the quickest way down, and we have a good head start. Soon it will be dark, too. . . . " the professor said. "Jack, you need to get out of those things—otherwise you'll die of cold." The professor nodded toward a compartment behind Jack's legs at the back of the boat. "Anything useful in there?"

Jack rummaged through the compartment's contents. "I don't think this boat has been used for a while. . . . "

There were a couple of dusty blankets and the canvas sheeting to fit over the metal awning. He shook out one of the blankets. It was dry enough but dusty and moth-eaten.

"I've got some spare things with me." Angus opened his small backpack, pulled out a T-shirt and fleece jacket, and handed them to Jack. "Try those."

Jack was grateful for the dry clothes and wrapped one of the blankets tightly around himself in an attempt to ward off the chill. Warming up, he looked around some more in the compartment. He yanked out a long, thin canvas bag. He undid the ties at either end, and out slid three wooden rods.

"Eureka!" the professor exclaimed. "A fishing rod. Maybe there's a reel."

Sure enough, hidden in the back of the compartment there was a reel with a line and, next to it, a small cigar box. Jack opened the box, and inside were eight fly-fishing lures carefully pinned to the bottom.

The professor had by now developed a more reliable stroke, and the oars slopped rhythmically in the water. Pushed on by the current, the boat made steady progress. There was still no sign of pursuit, and they all began to feel a little less edgy. Soon, they were listening to Angus's remarkable story.

"I need to tell you what happened after you escaped, Jack—by the way, pretty impressive, particularly the part when you squashed Belstaff." Angus grinned at the memory of their gym teacher impaled by the blast screen. "Never liked him anyway."

"What happened to him?"

"In pain. But OK. Unfortunately."

"I thought he was dead."

"No. I tell you, these VIGIL-support guys are tough. Anyway, I was pretty scared. Particularly after Gordon knifed poor old Pendelino . . . and then attacked me! And I'm even captain of the rugby team!"

"The Rector explained all that. He said they had to act quickly. . . . "

Angus looked at Jack blankly. "I don't know anything about that. But after the Rector, Tony, Gordon, and the others had made their plan to bring you back from 1914, the next morning two guys rescued me and Pendelshape—right from under the nose of VIGIL. There was a short fight, scary but no shooting, just karate and stuff, and then these men just blindfolded us and bundled us into the back of a van and we took off."

"Where?"

"Away from the school. And fast."

"But—"

"Wait, I haven't told you the rest. We drove on for a bit—but not that long. I was trying to keep tabs on the time, but it was tricky. I was rolling around the back of this van being driven at high speed, and getting really scared about what we'd gotten ourselves into."

"Tell me about it."

"So anyway, this journey went on for a bit longer. I don't know— maybe an hour, maybe more. We stopped a couple of times. . . . I think we changed cars or vans. I needed to pee but they wouldn't even let me do that. Whatever. Eventually we stopped. I was led out of the van and it was quiet, and dark, but I could tell we were near the sea. I could smell the salt air and hear waves lapping against concrete. Then we were in a boat. The engine fired up and we were off, slapping quickly along through the waves. And then we arrived somewhere, the boat was moored up, and I was taken up some steep stairs. I thought I was on another boat—but bigger. It was all pretty weird."

The professor was listening, but because of his central position at the oars, he had his back to Angus. He gently eased the boat into a shallow pool off the main current and then pulled in both blades and let the craft drift for a while so he could rest and listen.

"Then what?" Jack said.

"The blindfold came off . . . and there I was!"

"Where?" Jack asked. "Where were you?"

"Well, here's the strangest thing. You know when we were with Pendelshape that afternoon down in the control room and he was telling us all that strange stuff? I don't know about you, but I wasn't sure I was really believing any of it, and it was, like, when are we going to get out of here?"

"Yeah . . . "

"Right. So the room I ended up in looked just like the underground control room at the school with the Taurus. Then I found out it was a second time machine—another Taurus! But it's much bigger. You could fit a tank in it."

"So it's just as the Rector told us," the professor said, nodding to himself thoughtfully.

"You haven't heard the half of it, Professor. It was then that I met him."

"Who? You met who?" Jack was sitting on the edge of his seat.

Angus's eyes glazed over. He spoke in a hushed, reverential voice. "Him."

"Who?" Jack could hardly contain his curiosity.

"The Benefactor, of course. The inventor of time travel. The man with the biggest brain ever." Angus looked at Jack in awe. "Your dad, Jack. Your dad! I always wondered where you got your brains from."

Jack shrugged. "Right. I thought that's who you meant."

"Is that all you've got to say?" Angus's cheeks suddenly flushed red with anger. "You don't get it, do you? He rescued me and Pendelshape, then he sent me back using his Taurus to rescue you. I don't know what has happened to the others who should have come with me—maybe they got caught out with the time signal. Anyway, you should be grateful . . . and you should be proud of him. Your father is a great man. And he has sent us on a mission. Us! Don't you see?"

Jack felt himself getting angry now. "Not really. I haven't been sent anywhere. I pressed a random button to escape some people who were about to kill my history teacher and you, and who looked like they were about to kill me as well. Then I find out they're chasing me halfway across Europe. We turn up here and they tell me they're trying to protect me from, of all people, my own dad. Why? Because if he gets ahold of me, then there's apparently nothing to stop him from playing God with history—with consequences too awful to imagine. . . . "

There was a tense silence.

"Sorry," Jack said finally. He sighed. "To be honest, I'm not really sure who's right and who's wrong in this whole thing. I feel like a pawn."

Angus replied sheepishly. "Yeah—I'm sorry too, Jack. Maybe it's a bit more complicated than I thought."

The professor pulled on an oar to steady the boat and keep it from drifting into a sandbar.

"We'll get through this, boys," he said. "With my looks and your twenty-first-century brains, we can't fail." Looking at the professor's disheveled yellow hair, his muddied clothes, his round glasses, now with one cracked lens, and two bits of cotton ball still stuffed up each nostril, the remark sounded ridiculous. Angus and Jack looked at the professor, then at each other, and laughed.

The professor took up the oars again and rowed them out to the main channel. A fat orange sun was melting into the rocky horizon. Soon it would be dark.

"Probably time to try to find somewhere to rest for the night," the professor said. As they moved slowly down the gorge, they scanned each side for a suitable landing spot. The river was low at this point and twisted through a maze of large boulders, rocks, and an occasional gravel bank. There were several places where they could pull in and be well protected by the towering granite walls above. In some of the darkening pools off the main current, fish were starting to jump lazily at insects that buzzed above the surface.

They rounded the next bend in the river and spotted a large, deep pool to the left, where a low sandy beach rose gently toward the cliff wall. The professor maneuvered the skiff toward the shore, and they landed and got out, then yanked the boat as far up the slope as they could manage. He then scrambled back into the boat to retrieve the fishing rod Jack had discovered earlier.

"Shall we give it a try?" He looked at the pieces of rod and the reel and then at the box of flies. He looked as if he had no idea what to do next.

"Allow me," said Jack. He quickly assembled the rod, attached the reel, and threaded the line through the eyes in the rod.

Jack picked a fly at random and threaded a leader, which he had attached to the line, through the narrow eye of the hook.

"Ready." He looked at the professor. "Want a try?"

"It's not one of my skills, I'm afraid."

Jack took the rod confidently and stepped out to the water's edge, surveying the pool as he went. There was an occasional *plop* followed by telltale concentric ripples in the water as the trout fed in the fading light. He played out some line from the reel with his left hand.

"Here goes."

He flicked the rod once, and then repeatedly, until a large loop of line was whooshing back and forth through the still air of the gorge. Then he thrust out his arm, pointing the rod toward the last set of expanding circular ripples he had seen in the pool. The whole line raced forward across the river. The tiny fly, invisible in the gloom, presented itself just above the rippling water. There was a sudden disturbance, and a brown fish leaped up from the surface with a splash. Jack was taken by surprise, but took the strike. He felt the tug on the line as the trout struggled to free itself. Slowly, he reeled it in.

Angus danced on the bank, shouting, "You got him!"

"Hey, first time . . . what do you think of that? Never done that before!" Jack plonked the medium-size trout in front of Angus and the professor, delighted with his success.

But he had been lucky. It took him forty minutes before he landed another fish—losing two flies and having to rethread several leaders in the process. The professor busied himself with lighting a small fire from some driftwood on the bank and improvising a cooking grill. He piled up some stones on either side of the fire and looked around for something that they could use to suspend the precious fish above the flames. In a minute he emerged from the boat waving two metal anchoring pegs. With these, they skewered the gutted fish and then balanced them neatly above the fire, with either end resting on the stones. It wasn't perfect, but it did the job, and soon the fish were sizzling away. After twenty minutes Angus removed one and cut it open on a flat stone.

"Prof?" He offered a piece of the moist, pink flesh on the end of his penknife to the professor. The professor popped it into his mouth and sighed appreciatively. In five minutes the fish was gone.

Afterward, they wrapped themselves, mummy-like, in the blankets and the boat's canvas canopy. With the security offered by the gorge, their stomachs at least partly full, and the fire still giving off a modest warmth, their spirits were lifted. Although it was only just dark, Jack was astonished by the number and brightness of the stars that twinkled down from the Austrian night.

The professor gently urged Angus to complete his story. Angus leaned up from his canvas bedding on one elbow. The dying flames from the fire flickered across his face, creating lines and shadows where none existed—making him look older than he really was.

"In the short time we had together, your dad told me a lot, Jack. I don't want to upset you, but I really think you would be proud of what he's done. I'm not really sure I understand all this stuff, but after I met him, for the first time in my life, I was sure of one thing. A hundred percent sure."

"What's that?" Jack asked.

"I agree with him and Pendelshape about what they want to do."

"What do they want to do?"

"Change the course of history—stop the assassination of the archduke in Sarajevo and stop the First World War. Now that we're here, well, maybe we can help them do it."

Jack had never heard Angus talk about anything so seriously—it didn't sound like him at all.

"It's just what the Rector told us back at the castle," the professor said.

"Did he?" Angus was surprised.

"Yes," said Jack. "We should tell you what happened to us too."

He explained what the Rector had said—how the Rector and VIGIL had been astonished to learn of the creation of the second Taurus and how alarmed they all were about the possibility that his father might use it to make changes in history. He explained why Pendelshape had taken them into his confidence and how his attempt to snatch Jack to safety, away from the Rector, might have succeeded if the Rector had not arrived in the Taurus control room with Tony, Gordon, and the others.

"So you see, it's not as simple as you first thought. When you came to rescue us, I suppose we panicked and followed you, but maybe the Rector and VIGIL are right and Dad and Pendelshape are the ones who are wrong about all of this. . . . " Jack struggled to remember what the Rector had actually said about making changes in history. "It might mean that we would make history different—possibly worse." Yes, that was it. "And maybe the war would happen anyway: maybe it's even supposed to happen. Have you thought about that?"

But Angus was having none of it. "Jack, your dad and Pendelshape are right. I'm certain of it. Your dad talked all about how this war leads to the Second World War and how the whole of the twentieth century is a complete nightmare—and it all starts this Sunday in Sarajevo."

"This Sunday?"

"Yes. This Sunday, June 28, 1914—in Sarajevo. That's when the assassination happens."

"Today is . . . "

"Monday, June 22," the professor said. "So—only six days to go."

"Right," Angus continued. "You know I never paid much attention in Pendelino's classes. But the way your dad talked about it—it was real, I can tell you. And what is also real is that he has now made a way of changing it all and, well, making it better. If you talked to him, I think you'd get it." Angus shook his head and then lay back on the ground, exhaling slowly. "I think we need to help him do this. Your dad called it our destiny."

There was silence as they thought about the significance of what

Angus was saying. In the short time that he had known him, Jack's father had obviously made a big impression on Angus.

"Why did he send you—why not come himself? Did he at least send a message for me?"

"Not really. He sent me, I think, 'cause he knew that you would trust me. As I said, I was supposed to be supported by a couple of others—some of the guys that rescued us from the school—but something must have happened during the transfer. Your dad hasn't got as big a team as VIGIL, or guards like Tony and Gordon. Pendelshape stayed with your dad in reserve in case something went wrong. As for instructions . . . It all happened very quickly. We had one chance to rescue you. Your dad's Taurus was powered up, we finally got a signal and a fix on your time and location, and, of course, we were going to travel straight back again. We weren't supposed to hang around here. But then the signal went . . . "

"Not very reliable, these time phones," Jack said. "What does it say now?"

Angus sat up again and rummaged in the breast pocket of his fatigue jacket. He unzipped a padded pouch and took out his precious time phone. He cupped it in his hands carefully and flipped it open. Just as Jack's had, a very faint blue light illuminated the device from the inside, and they inspected the glowing readout.

Date: Monday, June 22, 1914
Time: 11:33 p.m.
Location: Southern Tyrol

"The yellow signal bar is still off," Angus said. "So we still can't use it. No surprise there."

"Did Dad or Pendelshape say anything else? You know—that might help us decide what to do, or where to get help, now that we're stuck here?"

"Not really—although he confirmed what Pendelshape said to us. Remember? That when they did the final testing of the Taurus at the school, Pendelshape, and I think your dad too, made some test trips back to 1914. Pendelshape chose the year himself—made some excuse that it was a period of history he was interested in."

Jack rummaged in his pockets. "Yes. I think I've still got the photo that he showed us." Jack fished out the black-and-white photo of the four young men of the Black Hand standing next to Dr. Pendelshape. They could just make out their gaunt, gray-washed features by the light of the flickering flame.

"There they all are. Pendelshape and the assassins."

"Funny to think that we're in the same time now—1914. This photo can only have been taken a few weeks ago, months at the most."

There was a pause before Angus continued. "And by choosing 1914, Pendelshape and your dad were actually starting to put their plan to change history into action. Pendelshape infiltrated the Black Hand—the assassination group—and gained their confidence. They always planned to return—"

"And somehow disrupt the assassination in Sarajevo."

"Right," Angus continued. "I think Pendelshape and your dad's plan was to infiltrate the group and support them, but then sabotage them at the last minute. You know, stop the assassination."

"And so stop the countdown to the war," the professor added. "Incredible."

"But then the final bust-up must have come, when VIGIL was about to do away with your dad, and he had to escape before he and Pendelshape could complete the plan. As far as VIGIL was concerned, the tests were complete and the Taurus was shut down. Without your dad to guide him, Pendelshape must have just hunkered down at school, got on with his life, and continued to pretend he was loyal to VIGIL."

Jack shrugged. "Well, that's all very interesting, but we're still nowhere nearer deciding what to do."

"Well, I know what your dad would want us to do now that we're here: help them complete their plan."

"But it's like the Rector said—that could have unexpected consequences," Jack said with alarm.

The professor weighed in: "Jack, I think your father is right. It's what I was trying to explain to you back at the castle. . . . "

"What?"

"As I said, Jack, it is a bit different for me. I am from this age. I am part of it. As a civilized person, living at this time, I should do everything to prevent the threatening war. I think if I know about it, I must act. I have a duty. Remember, nothing has actually happened yet." He shuffled nervously inside the canvas. "It sounds as if my own nation has an important part to play in the whole matter, and it sounds as if my nation will suffer—terribly."

Jack shook his head. He didn't know what to do. The embers in the fire were dying, and the last warmth of the evening evaporated into the twinkling Austrian night. They lay silently staring at the sky for a while longer. While Angus and then the professor gradually slid into a chilly slumber, Jack's head continued to buzz with unanswered questions and the choices he would still have to make.

Anna

They were up early, chilled by a dawn mist shrouding the river like a damp net from a lonely trawler boat. The fire from the night before was just a pile of soggy ash. Inside the canvas and blankets, Jack's bones had been aching, so it felt good to get moving and pack the boat to leave.

Soon they were pushing the skiff out from the bank and back into the river. The professor took his position at the center of the boat, manned the twin oars, and maneuvered them back out across the pool—the site of Jack's fishing triumph the night before. As the skiff rotated into the current, the mist unexpectedly parted and the gorge brightened for a moment in the morning light. Jack saw two birds circling way above them at the top of the gorge where the green pine forest fringed the cliffs. As he slowly shook off the fatigue from a restless night, he sensed a slight vibration in the heavy air of the gorge.

"Hear that?"

"Probably my stomach—that fish didn't have much impact," Angus moaned as he scratched sleep from his eyes. "When are we going to get some decent food?"

"Maybe not for a while," the professor said. "We have no choice but to keep following the river downstream."

Angus snorted grumpily and folded his arms around himself to ward off the chill.

Jack looked over the professor's shoulder, downstream, but the view of the main river was obscured by the maze of boulders and rocks. The vibration in the air seemed to be getting stronger, and he was sure that the current beneath them was increasing in strength. As the boat began to pitch in the water, occasionally a plume of white spray would whip up from the bow and spatter them.

"I hear something now too, Jack," the professor said, his brow furrowed. "Ahead of us maybe."

The vibrating sound was becoming louder—amplified by the canyon walls. The boat, now moving quickly, rounded a large boulder on a wide bend in the river, and to their horror, they were suddenly presented with the source of the noise. Rapids. For most of its course, the river had meandered through a network of boulders and pools. But just a hundred yards ahead it steepened and descended angrily in a white-water torrent that threw vapor high up into the gorge. The vibration in the air was now a deafening roar.

Jack and Angus braced themselves. The professor grabbed the two spare paddles from the bottom of the boat and tossed one to each of the boys. As the river dropped into the rapids, Jack thrust his paddle into the heaving water. The force of the torrent nearly tossed him clean out of the boat. He snatched the paddle back before trying a second time, this time compensating for the power of the water. His efforts made little difference, but miraculously, the current guided the boat between the large boulders that peppered the rapids.

Somehow the boat stayed upright, and as they progressed, they developed an uneasy technique for avoiding the worst of the rocks and the white water—the professor, in the middle, balanced the boat with the two large blades and prodded the occasional rock to avoid collision, and Angus and Jack tried to guide them with the small paddles from either end. Then, just as their confidence was starting to build, the gorge suddenly opened out over a wide, downward-sloping platform of glass-smooth rock.

The boat came up onto the lip of the precipice and then accelerated downward, water spraying from the bow. They could hear the hull scraping as the stone beneath tore into it. The boat slewed left, then right. Then they were airborne. The rocky outcrop had given way to a sheer cliff where a waterfall cascaded down into a smooth expanse of blue water. The skiff took off from the edge of the outcrop high in the air, propelled by the momentum gathered on its downward slide. They were flung free and wide from both the waterfall and the rotating skiff.

Day of the Assassins

If it had been Olympic diving, none of them would have scored highly for technique as they plunged into the lake.

Angus belly flopped badly onto the water's surface with a loud *smack*. He was quickly followed by the professor, who entered the water on his back, and finally Jack, who went in headfirst. Then, in the same order, the lake released them from its icy depths—bruised and confused—but otherwise unhurt. A moment later, their battered skiff also emerged, like a whale coming up for air. Astonishingly, although the boat had a bad list to port, it was otherwise intact. They made their way toward it and, with the occasional groan and grunt, helped each other back in before collapsing in a wet, panting heap. After a while, the professor eased his way, shakily, to his knees. He looked down at Jack and Angus.

"Great ride," he said, grinning from ear to ear.

Jack looked across at Angus and promptly threw up.

The lake was large—a couple of miles long. Behind them the waterfall cascaded unremittingly from the gorge above. The mountains to one side of the lake dropped dramatically toward the far end, where there looked to be a small village. To their right the land was flatter and heavily wooded, but it appeared as if there might be a decent landing spot. Leaning over the battered sides of the skiff, they used their hands to paddle to shore.

At last they pushed the skiff up onto a small stony beach where the lake met the wooded shoreline. A quick search of the boat indicated that almost everything had been lost in the final plunge into the lake. Angus unzipped the pouch in his breast pocket. The time phone was still there. He whipped it out and flipped it open. The yellow bar was still defiantly grayed out, but the distinctive lettering of the readout was glowing steadily.

```
Date:       Tuesday, June 23, 1914
Time:       8:17 a.m.
Location:   Achensee, Austria
```

"Looks OK," he muttered to himself with relief, placing the device carefully back into the zippered pouch. Jack and the professor were busy wringing out their clothes. The professor stopped for a moment and gazed across at the lake and the mountains beyond. He sniffed the air and said, "I think I know where we are. . . . "

"Achensee?" Angus asked.

The professor's face lit up. "Exactly! Achensee! How did you know?"

Angus tapped his head. "As you said, Professor, brains, twenty-first-century brains. We have silicon chip implants, you know."

The professor looked at him oddly and chose to ignore the comment. He seemed excited about where they had ended up. "We used to come up this way quite often on vacation. I know the spot well. It hasn't changed at all."

"So does that mean you know how to get us some food?"

"Better than that, I think. Nearby is the Mueller estate. I'm sure of it. It's been a while, but they used to be good family friends. I met Mueller when he worked in the diplomatic corps. The Muellers were quite big landowners around here." The professor scanned the oak woodland that fringed the lake, looking for an entry point or pathway.

Then, some way down the narrow beach, they spotted two figures emerging from the woods and marching purposefully toward them. The larger of the two, a round portly man with a red face, was shouting loudly in German. He was wearing some kind of strange hunting uniform. It included a felt hat adorned with feathers and a green high-collared jacket from the belt of which was suspended a dagger and, incredibly, a full-length sword. The outfit was completed with breeches and riding boots. His companion was a great deal shorter and thinner, dressed more modestly in knickers and a jacket, and was struggling to carry a large shotgun in one hand and a brace of rabbits hanging limply from a metal hook in the other.

The portly man strode confidently toward them, down the shallow bank and onto the pebble beach. The boys had little difficulty hearing what he was saying: "You cannot land here—no trespassing! No fishing. No hunting. No anything! This is the Mueller estate!"

The man got closer and his eyes narrowed as he focused on the group. Then, suddenly, the angry red face lightened a little.

"It cannot be . . . surely not?"

He advanced a little farther. The professor also moved forward, his hand outstretched, smiling. "Herr Mueller?"

"Pinckard-Schnell? I don't believe it."

The two men shook hands warmly, and Mueller, who was a daunting figure close up, immediately peppered the professor with questions.

"How on earth do you come to be here? It's been . . . how many years? Perhaps five? Why did you not tell me you were coming?" Then he paused for a moment, looking at Jack and Angus. "And who are these young men . . . and, my, you are wet. What has happened to you?"

The professor, forced to think quickly, responded, "My dear Mueller, we are so sorry to, er, surprise you like this. We, well, these are my nephews from England, and we are, well, the family is touring—yes, touring in the Alps. Well, we thought we would come up here for a couple of days. Show them my old holiday haunts. Left the others sightseeing in Vienna. Yes—Vienna. We thought we'd do a spot of early morning fishing, then maybe surprise you. I'm sorry, but we had a bit of a disaster with the boat. I was never much good at sports and that kind of thing, unlike you, Mueller. . . . "

Angus and Jack winced at the professor's story. He had to make it up on the spot—and it wasn't very convincing. But the truth would have been even less so. Mueller looked at the three of them for a moment in exasperation and then broke into uproarious laughter. In fact he apparently found the whole thing so funny, he nearly fell over. Meanwhile his manservant just stood there and, a bit like his brace of limp rabbits, continued to look miserable. Mueller's laughter was infectious, and soon he had the professor going as well. Between the professor's high-pitched wheezing squeal and Mueller's booming guffaw, it was quite a contest. Mueller wiped a tear from his eye.

"Come, my friends, come. No time to waste. Oskar, your jacket, please. At least one of these fine fellows can be kept warm. Now, you must come up to the house at once and we will get you all sorted out. What about your things?"

"At the bottom of the lake."

Mueller laughed again. "Dear me, dear me. Well, that's too bad.

Come now, Marta will be so excited to see you all." And with that they plunged into the woods, following Mueller and Oskar, while Mueller chattered away happily, barely pausing for breath or for anyone else to get a word in edgeways.

Mueller's house was an impressive wooden chalet set in its own grounds, surrounded by woodland and overlooking the southern end of the lake. Larger-than-life Mueller and his diminutive wife, Marta, lived well, now that Mueller was retired. Their children had left home, but there were a number of servants around, and by all accounts the Muellers had an active social life among the upper class of the Achensee valley.

The most interesting and, Jack thought, rather gruesome, aspect of the chalet, was the stuffed wildlife. Everywhere you looked there were stags' heads, chamois and ibex heads, and other, more exotic, stuffed beasts. There were even two hollowed-out elephant hooves near the front door, and a pair of giant elephant tusks adorning the entrance. Jack had read that this kind of slaughter was not thought unethical at the turn of the twentieth century. In fact, it showed sporting prowess. According to Pendelshape, Franz Ferdinand himself had bagged thousands of game animals in his lifetime—not to mention hundreds of stags. Jack realized the irony that in only five days' time Franz Ferdinand and his wife, Sophie, were going to be similarly butchered in Sarajevo.

After some loud introductions, they spent the day recuperating. Marta managed to locate some of her sons' old clothes, and now Jack and Angus looked ridiculous in traditional Austrian garb, which would not have looked out of place in *The Sound of Music*. Marta inspected Angus's outfit and sneakers closely and remarked that she had not seen anything quite like them before, but assumed they were some sort of English fashion of the time. The professor faked a call, using Mueller's recently installed telephone, to Vienna to inform the family that they would be back a little later than they had originally planned. Despite Mueller's persistence, the professor managed to decline an invitation for the fictitious family to travel the long way to Achensee to join them for an extended house party.

By late afternoon, they were sitting in Mueller's grand conservatory overlooking the lawn that led down to the lake. It was very beautiful, the grand chalet with its flower-laden window boxes, surrounded by its own woodland looking onto the pristine lake with the white-capped mountains in the distance. Jack wondered what would become of the place in the twenty-first century. Maybe it was a ski chalet, or a rehab clinic for aging celebrities.

The professor and Mueller were trading stories about what had happened since they had last met. The professor had been working for the German military in a research job at the time, and Mueller, before he retired, had been an attaché with the Austrian diplomatic service. Mueller was now onto one of his favorite subjects—the "problem" of the southern Slavs and the Balkans. His small and patient audience was more than happy to nod and listen, while sampling freely from the large plates of cakes, sandwiches, and cookies that had been laid before them.

"Of course, we had no option but to annex Bosnia and Herzegovina in 1908, although in so doing we added a million Slavs to the empire—most of them peasants." Mueller puffed on a large pipe as he held court. "We had to show that we could still act as a great power, and we couldn't with a strong Serbia on our doorstep. You know it's not easy for us—a patchwork of so many nationalities. If we show weakness to one group, the whole Austro-Hungarian Empire could collapse . . . and that would be tragic." Mueller turned to Angus, who had just taken a large bite of cake, and boomed, "Do you know how long the Habsburgs have ruled, my boy?"

Angus's mouth was filled with cream cake. He tried to say "No," but it came out as a sort of *ooarg* sound, and bits of saliva and cake spluttered onto the tablecloth. Angus blushed, swallowed, and covered his mouth. "Er, sorry."

Mueller looked bemused, but pressed on. "Since 1273 . . . 1273, I tell you! You English talk about the British Empire being the empire on which the sun never sets, but that title first belonged to our mighty Habsburg Empire. We stretched across Europe to Spain and even South America!" Another large smoke ring wafted up into the air as Mueller exhaled. Jack nearly gagged.

"You're a true *Schwarzgelb*, Mueller," the professor said.

Mueller snorted in acknowledgment. "But we need to watch out! Now, after the Balkan wars of a couple of years ago, of course Serbia is much stronger. Turkey has lost most of its possessions in Europe, you know, Professor?" The professor nodded. "We have so many Serbs within the empire. Serbia is becoming stronger by the day, egged on by their wretched students and revolutionaries and those damned Russians. They have their eye on Bosnia and Herzegovina next. A direct threat to our empire . . . "

Mueller took another long puff on his pipe and then exhaled a curling wisp of blue smoke, adding sinisterly, "No, there's no doubt, we will need to teach Serbia a lesson sooner or later."

Mueller paused and, without warning, turned to Jack and Angus. "Politics, I'm afraid, my young friends. A bit boring for you, I think. Anyway, let us change the subject. Tell me now, what did you think of Vienna—isn't it a jewel?"

Jack and Angus had not anticipated this. Contrary to the professor's story, they had never been to Vienna in their lives. Jack looked at Angus nervously and blushed. He was stumped.

"Well? Has my friend the professor not shown you the Belvedere, Schönbrunn Palace, and all the other wonderful sights? Don't be shy. Come on, what did you think of it?"

There was a pained silence, then Angus suddenly blurted out, "It was cool."

Jack nearly fell out of his seat.

Mueller frowned. "Cool? At this time of year? I don't think so. It is typically very warm in June." He turned to the professor with a confused expression on his face.

"Professor? Was it cool?"

"Er, yes, Mueller. In fact, it was unseasonably cold the day we arrived, but, er, we did not stay too long, as we were so keen to visit the mountains. We are saving the sights for our return."

Mueller eyed the boys with a puzzled expression for a moment, but then accepted the explanation and moved on.

"Oh, I see. I see. Well, you have much to look forward to."

Day of the Assassins

Distracted, he withdrew a pocket watch attached to a chain from his breast pocket and grunted in satisfaction.

"Professor, I think it might be that time. How about a brandy?"

The professor sighed in relief. "Most kind, Mueller."

"Excellent! Anna, if you please?"

For the first time, Jack noticed that a young woman, a servant, had been waiting patiently at the entrance to the conservatory. She had a dark complexion and brown eyes. She appeared not to be listening to the conversation but staring straight ahead. Jack noticed that Angus was staring at the maid admiringly. But Angus's trance was broken as, with Mueller's order, she scuttled off to fetch the brandy. Jack thought it was strange to have someone in the room who was just an ornament—except when required to serve.

The brandy arrived, and the professor had the presence of mind to excuse Jack and Angus, who gratefully grasped the opportunity. Not sure what to do, Jack stood and did an awkward little bow and thanked Mueller. He nudged Angus. Having never bowed before in his life, Angus's attempt at the procedure was comical—as if he was lowering himself onto an imaginary toilet. They then left the room, trying not to appear in a hurry.

Mueller looked at them with curiosity as they departed.

"Friendly young men, Professor, your nephews . . . interesting, er, manners."

The professor shrugged. "English. You know what they're like."

Mueller snorted, took a gulp from his brandy goblet, and busied himself with refilling his pipe. "Anyway, Professor, speaking of the English, tell me about your work with the Royal Navy. . . . "

Angus and Jack made their way up the old wooden stairs to their bedroom at the top of the chalet. The room had a low-beamed ceiling and, like the rest of the house, extensive wooden paneling. There were twin beds on either side of the room and two old pictures of local hunting scenes. The horns of some unfortunate animal had been pinned to one wall. The window gave out onto a balcony with an elaborately carved balustrade. Beyond, shadows crept through the woodland as the sun sank below the mountains.

Angus flopped onto one of the beds.

"That was a near miss."

"You idiot. You could have said something better than that. 'It was cool.'"

"At least I said something."

Jack removed his jacket and lazily dropped it onto the floor before collapsing onto his own bed.

"Let's take a look, then."

"What—the time phone?"

"See if it's changed at all."

Angus took out the device. He flipped it open. They inspected the miniature readout:

```
Date:       Tuesday, June 23, 1914
Time:       7:47 p.m.
Location:   Achensee, Austria
```

"Five more days until the assassination," Jack said. "And no yellow light."

"We're still stuck. No escape."

"Does that thing ever light up?"

Suddenly, there was a knock at the door. Angus quickly closed the time phone and slipped it back into his pocket.

"I bet it's the Prof." Jack called to the door, "Come in!"

But it wasn't the professor. The door opened and the boys were surprised to see Anna, the maid who they had last seen being barked at by Mueller in the conservatory.

Angus sprang from the bed as if he had received a mild electric shock.

"I prepare room for sleeping," she announced in broken English.

Angus's face lit up. "Sounds like an excellent idea. . . . "

Jack rolled his eyes. Anna either did not understand the remark or just ignored it.

Jack said, "You really don't have to. We can . . . "

"No. My duty."

She moved into the room and stooped to pick up Jack's coat from the floor. Embarrassed that she felt it necessary to do so, Jack also reached down for the coat, trying to beat her to it. They both stooped simultaneously and there was a loud *crack* as their heads banged together. Jack winced. Anna clutched her head. Then she giggled.

"Nice one, mate," Angus said sarcastically.

"Are you OK?" Jack said.

Anna grimaced. "No—not OK. You are clumsy."

Angus laughed. "You've got that right—you should see him play rugby."

Jack put out his hand, "Jack Christie. Very pleased to meet you."

Anna smiled again and shook his hand gently. "I, Anna Matronovic."

Although she wore a maid's white smock and cap, she held herself with poise and looked Jack straight in the eye with a challenging self-confidence. Yet she couldn't have been more than eighteen years old. Close up, Jack could understand why she had caught Angus's attention. She had dark, hypnotic brown eyes and was exceptionally pretty; Jack stared longer than he probably should have. As he picked up his coat, a piece of paper slipped onto the floor. Again, Anna stooped to pick it up. As she did so, she glanced at the paper and a puzzled expression slowly crept over her face. She did not return it to Jack but studied it intently.

"What is this?" She finally asked. Her face was flushed.

Jack looked at the paper Anna was holding and suddenly realized what it was—the photo of Pendelshape and the plotters of the Black Hand. Jack had transferred it to the coat provided by the Muellers. Despite the drenching in the lake, it was still intact and Pendelshape and his "friends" stared back at them eerily.

"It's mine. It's just a photograph. . . . "

Anna's brow furrowed.

"Where you get it?"

Jack faltered. "A friend . . . "

Anna looked down at the photo again.

"You know the English teacher, Dr. Pendelshape? He said he would send help soon. You and the professor, you sent by him to help us . . . yes?"

Jack and Angus couldn't believe what Anna had just said. They looked at each other, stunned. "Hold on, what did you say? How do you know—?"

Anna ignored the interruption and carried on quietly, urgently. "I understand now. I must talk to friends. I go now. But you in danger here. Big danger. We must go soon." She was very agitated. "I get message to friends in Vienna, Belgrade, Doboj. You say nothing. We talk later."

And with that she ghosted from the room.

Jack fingered the edges of the photo nervously, looking back to the door that had closed behind Anna.

"She knows Pendelshape. It's incredible," he said.

"And what's this stuff about Belgrade?"

"Belgrade. Belgrade—doesn't that tell you anything?"

"No," Angus said stubbornly.

Jack sighed impatiently. He was a step ahead. "It's where the photo was taken. Belgrade is the capital of Serbia. Remember, that's what all this is about—Austria and Serbia are enemies. Just like Mueller was saying."

"But what's that got to do with Anna, and how does she know Pendelshape?"

Jack sighed. "Keep up, Angus. *Matronovic. Belgrade.* Anna's a Serb. What she's doing in the house of a rich Austrian like Mueller, though, I have no idea." But suddenly he had a realization.

"Of course! Matronovic."

Jack flipped the photo over. The names written in Pendelshape's distinctive scrawl could still just be made out—*Princip and Matronovic.*

"Dani, wasn't it? Dani Matronovic."

"You don't think . . . ?"

"Yes, Anna has the same name, Matronovic, and recognized the people in the photograph. Pendelshape said the picture was taken by Dani's sister—Anna!"

"Incredible!"

"Yeah, incredible all right. Anna is a Bosnian Serb working here, for some reason. She and Dani met Pendelshape when he traveled back, testing the Taurus, and now she must think we have been sent by Pendelshape . . . to help them." Jack exhaled slowly. "Angus, it looks like you, me, and the professor are going to have to make that decision we talked about."

"What?"

Jack sighed. "Come on, Angus, you were the one who was going on about it. What Dad said. It's what we talked about last night— up in the gorge."

"What, you mean try to stop the assassination?"

"Yes. Anna can probably lead us to the assassins. In fact, she is expecting us to help them—because of what Pendelshape promised when he was here. If we make contact with the assassins, we can probably somehow stop the assassination from happening. Just like Pendelshape and Dad want."

There was a pause before he added, "That is, if we want to get involved at all."

"Well, you know what I think already. I think we should," Angus said. "And anyway"—he grinned—"I'm happy to help Anna as much as she wants."

"Come on, Angus. This is serious. Listen, I know what Dad and Pendelshape want to do. And I also know that the professor agrees with them."

"So what's the problem?"

"I'm not sure. Maybe it's not as simple as that. I'm thinking maybe we should just wait until we have a signal on your time phone—if that's ever going to happen—and then we'll travel back to Dad and work it out with him. Or maybe just give ourselves up to the Rector again."

Angus jumped off the bed. "No way! If you do that, you're on your own. You saw what they did to me . . . and to poor old Pendelino."

"I'm not sure, Angus. Is it really up to us?"

"We're involved whether we like it or not. And anyway, if you'd heard what your Dad said about it; you'd know the right thing to do would be to help them. I think your Dad would expect you to."

"Maybe. But see, I'm not sure I know how we could stop the assassination even if it is the right thing to do. We have no idea how Pendelshape and Dad had planned to stop it."

"Well, I'm not hanging around for those VIGIL nutters to catch up with us again and lynch us!"

"I don't know, Angus. The Rector seemed to make sense at the castle. . . . He was OK."

"Yeah? Well, I'm sorry, but he wasn't sensible when I last saw him with his bunch of thugs back at school."

Jack had no answer.

Later, Jack lay back on his bed and stared up at the ceiling. He felt very tired and slowly closed his eyes. Images from the last two days flickered randomly through his head as he fell into a light sleep. In his dream Angus and the professor were marching ahead of him down a muddy track. He was trying to keep up, telling them to slow down, to wait, but they kept going and going and seemed to know exactly what they were doing. Coming toward them on the same track marched a column of bedraggled men. On the horizon, way beyond, the air lit up with white-and-orange flashes of artillery fire. The earth rumbled beneath their feet. The line of men stumbled on past them. Their uniforms were dirty, bloody, and torn. Each one of them rested a hand on the shoulder of the soldier in front of him. Then Jack noticed that they were blindfolded—a single grubby white bandage around each head.

Without warning, as he hurried after the professor and Angus, one of the soldiers stopped, broke from the line, and squatted down in front of him. His face was dirty and lined—the pale skin hanging heavy with fatigue. Then, to Jack's surprise, the soldier put out one hand toward him and his lips curled up into a weak smile. Suddenly, to Jack's horror, the blindfold was whipped away and he found himself looking straight into two bloodied pits where the eyes should have been.

Muellered

Jack woke with a start. His sheets were wet with sweat. The room was dark. It took him a moment to understand where he was. He heard a gentle knocking at the door, and then a young woman's voice whispered, "Jack! Jack!"

Coming to his senses, he crept to the door and opened it a fraction. Two big brown eyes peered back at him. It was Anna.

"Wake your friend and listen carefully. I have plan."

Mueller had decided that he would drive them personally from Achensee to the train station in Innsbruck. He wanted to show off his new Mercedes-Benz. Picking up where he had left off the evening before, he continued to chatter away, starting off by pointing out all the features of the large motorcar. Somehow they had all managed to squeeze in, together with Anna. Marta had been left at home and was a little tearful to see them go, but there was no room for her, and anyway, she was "afraid of motorcars."

The mighty machine took three hours to make its way down from the Achensee valley to the town of Innsbruck. They had to stop several times. Mueller's excuse was that the radiator needed a refill, or something under the hood needed adjusting. But his main objective was to rummage in the trunk for refreshment. These stops proved good opportunities for Angus and Jack to surreptitiously inspect the time phone. The distinctive yellow bar remained stubbornly blank, just as it had since they escaped from the castle.

The station was busy when they finally arrived. The massive black hulk of the Vienna train was steaming gently alongside the platform as people boarded. Mueller had kindly supplied them with a small basket of food for the trip, and he had even given the professor some money to replace what had been lost in the lake. As they prepared to board the train, Mueller shook each of their hands warmly. Anna stood a little behind Mueller, eclipsed by his massive bulk.

They climbed aboard and found a compartment all to themselves. It was small and smelled of coal smoke but comfortable. They spread themselves out on the neatly upholstered bench seats. Mueller was also sending Anna to Vienna—with a long shopping list—but she had been banished to one of the third-class carriages farther down the platform. Soon, the train was rumbling through the Austrian countryside, which looked greener than ever. It was hard to believe that this was a country on the brink of war.

The professor was relieved to have extracted them from the Mueller household without arousing unnecessary suspicion.

"You did well, boys."

"Funny chap, Mueller," Jack said.

"We were lucky. He and I go back a long way. He—"

Jack interrupted, "We should explain, Professor. Anna, the maid, she's not what she seems. She's a Serb."

"A spy," Angus added.

The professor looked shocked. "What? What do you mean?"

Jack took Pendelshape's photograph from his pocket and handed it to the professor.

"Remember this, Professor? Anna took this photograph."

"What?" the professor exclaimed. "But . . . "

Jack pointed at one of the figures in the picture. "That's Anna's brother, Dani. He is a member of the Black Hand. They are a Serb underground movement."

"Incredible!" The professor held the photo level with his eyes. "So how on earth did Anna come to be working in Mueller's house?"

"She was placed there to keep tabs on him. Remember? You told us he worked for the Austrian diplomatic service. Anna says he still has senior contacts, apparently. There is a large network of informants, like Anna. They're everywhere. But the main point is"—Jack took the photograph from the professor and held it in front of them so they could all study it properly—"that Anna and her brother, Dani, know Pendelshape."

They all looked at the photograph closely.

"This morning Anna explained to us who they all are," Jack continued. "The photo was taken in Belgrade when Pendelshape, my dad, and the rest of the VIGIL team originally tested the Taurus, just before Dad disappeared. Look—there's Pendelshape. Anyway, that one is Gavrilo Princip, the man who shoots Archduke Franz Ferdinand this Sunday in Sarajevo . . . four days from now."

"So how do these plotters know Anna's brother? How is he involved?"

"Part of the Belgrade café set, but that's not all." Jack looked at Angus nervously. "Anna and Dani's father was murdered. Anna didn't tell us the whole story, but the Austrian authorities did nothing about it."

"So Anna and Dani don't like living under Austrian rule?" the professor asked.

"Hate it. Anyway, it seems that Pendelshape quite easily penetrated the plotters' circle by traveling as an English academic with a big interest in the southern Slavs. He pretended to be sympathetic to them, gave them money, that kind of thing. They were grateful for Pendelshape's support—being so poor and eager for any help that they could get to fight the Austro-Hungarian Empire."

"Wait," the professor said. "I thought your teacher, Pendelshape, and your father wanted to stop the assassination and the war . . . not help the Bosnian Serb conspirators who trigger it."

"You're right, Professor," Jack said. "Angus and I talked about it last night."

The professor raised his eyebrows expectantly.

"Using their knowledge of history, Pendelshape and my dad wanted to get the trust of the conspirators, infiltrate the group, and then, at the last moment, disrupt the entire plot, stop the assassination, and thereby prevent the war from starting. It's quite the opposite of what Anna and Dani think."

Angus added, "Yeah, and Anna and Dani were taken in by Pendelshape. He must have impressed them, because they trust him completely."

"So Anna now trusts us as well."

"And Anna thinks that Pendelshape was a friend and will be returning soon to help them," the professor said.

"Yes, but Pendelshape isn't a friend at all. He was going to blow the whole thing. He was going to betray Anna and Dani. But Anna thinks we have been sent by Pendelshape. She thinks our guise as English boys traveling abroad with our German uncle is a good one. Mueller thinks she is going to Vienna to do some shopping for him, but when we get there, she'll meet us at the station and then she wants to take us to Dani. After that, she didn't say. But she assumes we have instructions from Pendelshape to help them. Her first job is to get us to the assassins."

As Jack explained it all, the professor's eyes flashed in anticipation. "Well, this is our chance!" He nodded. "Yes, we now have a way in— a way to stop this horrible war from happening, just as your father and Dr. Pendelshape intended!"

After many hours the train slowed as they at last approached Vienna—the center of the Austro-Hungarian Empire. The professor and Angus were slumped in one corner of the carriage, the gentle movement of the train having rocked them to sleep. Jack craned his neck—sure enough, they were rumbling toward a large station.

"Wake up—we're here!"

The professor and Angus came around, eyes blinking. The train creaked to a gentle halt with a loud hissing of smoke and steam. Doors swung open onto the hubbub of the platform.

Angus studied their new surroundings. "Vienna, eh? Cool."

"I've heard that before," Jack said.

Anna pushed through the throng that was emerging from the third-class carriages and greeted them with a warm smile. She had jettisoned her maid's outfit, and her long hair flowed loosely—a first gesture of freedom. There would be no return to the drudgery and humiliation of life in the Mueller household for her.

She looked around furtively. "You need to follow me," she said quietly.

But they had no time to obey.

At that moment, they were surrounded by five uniformed officials. Out of the shadows, a sixth man appeared. He wore a simple double-breasted suit and a straw boater. He was a thin, wiry man, and he spoke English with a strong foreign accent.

"Welcome to Vienna," he said. "I hope you had a pleasant journey from Innsbruck? We have been expecting you. Please, let me introduce myself—Friedrich Kessler. I work for the Austrian government."

Schönbrunn Shenanigans

The professor started to speak. "What is the meaning—?" Kessler put his finger to his lips. "Please, Professor, no trouble now. If you would like to come with us, I assure you, you and your, er, family, will come to no harm. No harm at all."

They were marched through the station concourse, causing a flurry of heads to turn in the crowd.

"What's this all about?" Angus whispered.

"Well, one thing's for sure: these guys: don't look like VIGIL agents, more like army guards or something," Jack replied.

"That's exactly what they are," the professor said out of the corner of his mouth.

But Anna, for one, was not going to hang around for confirmation. Suddenly, she elbowed the guard next to her in his solar plexus and then bit his hand—hard. She writhed free and made a dash into the thronging crowd on the concourse. One of the guards raised his rifle. But it was too late—Anna was gone.

Kessler swore and harshly reprimanded the guards, who now gripped Jack, Angus, and the professor firmly by the arm, so they couldn't try a similar stunt. They were bundled unceremoniously into a waiting van outside. The professor protested again but was ignored, and the van rumbled off with the trio and two guards in the back.

The professor rattled the mesh that separated them from the driver's cabin.

"What's happening? Where are you taking us?"

Kessler replied evenly, "Please calm down, Professor. All will be explained shortly."

The van rumbled along, and from their cramped position inside, it was difficult to make out their direction through the streets of Vienna.

Jack was scared. "What's going on, Professor?"

"No idea, and I don't know Vienna well, but if these are Austrian officials, there are a limited number of places they could be taking us: a police station, maybe one of the jails, maybe even the Belvedere . . . "

"Or maybe, there." Angus pointed through one of the slit windows. Through the narrow aperture they caught sight of the most incredible building that Jack had ever seen. In books he had seen pictures of the Palace of Versailles, outside of Paris, but this seemed to eclipse even that.

The professor nodded knowingly. "Schönbrunn. It's Schönbrunn Palace. The home of the Habsburgs. This is where the emperor lives."

"Looks like they have plenty of rooms."

"One thousand four hundred and forty-one at the last count," the professor said.

"Why do they have so many?" Angus asked.

"Because they can," Jack replied.

They came to a stop, and the guards bundled them out of the van. As the modest entourage filed around the outskirts of the palace, Jack craned his neck to get a better view of the magnificent building. From whichever angle you looked, it exuded splendor. Jack had seen wealth in his own time, of course, and had heard people bemoan the gap between the rich and the poor, but he had never seen wealth like this.

They were led through an entrance at the rear of the palace, up some stairs, and then through an increasingly ornate series of passages and state rooms. Finally, they entered a vast gallery. It must have been at least fifty yards long and it stopped Jack in his tracks. Along one side, a series of massive arched windows displayed the formal gardens beyond. Opposite these, huge gilt-framed mirrors reflected the light to make the whole room appear even larger. Above them, the ceiling was painted with three grand frescoes between which hung crystal chandeliers that looked like oversized wedding cakes.

"The Great Gallery," the professor murmured.

Jack was stunned by the extraordinary opulence. The place was making him feel very small. Halfway down the gallery, they were ushered into an unusual oval-shaped room. Lacquered compartments of varying shapes and sizes were set into white-painted wooden panels in the walls. Each compartment was framed in gold and housed its own piece of blue-and-white porcelain sculpture. Kessler gestured for them to sit at an ornate table and spoke for the first time since their hurried journey from the station.

"Count Sieghard will join us shortly. In the meantime, I will ensure that you receive some refreshments." He said no more and slipped quietly from the room.

"Count Sieghard," Angus whispered. "Who's he?"

They didn't have to wait long to find out.

The guards stationed by the door flinched slightly as a tall, gray-haired man swept into the room. The two guards quickly disappeared, closing the doors behind them. The man was dressed in a high-collared double-breasted jacket with two columns of brass buttons and elaborate gold braid around the collar and cuffs. His trousers had a twin red braid down each side. Whoever he was, he was important.

He settled himself down at the end of the table, and they got a closer look at his face. He was perhaps in his forties, with finely chiseled features and a good head of silver hair, which gave him an air of distinction. Jack thought there was something unusual about the man's face, something that made him seem a little out of place. But for the moment he could not quite make out what it was. Then he realized. All the men he had encountered on his journey so far— Mueller, Kessler, the people in Innsbruck and at the Vienna station— had mustaches. Some of them had real handlebar jobs. But this man had no mustache, which put him quite out of place with his surroundings. In fact, he would have been much more at home in London wearing a pinstriped suit.

The professor bravely managed to find his voice again. "Sir, I don't know who you are, or why we are here, but I am a member of—"

Count Sieghard raised his hand. It was all that was needed to silence the poor professor on the spot.

"Please, Professor Pinckard-Schnell," he spoke smoothly in crisp English with effortless confidence. "Of course, we owe you an explanation . . . and to you as well, Jack and Angus." He smiled. "My young time adventurers."

Jack and Angus exchanged glances nervously.

"I'm afraid that your friend, Herr Mueller, has somewhat turned you in."

The professor frowned. "Mueller? What has—?"

"Yes, Professor, I know he appears to be a complete idiot . . . and of course to some extent he is. But he is still a loyal idiot. Mueller didn't like what he was doing. But nevertheless felt he had to do it. I'm afraid he betrayed you. I don't think Herr Mueller really bought your story of being on holiday in the Alps. And, of course, word has gone out among our network, so we have been looking to pick up a man and two, er, younger men, with your description for forty-eight hours now. Mueller *is* an ex-member of the Austrian diplomatic corps, and he was able to correctly identify you when you appeared on his land. I'm afraid he had no choice but to turn you in."

"So we are being held by the Austrian government? May I ask for what possible reason? We have done nothing wrong, and may I add, I am a citizen of the German Empire!"

Sieghard waved his hand dismissively. "Yes, yes, Professor. Please don't waste my time."

The professor fell silent.

"I should introduce myself properly. This might make things a little clearer for you. You have probably heard my name by now. I expect my colleague, your rector in fact, boys, may have referred to me. I chair VIGIL, and I have played a modest part in a not unimpressive scientific achievement. . . . " He smiled for the first time. It was a little disconcerting. "The invention of time travel.

And it has been my dubious pleasure, along with your rector and the rest of our team, to try to prevent your father, Jack, from doing something completely mad. My real name, of course, is not Count Sieghard at all, but Inchquin. Counselor Inchquin."

It took a few moments for them to take in what Counselor Inchquin had said, and it slowly dawned on them. Here was the Rector's boss: the man who chaired VIGIL and directed the whole secret operation. He was the one who was responsible for having them chased halfway around Europe. He was, in fact, the man who controlled time travel.

"Yes, I know it must all seem rather confusing . . . so perhaps I should explain. First of all, you've probably gathered that you are at Schönbrunn Palace. The home of the Habsburgs and the center of the Austro-Hungarian Empire. The current occupants might be alarmed to find that in our time, nearly a hundred years from now, seven million tourists a year tramp through the palace and its gardens. But anyway, how did I come to be here?" He nodded as if to say "good question."

"Well, with the significant benefit of hindsight and VIGIL's encyclopedic knowledge of history, it has proven quite easy to insert myself into the apparatus of the Austrian bureaucracy, acting as a visiting foreign diplomat. Although I have no executive role here— that would be far too intrusive in terms of my impact on the future course of history—I have a temporary position that allows me to know what is going on. Call me a special agent, if you will. And, of course, knowing the personal history of some of the key players will make it a little easier for me to 'influence,' if I must, and tidy up any damage that your journey might cause. Hindsight is a wonderful thing." He paused. "Yes, I have access to them all: the Austrian premier, Count Sturkh; the Hungarian premier, Count Tisza . . . " He shrugged, "And, if I were to need it, an audience with the Emperor Franz Joseph himself could be easily arranged." He sighed with satisfaction. "Now that we understand what Pendelshape and your father are up to, we have had to put in place contingency plans. Thus my rather unusual presence here. But currently, we have no need to do anything. Everything seems to be moving along quite nicely.

Just as the course of history intended. And that is exactly how it should be."

Inchquin now looked at them more gravely. "This war will happen despite the antics of my old colleague, Christie, and the turncoat Pendelshape."

The professor finally spoke up: "Counselor Inchquin, I think I speak for the boys here as well as myself. We have no wish to become embroiled in something we do not understand. We have become involved in this simply by chance. We are innocent victims. All we wish is to return to our lives."

"Do you really think there is such a thing as 'chance,' Professor?" Inchquin snapped. "History is determined. There is a required course of events, and we meddle with them at our peril. Although you protest to be innocent bystanders, I am afraid that you are involved whether you like it or not. We must therefore consider very carefully what we do next. I think the Rector explained the VIGIL Imperative and the delicate role we in VIGIL must play in terms of preventing and controlling interventions that are made in history. And this is not helped by fools like your father, Jack," he added bitterly.

The professor tried to stay calm. "Counselor Inchquin, we have no desire to interfere with your plans."

Of course, Jack knew what the professor really thought, and that this was a lie.

Inchquin shrugged. "Sometimes, desperate times call for desperate measures. We are dealing with matters of utmost importance, and now we must take executive action."

"What does that mean?"

"It's just as the Rector explained to you. While we have you, we can protect you from your father. You are the only hold that we have over him. I'm afraid that you will be incarcerated here until we can get a time signal to send you back home. From there on, you will need to be protected at all times from him. But until we can get you home, we must limit your contact with the outside world, though . . . " he added with a little more warmth, "we will try to make your stay as comfortable as possible."

"You're going to lock us up again?" Jack said.

"It is for your protection."

"What about the war?" the professor said, his voice rising in agitation. Inchquin looked at the professor. "What about it? When Princip pulls the trigger in Sarajevo on Sunday, four days from now, the cogs of history will grind inexorably forward and we will have our war. I will stay here to ensure that the diplomatic process is smoothly executed. And you will stay here, Jack, to ensure that neither your father, nor Pendelshape for that matter, do anything stupid. If they do, I fear your father may find himself without an heir."

Inchquin's words hung ominously in the air. There was no emotion, no histrionics. There didn't need to be. He held all the cards. "Ah, one thing I nearly forgot. Your time phone, Angus." Inchquin held out a hand. "If you please." Angus reluctantly removed the precious device from his pocket and slid it over the table. Inchquin eyed the time phone in his hand.

"Thank you." He nodded. "I must say, very impressive of your father, Jack, to re-create all this. And he was certainly taking a risk by giving this to you, Angus. He must have known it might fall into our hands. But that's just like him. Brilliant—but impetuous. A risk taker. He hasn't changed. But now, finally, I have a time phone that is linked to his Taurus. We can use it to give him a little surprise." He flipped open the time phone and peered at the display. "As I thought. No signal. But there will be at some point, and then we'll be able to locate your father and his Taurus and get rid of this whole annoying problem once and for all."

Inchquin got to his feet. The meeting was over. He clapped his hands and the guards reentered the room to usher them back through the Great Gallery and into the bowels of the palace to begin their imprisonment. Inchquin stopped at the door to acknowledge their departure. The professor and Angus were escorted away, and a third guard was about to take Jack when Inchquin unexpectedly touched him on the shoulder.

"Jack, one last thing. How is your mother?" Under the circumstances, Jack felt this to be the strangest of questions. He didn't really know what to say. "She's fine. I hope." Inchquin smiled. It was an odd smile —there may have been even a hint of warmth there, warmth that had been absent from the earlier conversation. But it also hid a tinge of embarrassment, perhaps guilt. He said quietly, "That's good, Jack, that's good. She has been loyal to us, and she and I, well, since Geneva and through all this turmoil, we have become good . . . friends." He paused and grimaced slightly. "This is not easy. Not easy for any of us. But I want you to know that we are doing the right thing. We are not monsters. I just hope your father sees sense. I really do, Jack. . . . I really do."

The words lingered briefly in the air. But Jack had little time to consider their meaning before he was marched off with the others. As they made their way from the Great Gallery, a small group appeared ahead of them. Their escorts suddenly halted and gestured for Jack, Angus, and the professor to follow suit. In unison they dropped their heads in a bow. In the center of the group ahead was an old man. He was dressed like Inchquin, the same light gray double-breasted tunic with brass buttons, high braided collar, and gold-braided cuffs. An insignia of some high office dropped from his neck, and a number of impressive medals hung from his left collar. He was balding but had a fine white mustache and white mutton-chop sideburns. Although the man was old, he was tall and had the straight back of a horseman. He carried himself with an air of superiority. Suddenly Jack realized that he was gazing upon the emperor himself—Franz Joseph.

As the entourage crossed their path, the emperor glanced over and, for a split second, Jack caught his sharp blue eyes and realized that he was looking into a different era. An era when God gave power to the few, who in turn took on the responsibility of ruling. He realized that although he and the emperor were both human, they were a whole world apart. And in a way, this pending war would be the very thing that made Jack so different from him. It was going to be the great watershed between the old and the new. The emperor turned his head away again. He had not even registered the odd presence of Jack and his friends, chaperoned by Inchquin and his helpers. He was not to know that in only four days' time his own nephew would be assassinated in Sarajevo, triggering a chain of events that would lead to the end of his mighty empire.

Incident at the Orangery

Jack, Angus, and the professor were led back into the depths of the palace. The building was endless. You could have fit a hundred Cairnfields inside this place and still have have had room for the yard.

At last they were deposited in rooms close to the servants' quarters on the ground floor at the rear of the palace. There was a small bedroom with two bunk beds and a larger living room furnished simply with a table and four wooden chairs. There were no windows, only a couple of metal-grilled skylights. Two guards had been stationed outside the door. This was to be their home until . . . well, until they were told otherwise. Jack took the chance to wash in the small bathroom that adjoined the bedroom. A strange array of early twentieth-century bathroom accoutrements had been supplied, and although he was unsure what a number of them were for, he did identify some soap, which took forever to lather.

He peered into the mirror. Somebody stared back, but it didn't look much like him. His eyes seemed to have turned a dullish gray, and his blond hair was greasy. He rubbed his tired eyes, as if tuning an old TV set, trying to improve the image before him. He remembered what Inchquin had said about his mom—*becoming good friends*. It hadn't really registered at the time, but now the remarks combined uneasily with his mom's guarded attitude toward his father and her unwillingness to trust Jack with what she had known all along. He frowned. Was there something else his mom hadn't told him? Jack felt a sudden stab of despair. He sat on the edge of the bathtub. Here he was, stuck nearly a hundred years in the past, with no obvious way home. He was a pawn in a battle in which he was unsure which side was right and which side was wrong. It was a battle that had torn his own family apart. It had meant that he had to grow up without a dad and with a mom who felt she couldn't tell him the truth. Jack put his head in his hands. But he didn't cry.

When he emerged from the bathroom, the professor had his head propped up on two pillows as he read Jack's history book, which he had somehow managed to hold on to. Angus sat at the table fidgeting with a splinter of wood, trying to remove some dirt from under his fingernails. There had been no discussion since the meeting with Counselor Inchquin, and the naive excitement that they had shared on the train journey from Innsbruck was long gone.

As they slowly prepared for bed, they heard muffled voices from the servants' quarters outside their rooms. Then the door to their living room swung open. A small posse of guards marched in, followed by Inchquin. He was holding a time phone.

"Sorry to disturb you, gentlemen," he announced. "However, we have our time signal—much sooner than we anticipated. This is our chance to send you home and to pay that little visit I promised to your father, Jack. Come—we must get down to business immediately."

Inchquin took a step over to the table, gesturing for them all to gather around. But one step was as far as he got.

There was a deafening explosion, and a powerful shock wave hit them like an express train. Jack was propelled backward and landed awkwardly on the stone floor, a cloud of dust and plaster fragments spraying over him. He spluttered uncontrollably and raised his head, trying to peer through the swirling dust. The brick wall on the far side of their room had collapsed. It was now just a smoking heap of bricks. Jack pulled himself shakily to his feet. Angus and the professor were in front of him, shouting and pointing, but all Jack could hear was a loud ringing in his ears. He tried to shout back, "I can't hear you!" but his words came out as a muffled booming in his own head. They pointed again, and Jack could see the silhouette of two figures appear in the large hole that had been created in the wall by the explosion.

Beyond the figures, Jack could make out the palace grounds and the vague shape of trees. The two figures were gesturing wildly at them. They were being rescued!

He rushed forward, following closely behind Angus and the professor who had already made it out into the garden. As he moved through the living room, he spotted Inchquin. He had caught the full force of the blast and was lying on the floor, moaning. He was hurt—hit by a piece of flying mortar—and his face was white with dust and plaster. Dark blood, oozing from a wound on his forehead, was starting to mix into it. Lying next to Inchquin, seemingly untouched, and still open and glinting on the stone floor, Jack spotted Angus's time phone. He snatched it up, then clambered over the debris that was strewn across the floor and through the ragged hole created by the explosion. From out of the shadows two more rescuers dashed forward. One was a man—large and stocky. As they approached, Jack could see they were both carrying rifles. The second figure was smaller, slimmer—a young woman. In the darkness, he could just see her smile, and she put out her hand to greet him. The big brown eyes and wide face were unmistakable.

"Anna?"

"Nice to see you again, Jack Christie. Sorry about our bomb. We wanted a little bang, but we make big bang. This is my brother, Dani, and friends—Vaso and Goran. We thought you needed help, so we came."

"But how did you . . . ?"

As he spoke, she stopped smiling. There was shouting as the guards regrouped in the room behind them. A shot rang out and whistled past Jack's temple. In one fluid motion, Anna raised her rifle and, aiming over Jack's shoulder, closed one eye and squeezed the trigger. The rifle bucked violently in her slender hands, and the gunshot exploded right beside Jack's ear. Instantly she slipped back the bolt, released the used cartridge, and smoothly refilled it with a fresh round from her belt. She fired again, without hesitation. The guards dived for cover.

Anna and Dani hurried the three of them onward.

"Quick—this way!"

Jack's head was ringing like a fire alarm—first from the crude bomb that their rescuers had used to blow a hole in the wall and now from the rifle that had just discharged an inch from his ear. Another shot rang out and whistled over his head. One thing was certain: if they hung around in all this confusion, one of them was going to get killed. Anna and Dani dashed off into the palace grounds, and they had no choice but to follow. But right ahead, the air shimmered. There was a flash of white light, and close in front of them, a VIGIL guard appeared. There was another flash and another VIGIL guard appeared.

Jack groaned. He couldn't believe it—Tony and Gordon.

Tony leered at them through the gloom. "Evening, all," he said, and readied his APR. "Let's just all hold our horses, calm down, and not try anything silly."

Tony and Gordon were not alone. Soon the grounds outside the palace were alight with blinding flashes as guard after guard appeared—each armed and dressed in VIGIL's telltale flak jackets. At least ten guards fanned out in front of them. Inchquin must have planned for reinforcements to travel from the Taurus as soon as there was an available signal. He planned to secure and protect Jack once and for all before executing the raid on his father's base.

Inchquin had dragged himself to his feet and was issuing orders. The palace guards in their bright uniforms and plumed hats emerged from the hole in the wall and approached them from behind. With Tony, Gordon, and the other VIGIL guards in front of them, they were now trapped. Jack looked at his friends. Angus was standing with his fists clenched defiantly by his sides. The professor, yellow hair messy as ever, was following the proceedings with a detached curiosity, as if he were observing a strange experiment. Anna was grim faced. The reckless confidence she had shown a moment before had vanished. She lowered her rifle, realizing the hopelessness of their situation. Her lower lip was trembling in fear. She knew what the Austro-Hungarian Empire did to traitors. Jack suddenly felt a pang of sympathy for her, and as they stood there, he did something that surprised him. He took her hand and gently clasped it in his own. She looked at him a little oddly and opened her mouth to say something.

But his tender gesture of solidarity was short-lived. A single gunshot rang out from the group of palace guards behind them, and Jack felt a warm substance splatter onto the side of his face. Beside him, the professor's legs seemed to give way and he collapsed onto the ground in a heap. They heard Inchquin scream an order.

"No shooting!"

Too late. Jack looked down at the professor uncertainly. Dani dropped to his knees and held the professor so that his face was turned upward, his open eyes staring unblinking at the moon. The side of his head, where there had been curly yellow hair, was now just a dark mess.

Jack had read about death, seen it on TV, and experienced it a million times on a hundred different computer games. This was horrifically, gut-wrenchingly different.

They heard Inchquin commanding them to put their weapons down and their hands up. They had no choice. One by one, Dani, Anna, and their two companions placed their weapons on the ground and reluctantly raised their hands. Jack was about to raise his own when he realized that he was still clutching Angus's time phone in one hand. Through the dark mist of his despair, a pinprick of light suddenly appeared. Of course! Jack peered down at the time phone and flipped it open. Sure enough, the bar was lit up—an intense yellow light. In his hand he had a time travel machine. It had a signal, and it was linked to his father's Taurus. Maybe, just maybe, he could use it, somehow, to bring the professor back. With one finger he started to tap out a message. Behind them, Inchquin and the guards were now cautiously approaching their little huddle. Jack hurried.

VIGIL attacking. Need help. Hurry. Jack

He pressed a button and the message was gone. Inchquin was nearly upon them, and he continued to bark orders to both the VIGIL guards and the palace guards. He was probably furious that a lack of discipline had resulted in the professor's unseemly death. Probably more mess in the space-time continuum that they would have to clear up later.

There was a sudden *bleep*. Dad had replied!

Rescue imminent; hold tight. Proud of you.

"Yes!" Jack hissed. As Inchquin approached, he flicked the time phone shut and slipped it back into his pocket. He didn't have long to consider what form his father's rescue attempt would take, because off to their right, there was another flash of light. For some reason, this flash was brighter than those that had signaled the arrival of the VIGIL guards. Everyone turned to see what had caused it, but there was nothing but the outline of the bushes and trees of a large thicket, some way off. For a moment everything was still. Then they heard a loud mechanical grinding. The earth shook, and the grinding noise was joined by the guttural roar of an engine. A very large engine.

Suddenly the bushes at the front of the thicket collapsed, and a huge dark object emerged, crawled halfway across the lawn in front of them, and stopped. The distinctive shape of the metal behemoth was clear. Jack knew at once what it was and understood exactly how his father proposed to expedite their escape. Their little party at Schönbrunn Palace had a gate-crasher. But this was not any old gate-crasher. It was a Mark II Tiger tank of the German Wehrmacht. The biggest, heaviest, and deadliest tank from World War II. And it wasn't there for the lemonade and cupcakes.

Then all hell broke loose. The 7.92-millimeter forward machine gun on the Tiger opened up, and bullets ripped across the lawn and into the mass of guards, who leaped for cover. At the same time the muzzle of the Tiger's massive 88-millimeter main gun flashed and a shell whistled over their heads, narrowly missing the VIGIL guards and embedding itself in the nearby wing of Schönbrunn, which promptly collapsed in a pile of rubble as the high-explosive shell discharged.

The VIGIL guards returned fire, but their APRs were useless against the armor of the seventy-ton Tiger. Its machine gun continued to rattle away as the main gun found its range. The muzzle flashed again, and a second shell pumped straight into the melee of VIGIL guards.

Jack's father had been one step ahead. Inchquin had been about to use the location codes on Angus's time phone to carry out some sort of assault on his father's base using the assembled VIGIL guards, but Christie had gotten there first. Even before Jack's message, he must have anticipated that help would be needed and, when the moment came, had taken advantage of the available signal to send help in the form of a tank. But now this wasn't looking like the best of plans. Jack, Angus, and Anna were caught in the middle with Dani, Vaso, and Goran standing by—they had Inchquin and the Schönbrunn guards behind them, Tony and Gordon and the VIGIL guards in front of them, and a Second World War tank off to one side. The professor lay by their feet—dead. It wasn't looking good.

Jack spotted two of the VIGIL guards fiddling with a large tubular device—some sort of bazooka. One of them hoisted it onto his shoulder. The weapon bucked, and its shell fizzed like a firework as it shot across the lawn. It smacked plumb into the side of the Tiger and there was an ear-splitting explosion. The 180-millimeter armor of the Tiger had been punctured, and its machine gun abruptly stopped. Yet someone in the tank had survived. The gun turret swiveled toward the two VIGIL guards, who were desperately reloading the bazooka. The tank's massive gun aimed toward them, but just as the muzzle flashed and recoiled, releasing a third shell, a second antitank round fizzed from the bazooka toward the Tiger. It was too late for the VIGIL bazooka crew. They were vaporized as the shell exploded just in front of them. But almost instantaneously the second antitank round ripped open the Tiger's armor and buried itself in the engine compartment. The rear of the Tiger erupted in a huge orange fireball. In a moment, the turret hatch swung open and a figure emerged, briefly silhouetted against the fierce flames rising from the Tiger. Even at a distance, the portly figure was immediately recognizable to Jack and Angus.

"Can't be," Angus said.

"It's Pendelshape. Dad sent Pendelshape back," Jack confirmed, awestruck.

"In a tank," Angus added unnecessarily.

Pendelshape leaped from the turret into the gloom and was gone.

"Come on!" Anna shouted.

As one, they dashed farther into the grounds. Jack's eyes had adjusted to the darkness, and he could now make out the elaborate matrix of Baroque-style pathways and hedges. Anna led them through it at a heart-burning pace. He had a nagging feeling that, with his lungs, he wouldn't be able to keep up. But surprisingly he found himself breathing deeply and actually managing to keep up with Anna. Suddenly, Jack felt a tremor in the earth. He glanced around and saw large shadows behind them. Lancers from the palace—on horseback. They hadn't wasted much time. Anna shouted to her brother.

"Dani, what do we do?"

"Split up—as we planned. You and I take the English boys. Vaso and Goran split off."

The lancers were already only a hundred yards away and bearing down on them.

Dani and Anna whisked Jack and Angus off the main path and into a narrow, hedged passageway. Vaso and Goran disappeared in the opposite direction.

Behind them, the horsemen came to a sudden halt in a maelstrom of dust, scraping leather, and metal. They had been temporarily caught off guard by the split of the group, but it wouldn't be long before they were back on their trail. Dani led them out through an archway in the hedge. Ahead of them was a wide grass bank that rose gently to a long low building with a series of archways built into the walls.

Anna egged them forward. "Come on!"

Behind them, one of the lancers had managed to force his horse through the narrow passageway and was hot on their heels. Anna raced toward the low building with Dani, Jack, and Angus following closely behind. Anna took her rifle and thrust the butt hard into the large glass window of one of the arches. It shattered instantly.

Anna jumped through the gap and they followed her. They started to run. The building was so long that they could barely see from one end to the other. It was mostly empty, although there were some large tables set in rows and, bizarrely, a section of manicured trees in large boxes. The atmosphere was different in here. It was warmer than outside and more humid and there was a fragrance in the air—a citrus smell, like oranges. That's where they were: inside a massive orangery. Most of the trees must have already been moved to the gardens for the summer. But before they had a chance to gather their wits, there was another loud crash. They wheeled round. A tall figure sat astride a black horse. One of the pursuing lancers had burst through the large broken window and skidded to a halt in the central aisle of the orangery. His steel helmet glimmered and the long feathered plume quivered in its crest. The horse bucked, and the horseman wheeled around expertly to face them. He was balancing a pole in his right hand. At one end Jack could make out a small metal spike. In a flash, the lancer dug his heels hard into the flanks of the black horse. It reared . . . and then charged.

They could feel the floor beneath them rumble as the four hooves pounded forward. The horseman skilfully maneuvered the lance so that it pointed at a slight angle down to where they stood. In seconds he would be upon them. Jack and Angus dived for cover. But Dani was too slow. Jack saw the lance pierce his chest, and Anna screamed in horror as her brother slumped to the ground. The horseman withdrew the lance from Dani's body. His horse snorted as the lancer turned for a second attack. Anna climbed, catlike, onto one of the long tables. From her elevated position, she leaped out at the horseman, landing on his horse's rump. The horse reared up in surprise, its front hooves kicking out wildly. First Anna, then the lancer tumbled backward onto the stone floor. They watched as the lancer landed awkwardly on his head. He didn't move. His lance spun from his hand, and its metal tip shattered free from the wooden pole as it hit the floor. Jack and Angus rushed over to Anna, who groaned, opened her eyes, and shakily pulled herself up into a crawling position. She crept over to where Dani lay and cradled her brother's head in her hands.

First the professor and now Dani. Dead.

In the dim light, something caught Jack's eye. He peered down and the metal lance head glinted up at him. It was exactly the same size and shape as the lance head he had discovered in his father's workshop at Cairnfield and presented to Pendelshape. The Schönbrunn raid was not a historical myth. Jack knew now—because he had been part of it. In fact, his trip back to 1914 had caused it.

Anna turned from her brother and stared up at Jack and Angus. She had a strange, questioning look on her face. Then the shock of her brother's brutal death hit her, and she started to rock violently back and forth, cradling his head, sobbing uncontrollably. Anna was in a place beyond comfort, and for a moment Jack and Angus just stared down, not knowing what to do.

Suddenly they heard voices from outside. More guards.

Angus looked at Jack, desperation on his face. "What do we do now?"

Jack fumbled in his pocket. "Time phone! Maybe we still have a signal . . . maybe we can get out of this mess, once and for all."

He held the device in his hand and flipped it open, but the yellow bar had turned gray. The signal had vanished.

"No good," Jack groaned.

At the end of the orangery, the guards were starting to scramble through the shattered window. Soon they would be upon them.

"What's this?" Jack had noticed something else in the time phone's readout.

"Another message! Must have been sent just before the signal was lost."

Have lost contact with P-shape. Rescue may have failed. Can only help when time signal. If P-shape alive, he will help you.

In frustration, Jack snapped the time phone shut.

Next to them, Anna kissed Dani lightly on one cheek and rested his head, finally, on the stone floor. She looked back down the orangery, where they could now see the shadows of the guards approaching. Then she got to her feet. She had stopped sobbing. She was cold and emotionless. There was steel in her voice.

"Now I want one thing . . . only one thing: justice."

It took them two hours to creep from the grounds of Schönbrunn Palace and make their way cross-country to the prearranged meeting place. They worked their way through thick woodland. Eventually they arrived at some farmland, where a rustic timber barn nestled between the edge of the wood and the fields beyond. The crude structure was raised from the ground on four wooden stilts and, in the gray light, Jack saw that a large stone rested on each stilt. The smooth surface of the stones was meant to deter rats and mice. Gingerly, Anna approached the wooden ladder that led to the elevated doorway. She climbed up and levered open the door. Soon all three of them were safely inside. It was clear that this was to have been the rendezvous point with Vaso and Goran. But, worryingly, there was no sign of them. They had no idea what had happened to Pendelshape either, following his escape from the burning Tiger.

Anna curled up in a corner and for a while remained motionless. Finally, perhaps seeking comfort from distraction, she pulled some bread and cheese from her bag and parceled it out. They sat and tried to eat, but Jack's mouth was dry and the bread and cheese tasted like a papery ball. When Anna finally spoke, her voice was strangely calm.

"So, you will help us—as we planned, yes?"

It was clear what she meant. They had not staged the rescue from Schönbrunn for fun. Dani's death was not to be in vain. They were still expected to travel to Sarajevo to help in the assassination attempt and help Anna find justice.

Zadok the Priest

"Doboj, eh? I tell you what, they've got some funny names around here."

Jack could not summon the energy to respond to Angus. The night in the third-class railway carriage had exhausted him. Anna scanned the thronging crowds from the steps of Doboj's main railway station.

"There!" she whispered.

Farther up the street stood a pony and hay cart. A dark-skinned boy—he couldn't have been more than ten years old—was perched high on a wooden seat at the front of the cart.

"Our transport."

"It just gets better and better," Angus groaned.

Soon they were slumped on the hay in the back of the cart and the contraption rumbled off.

Jack reflected on their escape from Schönbrunn and their four-hundred mile journey from Vienna to Doboj, which was one hundred miles north of Sarajevo. It had been long and exhausting. On Thursday afternoon Anna had managed to get them aboard a train from Vienna to Belgrade and then on to Doboj. The Bosnian Serb underground network was proving to be remarkably pervasive and efficient. Jack had lost count of the times Anna had started a sentence with the words *I have a friend who . . .* or *I know someone who . . .* The valuable train tickets had been procured from just such a source—a young train porter who was part of the network and also, as Jack was starting to notice, one of Anna's many male admirers.

Since Schönbrunn, and the final message from Jack's dad, the time phone had gone back into hibernation and the yellow bar had remained stubbornly unlit—making any pursuit by VIGIL very unlikely. It also meant that there had been no communication with Pendelshape. There was still the risk, however, of being picked up by the regular Austro-Hungarian authorities—but so far they had avoided this fate.

Jack had begun to understand more about Anna as they rumbled south. Her desolation over the loss of her brother became buried under a brooding and renewed hatred of her Austro-Hungarian masters. Jack had persuaded her to tell them how she had orchestrated the daring rescue from Schönbrunn.

She had explained: "We are planning a raid in Vienna for long time. It is the heart of the Austrian Empire. We had plans already. After I meet you, and realize you are sent by the English teacher, Dr. Pendelshape, I know we must protect you . . . get you to Zadok to help us in Sarajevo. After the capture at Vienna station, we activated the Vienna cell. We know where they take you, so we organized raid."

"You took a big risk to save us," Jack had said.

"We must. You sent by English teacher. You will help us." Anna's eyes had softened, just for a moment.

Anna had not explained, however, what form this "help" was supposed to take or exactly how he and Angus, in particular, could possibly bolster the cause of the southern Slavs. Clearly Pendelshape had mightily impressed them on his visit, and any connection with the "English teacher" meant access to great, if as yet unrevealed, powers. Of course, Jack had not explained to Anna the strange history of Pendelshape and how they had really come to be there. They had also pleaded ignorance about the battle at Schönbrunn. In the darkness, it had been confusing, and only Jack and Angus knew what had really happened. But even using the extraordinary powers of VIGIL, Inchquin and the Rector would surely have their work cut out to minimize its historical impact.

But Anna was interested in only one thing. There was no question in her mind as to the righteousness of their mission in Sarajevo. Nothing would persuade her to deviate from her chosen path. Now she was doing it for her brother, as well as for her family and her nation. To have this certainty, Jack thought, must be good. It would make everything so . . . simple.

Jack recalled the conversation that he and Angus had had with Anna during a sleepless stretch on the long journey from Vienna.

"Anna, why do you hate them so much? Why do you want to kill the archduke?" he had asked. There'd been a pause. A shadow had passed across her face and her eyes had moistened.

"You need to understand who I am . . . where I am from." She had spoken softly—in monotone. It was almost as if she had been trying to distance herself from the words that came out of her mouth. "My family is poor. Some years ago my father had an argument with neighbor. One day there was knock at the door . . . my father was murdered"—Anna wiped a tear from her eye—"in front of me. And Dani." Jack was speechless, but he heard the bitterness in her voice. "To the authorities, it was just another peasant dispute. They do nothing. This 'great power.' And for this we could never forgive. Then they take Dani. And now I want justice."

The gentle rocking of the pony cart finally put them all to sleep but Jack woke up as one of the cart wheels hit a pothole. He didn't know how long they had been going, but it must have been some time, because the dust and smell of the coffee shops of Doboj had long since gone. Now they were surrounded by verdant woodland and the road had changed to a rutted and bumpy track.

Jack pulled himself up from the hay, and the grubby-faced boy at the front turned and flashed him a toothy grin. They were in hill country, and occasionally through a gap in the trees Jack spotted the ragged outline of the mountains. He breathed in the fresh air. Anna and Angus still slept soundly in the cart, and, Jack noticed, one of Angus's arms had fallen across Anna's waist as they lay side by side. Jack rolled his eyes.

"So how long now, Anna?" Jack said the words deliberately loudly, almost shouting, to wake his two companions. Both Anna and Angus jerked up their heads, disorientated and confused. Then Angus's face turned red and he snatched his arm away from Anna. Anna giggled. It was the first time that Jack had seen her smile since Schönbrunn. She pulled herself up onto her knees, scanning the track and surrounding country. Content with their progress, she leaned over to the boy, ruffled his hair, and said something they didn't understand.

"We are nearly there."

Sure enough, they rounded another bend, and the woodland abruptly thinned out as the path led into a small valley surrounded by gently rolling hills.

"That's it."

They followed Anna's eyes to one side of the valley, where there was a raised plateau. Then they saw it.

"A church?" Angus asked.

"Monastery," Anna confirmed.

As the old wheels of the cart creaked onward, the monastery came into full view. Jack had visited a couple of famous ruined abbeys near home—Dryburgh, Melrose. Their ruins suggested something much grander than the building in front of them now. The whole structure was enclosed by a large, circular outer wall. Built into the front was a large bell tower with a pyramidal roof and an arched gateway leading into a main courtyard, with overgrown gardens and a small orchard beyond. On either side of the tower were simple two-story structures built into the curved outer walls. The white stone had turned gray in many places, and some parts of the outer wall had collapsed completely. There was a large hole in the sloped roof of one of the buildings, exposing the beams within. The place may have once been well kept, but now it was in ruins and probably deserted. Nevertheless, surrounded by the hills and woods, and with the tower glinting in the late morning sun, it possessed a peaceful beauty.

Just as the cart approached the arched entrance gate, Jack had a powerful sense of déjà vu.

"You know, I think I recognize it . . . this place." Suddenly the memory was there. "Got it!" He jabbed Angus in excitement. "It's the picture! The picture of the old church—you know, stuck to the map of Bosnia in Dad's workshop at Cairnfield, remember?"

Angus screwed up his face. "You know what? You're right. Definitely. Definitely this place."

But neither of them could explain it. "Does that mean that Pendelshape or Dad has been here before?"

They stepped down from the cart, but the swaying sensation continued to stay with them. Anna handed the boy some coins and ruffled his hair a final time.

Suddenly, through the entrance, a tall thin man with long dark hair and a beard appeared. Anna squealed in excitement and rushed forward to hug him.

"Zadok!"

The man beamed and held Anna in his arms. "We received your message. We are ready." Zadok held her away from him to look into her eyes. "But Anna . . . I am so sorry to hear of your loss."

Anna fought back her grief and chose not to respond to the remark. She gestured to Jack and Angus.

Zadok stepped forward and smiled. "Ah, you are the ones we have been waiting for. Sent by the English teacher. We are honored." Zadok then did something that completely astonished Jack and Angus. He lowered himself to one knee before them and kissed each of their hands in turn.

Jack was embarrassed. "It's OK, er, really. You can get up."

Zadok rose to his feet.

"I am Zadok. Zadok the priest." He paused theatrically. "We were promised help. Help has come. This is a happy day. Come. You must eat after your long journey."

They sat at one end of the old refectory and, through the broken windows, Jack inspected the small, white stone chapel in the center of the overgrown monastery grounds. Beyond lay the remains of the cloister that curved around the inner wall on the far side. It was very quiet. Zadok was alone and explained that he had only come up the night before "to prepare everything," as he put it. He and Anna had cooked a simple stew with vegetables that they served with bread, and now the empty plates rested in front of them.

"Zadok is from my village," Anna explained. "But you're not really a priest, are you, Zadok?" She smiled.

"No?" Jack asked.

"No. When the English teacher came, he seemed to think it was funny that I was called Zadok. Not a Serbian name. He called me Zadok the Priest. It's from the Bible."

Jack looked puzzled. "When did you meet Pendel—I mean, the English teacher? What did he do?"

"Dani, Anna, and I first met the English teacher in Belgrade." Zadok's eyes twinkled in excitement. "We were not sure at first why an Englishman would want to help the Bosnian Serbs in our cause. We thought he might be a spy . . . but he knew so much. He knew everyone; he knew everything. It was incredible. On his first visit, he warned us that the Austrian police had identified one of the Black Hand and were going to arrest him. He proved to be right, and we were able to save him. It was almost as if the English teacher could predict—"

"The future?" Jack finished Zadok's sentence.

"Yes, Jack. Exactly."

"On his second visit, he brought plans."

"What plans?"

"Some of the others—Princip, Ilic, Apis, Grabez, Cabrinovic— had an idea to organize a major blow to the oppressors."

"You mean the planned assassination of Franz Ferdinand when he visits Sarajevo—the day after tomorrow?"

"Yes, this was what was finally decided. And the plans are now in place. But the English teacher suggested that we split into two groups. We should operate separately from Princip, just in case one of the groups was infiltrated. Dani, Vaso, Goran, and I would form the second group. It was a good idea." His face darkened. "But then we heard that Vaso and Goran were captured at Schönbrunn, and Dani . . . " Anna flinched at the memory and Zadok held her hand gently over the table.

"Were there any more visits by the English teacher?" Jack asked.

"Yes, one last time—only two months ago. He said we needed a base, near Sarajevo."

"This place?"

"Yes, a ruin now, of course, so no one comes up in these hills."

"And help?"

Zadok looked at Jack and Angus and smiled. "You two, of course . . ."

Angus looked at Jack again with a worried expression on his face.

"Did, er, the English teacher . . . well, was he specific about the kind of help that we would provide?"

"No. He had to leave urgently. It was always the case. On each visit he would arrive quite suddenly and then just disappear. I think it was his way of not arousing the suspicions of the authorities. He just said that near the time, June 28, the date of the planned assassination, he would send help." Zadok smiled knowingly. "We now know what he meant. He sent you. Two boys and an uncle—the professor. He must have thought that nobody would suspect you." He paused and got to his feet. "And now that you are here, you can tell us how it all works."

"How all what works?"

Zadok smiled. "The English teacher has planned well. He has given you only the minimum amount of information you require and no more. This is so that if you fall into the hands of the authorities and are questioned or tortured, the plan will still be kept secret. Come, I will show you, and then you can explain."

Zadok led them from the table, leaving the empty plates. They followed him down the cloister and past the old chapel. They took the path through the old orchard at the back of the grounds to what looked like some garden sheds. Zadok took a giant key and unlocked an old oak door. The air inside was dry and dusty. Zadok lit a small lamp and the contents of the shed were revealed in shadowy outline. At one end there was a large cupboard. Zadok took another key and turned it in the lock. The cupboard door creaked open to reveal its extraordinary contents in the flickering lamplight.

Angus and Jack couldn't believe what they saw.

Arms Cache

A rack of six assault rifles—but they didn't look like rifles from the First World War.

"What are they?" Jack asked.

"L85A2s," Angus replied matter-of-factly.

"What?"

"British army assault rifles. Not the old SA80s, either."

"So they're modern?"

"Yup. British standard. Accurate to a quarter of a mile. Ninety-five point six percent reliability rating. Probably the best standard assault rifle in the world."

Jack shook his head. "And you call *me* a nerd."

Zadok opened a second cabinet. It was a veritable arsenal. There were two grenade launchers, two boxes of hand grenades, and several ammunition clips.

"You've got enough stuff here to wage a small war, not just kill some archduke with a funny hat."

"The English teacher has been generous. We are behind the times here, I think. We had no idea such weapons existed. And over here . . . "

Zadok moved to the far end of the room and with an extravagant flourish swept away a dust cover.

Angus's jaw dropped. "Unbelievable . . . "

"What are they?"

Angus lowered his voice reverentially. "Before you stand two Harley-Davidson MT350Es. American army issue. Rotax engines— four stroke, thirty brake horsepower, eighty miles per hour top end. . . . " He turned to Jack. It was as if he was having some sort of religious experience. "Jack, they've even got gun carriers."

"So," Zadok said, scarcely able to control his excitement, "the English teacher said you would know."

"Know what?" Jack asked.

"How it all works."

Angus smiled, eyeing the bikes. "Oh, yes, Mr. Zadok, we know how it works all right."

"Excellent. The English teacher said this equipment is all modern English design, the very latest and very best. I am not a military man, so I am afraid I have no idea where to start. But I suggest that Anna and I leave you here to check that everything is in working order. Then you will be prepared to carry out the English teacher's instructions. Anna and I will make preparations for the journey to Sarajevo. We should leave after nightfall."

Anna and Zadok left them alone in the dingy outbuilding with its extraordinary array of twenty-first-century firepower.

Angus turned to Jack as soon as they had gone. "I hope you know what's going on, 'cause I don't."

Jack was concentrating hard. "So, Pendelshape made three visits. Probably in quick succession. On the final trip they brought all this stuff with them and set up this arms cache."

"But why?"

"It's just as we said, Angus. Pendelshape and Dad's plan was never to help the assassins. Anna and Zadok still don't know it, but the real plan is to betray them. They were going to stop the assassination."

"But why do they need all this?"

Jack shrugged. "Kind of makes sense. The bikes are to get to Sarajevo easily and quickly. The weapons need to be good and reliable, just in case anything goes wrong. Remember there are seven potential assassins from the other cell who are also making their way to Sarajevo . . . and a whole network of supporters. I guess Dad and Pendelshape needed to be sure that if it turned ugly, they would be ready. Remember, they might need to hold out without a time signal for quite a while. And not only that . . . "

"What?"

"Well, Pendelshape and Dad knew that they might not only have to take on the other assassins. They were probably more worried about—"

"VIGIL."

"Right. They couldn't be sure that VIGIL, the Rector, and Inchquin wouldn't find out about their plan, and maybe even spring a trap for them in Sarajevo. So, all this stuff"—he waved around at the equipment—"was just in case they ran into difficulties. One thing's for sure: Pendelshape and Dad were taking a big risk bringing all this stuff back here."

"Why?"

"Like the Rector said, making any intervention in history may have unforeseen consequences. I would have thought that bringing some of this modern weaponry back here, even though it is hidden in these ruins, would be a risk. Someone might find it." Jack's mind raced ahead. "The Austrian army, or the German army, if they got ahold of one of those guns, or one of the bikes, they wouldn't understand what they were at first, but they might work out a way to copy them or something. . . . "

"Could give them an edge—a military edge."

"Yeah, these guys are not stupid. If they got ahold of all this, then maybe they could win the war. All of history would change. We'd be living in a very different future. Did they really think about all these possibilities when they did the computer modeling of how the future might change?"

"I hate to admit it."

"What?"

"I was wrong, Jack. And I think your Dad and Pendelshape are wrong."

"I think I agree with you. It all sounds too risky. But not only that . . . " Jack turned to Angus, shaking his head. "Ever since we've been on this crazy trip, death and destruction have followed us around. It doesn't feel like we're supposed to be here. Doesn't feel right."

"I'm with you on that." Angus picked up a pebble from the dirt floor and flicked it at the wall. "And there's Anna. We can't betray her, can we?"

Jack got to his feet, dusting himself off. "No, Angus, I don't think we can. In which case, Dad's not going to be happy with us."

Angus shrugged. "Just say we felt we didn't belong here. You know, none of our business." He reached into his pocket to retrieve the time phone.

"Don't tell me. Still dead, right?"

Angus flipped it open. "Dead—apart from the usual stuff."

Date: Friday, June 26, 1914
Time: 6:03 p.m.
Location: Ozren, Bosnia and Herzegovina

"Still on our own."

"Apart from Pendelshape."

"Yeah. If he's still out there. But we're doing the right thing coming here with Anna. Pendelshape will come to this place, or to Sarajevo. He'll know that's where Anna will be taking us."

"Well, I hope he pops up sooner or later. I want to hear him explain himself—properly this time."

"Right." Jack nodded at the two Harleys. "Will those things work?"

Angus looked them over. "Incredible. Keys in the ignitions . . . " He unscrewed the fuel gauge of one of the bikes and peered in. "Full tank of gas. They look like they've never been used." He grinned at Jack. "What do you think?" He continued in an exaggerated American accent, "Shall I fire up old Mr. Haawg?"

Soon they had managed to haul both bikes out of the shed. Angus deftly climbed aboard the nearest. "Here goes!"

He turned the ignition and the engine fired immediately. "Bingo!" He revved the engine. "Nice sound. Better than my two-stroke bike back home." He revved a couple more times and then cut the engine. He shrugged. "So they work. What next?"

"Let's go back up and think about it, then decide what to do."

They walked slowly from the shed, returning up through the small orchard. The long grass swayed gently in the early evening breeze. At this point the circular outer wall of the monastery was much lower and they could see over it across the untended fields toward the woodland beyond. Angus paused to take in the view.

"It's nice here. A little like home. Hotter, though. Look over there—they've even got sheep."

Jack cocked his head. "Miss them, do you?"

"Ha, ha—I'm in stitches."

Jack stopped in his tracks. "Hold on, Angus. What did you say?"

Angus looked at Jack blankly.

"Sheep. You mentioned the sheep." Jack smacked his forehead. "What an idiot I've been!"

"What are you talking about?"

"Sheep. Your sheep farm back home. Your home . . . your family . . . your dad . . . your great-grandfather. You know—on the mantelpiece—Ludwig?"

Angus was staring at Jack as if he were crazy. "What are you talking about?"

"Ludwig. You said that he met your great-grandma, Dot after he was captured by the Brits in the war. This war coming—the First World War."

"Yeah. So?"

"We've been so focused on my dad and Pendelshape on one side, wanting to stop the war, and the Rector, Inchquin, and VIGIL on the other side, trying to make sure nothing disturbs the past, and worrying about who's right and stuff. But that doesn't matter!"

"Doesn't it?"

"Well, yes, it does, of course. But there is something else, much more important—to us. In fact to you, mainly."

Angus was none the wiser.

"Let me spell it out. No assassination equals no First World War equals Ludwig doesn't become a German soldier equals he doesn't get captured by the Brits equals he doesn't meet Great-Grandma Dot equals they don't get married equals they don't have kids equals you don't exist equals bye-bye, Angus."

Now Angus got it. He had a look of panic on his face.

"What will happen to me?"

"No idea. Maybe you'll go up in a puff of smoke or be zapped by lightning or, more likely, you just won't exist."

"I don't like that idea much. I mean, I quite like existing."

"Exactly—mind you, it's tough on the rest of us."

"So . . ."

"So, that seals it. Unless Dad and Pendelshape know something that we don't, messing with history will have consequences. And in this case one consequence that we know of for certain—you won't exist. I can't believe we didn't think of that before."

Angus tried to assimilate the consequences of what Jack had said. He looked thoughtfully at the scrawny sheep chewing away on the hillside and then lowered his eyes to the trees that fringed the far side of the fields.

He frowned. "What's up?"

Jack followed Angus's gaze and suddenly his eye caught a glint of metal from within the woods. He narrowed his eyes. There was something there.

"People. There are people in the—" But before he could finish the sentence there was an explosion, and a plume of mud erupted from the field just outside the monastery wall.

A moment later there was a second explosion. This time closer. A whole section of the monastery's outer wall was blown apart. Ahead, Zadok and Anna were running toward them, shouting.

"Soldiers! The Austrian army's here!"

A third shell whistled overhead and landed in the refectory building, which promptly collapsed.

"They've got artillery. We've got to get out of here!" Angus shouted. "Only one option."

"You mean the bikes."

Jack's heart sank. He remembered his motorbike experience back at Angus's farm. It hadn't gone well, and the Harleys were bigger and heavier. And there was another difference—on Angus's farm they hadn't been under artillery bombardment.

The field gun in the trees had found its range, and its crew was now delivering projectiles into the monastery with impressive regularity. The troops in the wood stayed low. They wanted the occupants of the monastery cowed into submission before they moved in. They were not in a hurry.

Angus had his bike going. Jack copied Angus but felt very precarious perched high above the ground on the seat. It took all his strength to hold the machine at an angle so that one of his feet could touch the ground. With a light push from his left foot, he checked neutral and turned the ignition. The Harley roared to life beneath him.

"Let's go!" Angus yelled.

They powered back up the path through the orchard toward Anna and Zadok. Angus halted his bike expertly next to Anna and scooped her up to ride behind him. Jack realized that he was expected to repeat the procedure with Zadok.

"Angus, I can't manage a passenger!"

Angus swiveled around. "You have to!"

There was another explosion, this time in the bell tower. With a muffled, distorted clanging, rubble and timber crashed down around the old bell. The whole structure swayed, but for the moment the tower and the arched entrance beneath stayed intact.

"Come on, then."

Zadok clambered aboard. The extra weight dampened the suspension and made the bike lower and marginally easier for Jack. He pulled in the clutch lever, kicked down to select first gear, and pulled back the throttle. The engine roared. Angus was already away, heading for the archway with Anna clinging on behind him. Jack let out the clutch lever, but this time far too quickly, and the whole machine jerked forward, the engine immediately stalling. He groaned.

There was a sharp whistling through the air and another explosion, so close this time that it peppered them with great clumps of dirt.

Jack was starting to panic. He could feel Zadok's heavy breathing on the back of his neck. Again he selected neutral, turned the ignition, and the four stroke burst back to life. He stabbed down on the gear pedal a second time. Now they could hear voices. The soldiers were emerging from the gun position in the woods and gingerly picking their way across the open fields toward the burning monastery. An officer barked orders. Jack's palms were sweaty, and he was having difficulty holding on to the handles. Through a supreme effort of self-control he pulled back the throttle, more gently this time. The engine tone increased, and he let the clutch out carefully. The back tire spun momentarily on the gravel path, and then, miraculously, it gripped and they were off. Jack was exhilarated. He twisted the throttle some more, and the bike responded eagerly. He pulled in the clutch again and kicked up into second. They were in business.

Angus had stopped under the archway, revving his bike. It provided momentary cover from the bombardment and a temporary blind spot from the approaching soldiers. Both Angus and Anna craned around to check on Jack and Zadok's progress.

"Come on!" Angus shouted.

Jack drew parallel with Angus's bike, and the two of them paused beneath the stone archway. They looked back at the monastery. Fire was taking hold everywhere. A final shell whistled in over the heads of the approaching soldiers in the fields and slammed into the shed that housed the arsenal. There was a moment of quiet and then the whole structure wobbled briefly before the final explosion.

"There goes the arms cache."

"And with it the evidence Pendelshape was here."

"You ready for this?" Angus asked.

"No," Jack replied.

"Well, you'll have to be. We've only got one chance. Soon as I say go, let's hit it. Hard."

Angus twisted his throttle.

"Go!"

Angus redlined each gear in turn as he and Anna screamed off down the path away from the monastery gate, a plume of dust rising high into the air behind them. Jack, trying not to think, crouched low on the bike, gunned his engine, and set off in pursuit.

Day of the Assassins

To the right of the farm path leading to the monastery, soldiers were fanned out across the fields, about twenty of them. As soon as they saw the bikes, there was wild consternation. But Jack and Angus were quick. In ten seconds the path would lead them into the forest. They had a clear run. But suddenly three uniformed soldiers emerged from the woods onto the path thirty yards dead ahead of them. They were staring straight at the two bikes bearing down on them and fumbling clumsily for their rifles. Jack's heart sank, but then, only ten yards ahead of him, he heard Angus drop a gear and the four-stroke MT350 wailed. Suddenly, the front wheel of Angus's bike popped high into the air. Standing proud on the footrests, with a rather surprised Anna clinging desperately to his torso, Angus pulled a twenty-yard wheelie straight at the unfortunate soldiers, who dived for cover. In five seconds it was over. The front wheel touched down again, and Angus was into the cover of the woods, closely followed by Jack, who now sported a very wide grin. He heard Zadok behind him whoop in delight, and he slapped Jack on the back as they powered on.

"Well done, my friend!"

Suddenly there was a crack behind them, curiously muffled by the dense woodland and the roar of the bike engines. One of the soldiers had risen from the mud and just managed a single rifle shot. It caught Zadok square in the back with the force of a pile driver. For a moment, Jack did not know what had happened. He twisted around, but Zadok was already slumped behind him, the pressure of his grip around Jack's torso weaker.

"You must go on, Jack. I have done my part. You go."

With a supreme effort, Zadok rose from the saddle and pushed himself free from the moving bike, landing in the ditch at the side of the path.

Jack looked back in horror and brought the bike to a sharp halt. Zadok was still breathing and looked up at him weakly.

"Go!" He groaned.

The soldiers were now running hell-for-leather down the path toward them. One was kneeling and aiming his rifle. It bucked in his hands, and Jack felt the bullet whistle past his head. Ahead, Angus had gone, leaving only exhaust fumes in his wake. Jack couldn't wait.

"I'm sorry, Zadok."

Jack revved the engine, dropped the clutch, and powered off down the woodland path in pursuit of Angus and Anna.

Sarajevo
Showdown

This was the day. Sunday, June 28, 1914. Archduke Franz Ferdinand and his wife Sophie would soon pass right before Jack and Angus in a procession of cars on their royal visit to Sarajevo. The town of Sarajevo was set in the center of a great bowl surrounded by mountains—the lower slopes wooded, the higher ones heathland. Jack thought he would be entering a European-looking town, but he had been struck by the number of mosques. This really felt like a divided city. People spoke different languages and wore different clothes from one another. Even at night their customs were varied. Anna had explained: "The clock of the Catholic cathedral strikes at two a.m. A minute passes and then the bell of the Eastern Orthodox Church rings. Later, Sahat Tower, near Beg's Mosque, rings. It strikes eleven times, Turkish time. Even when everyone is asleep, the counting of the hours shows we are all different."

Jack, Angus, and Anna had made good their escape from the monastery. Anna knew the hills well and had found them a shepherd's hut above Sarajevo where they spent a fitful night. Early on Saturday morning, they had sunk the two bikes in a woodland lake. As the last bubbles floated to the surface, Jack had thought that Angus was going to cry. They had walked the remaining distance to Sarajevo. With the raid on the monastery and the death of Zadok, the second assassination cell, set up by Pendelshape and Jack's father, had been fatally compromised. Anna had decided to take a risk and contact the main assassination group in Sarajevo, following a prearranged emergency plan. Jack and Angus had little choice but to follow.

Their rendezvous was with only two of the gang—Princip and Ilic. It took place in the run-down Café Miljacka in a dusty back street. Jack had not known quite what to expect from his first encounter with the assassins, particularly Princip, about whom he had heard and read so much. Here was a man who was unknown to the world now, but within twenty-four hours would become a household name. The meeting was inauspicious. Princip was skinny and somewhat disheveled, with dark eyes and a thin mustache. He was furtive and nervous. Communication was difficult. A package was handed over at the meeting. Inside was one of the few pistols that had been smuggled into Bosnia with the gang. It wasn't clear from the meeting what Jack and Angus's role was to be, but it was obviously assumed that, because of their association with Pendelshape, if all else failed, they would intervene in a way that would ensure that the Black Hand would succeed. After only twenty minutes, the meeting ended.

Now, standing behind a growing crowd of people on the Appel Quay, Jack thought it incredible that he knew precisely the course of events that was about to unfold. He was already aware of every detail of the Archduke Franz Ferdinand's visit—he had seen it all in Point-of-Departure. In just a few minutes, Franz Ferdinand and his wife, Sophie, would die.

Suddenly, in the distance, they heard a muted explosion. A ripple of consternation ran through the crowd. Voices were raised; there was confusion. A car drove rapidly down the road, then a second. There were a few muted cheers as a third car passed. Jack caught a fleeting glance of hat feathers and finery over the heads in front of him. Then the archduke and Sophie and their pursuing entourage were gone. There was a rumor in the crowd that a bomb had been thrown at the archduke, but the would-be assassin had been mobbed by the crowd, and the archduke was bravely continuing with the tour.

After a while, out of the corner of his eye, Jack saw the unmistakable figure of Princip furtively cross the Appel Quay and disappear into Moritz Schiller's delicatessen. Since the entourage had already passed on its way to the presentation at the town hall, Princip must have thought that he had missed his opportunity and decided to get some lunch. Jack followed Princip and took up a position next to the shop, just back from the road. Angus followed a few paces behind. Jack scanned the crowd. If VIGIL guards were in Sarajevo, they were well hidden.

"Jack, we must do something!" The urgent voice startled Jack.

It was Anna. She had left her position by the Cumurja Bridge. She was out of breath. Her face was flushed and her dark hair disheveled.

"Our bomb missed. Cabrinovic is captured. The others have fled. It is only us and Gavrilo left. . . . " She was distraught.

Jack reassured her. "It will be OK."

She looked pleadingly into his eyes with the same desperate expression on her face that she had had as she held her brother's lifeless head.

The mayor's car rumbled around the corner and passed them as it turned onto Franz Joseph Street. It was leading the procession back from the presentation at the town hall. A second car followed carrying the archduke and Sophie. The big headlights and fender of the Graf und Stift lumbered around the corner from the Appel Quay. It was slowing down—the driver had taken a wrong turn and was not following the route straight out of Sarajevo as had been arranged following the earlier bomb assault. They could clearly see all the occupants, including, in the rear, perched up high, the archduke and, to his left, Sophie. A man was leaning over to the driver telling him something.

Gavrilo Princip emerged from the delicatessen, a sandwich in one hand. There was a look of astonishment on his face as the archduke's car ground to a halt, delivering Princip's target to within a few feet of him. He dropped his sandwich and reached into his coat pocket. He quickly looked around, and as he did so, just for a split second, his dark, wild eyes caught Jack's, only feet away. Jack felt a sudden twinge of doubt. He could stop Princip right then and there. His mind flashed back to the family holiday when he was small—the visit to the war graves. He remembered the endless sea of white crosses, and in his head, the image fused with the pictures of the war from his father's history book—all the horror and suffering laid out in black and white. He could feel the pistol that had been given to him the day before nestled next to his chest. He could shoot Princip now. He slipped one hand into his inside pocket and felt the cold metal. His fingers closed around the weapon.

Suddenly, from across the road, two burly police officers broke from the crowd and advanced toward Jack. They had spotted the suspicious movement of his hand, and taking no chances, they were now moving menacingly toward him. Jack spotted them and quickly snatched back his hand, leaving the gun snugly in place. But Princip had ignored Jack and had already turned toward the archduke's car. He leveled his pistol, then he fired—two shots in quick succession.

Sophie slumped onto the knee of the archduke. For a moment the archduke remained upright, but then blood from his neck wound started to spurt from his mouth, and he listed into unconsciousness.

Chaos. The crowd quickly realized what had happened and turned on Princip. Jack, Angus, and Anna were engulfed by the angry crowd, and Jack felt himself being jostled and harried. The officers were wading into the melee to make sure no one escaped.

"Run!" Angus shouted.

He lowered his head and barreled through the crowd. Jack and Anna followed in his wake. The crowd thinned, and in an instant they broke free into the open street. For a moment Angus hesitated, not knowing which way to turn. Anna took up the lead. Jack stole a glance behind him and saw that two officers were hot on their heels.

"Down here!"

Anna sprinted down a dusty side street where a market was in progress, with Jack and Angus following closely behind. Quite unexpectedly, a cloaked figure stepped from the shadow of a doorway, into their path. They clattered straight into him. Without hesitation the man bundled them through the doorway and into a small storeroom. The man checked up and down the street, then, satisfied that the pursuers had been temporarily shaken off, stepped back into the room and closed the door behind him. His hair

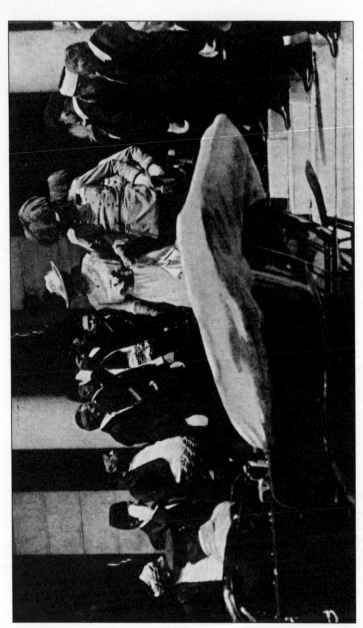

The archduke and Sophie leave the town hall moments before they are assassinated

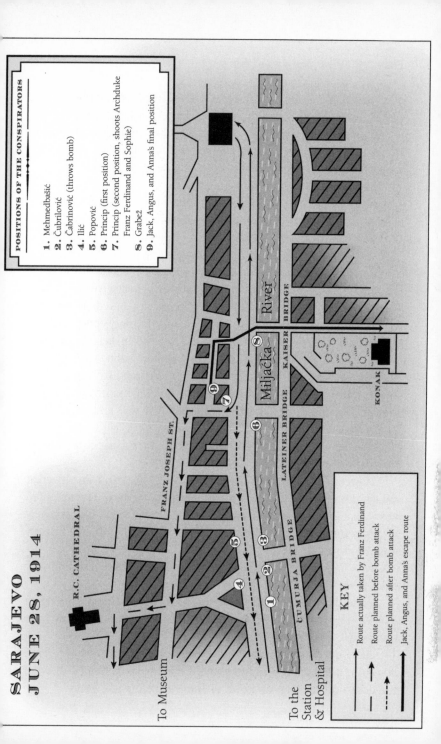

SARAJEVO
JUNE 28, 1914

R.C. CATHEDRAL

To Museum

FRANZ JOSEPH ST.

To the
Station
& Hospital

ČUMURJA BRIDGE

LATEINER BRIDGE

Miljačka River

KAISER BRIDGE

KONAK

POSITIONS OF THE CONSPIRATORS

1. Mehmedbašić
2. Čubrilović
3. Čabrinović (throws bomb)
4. Ilić
5. Popović
6. Princip (first position)
7. Princip (second position, shoots Archduke Franz Ferdinand and Sophie)
8. Grabež
9. Jack, Angus, and Anna's final position

KEY

→ Route actually taken by Franz Ferdinand
→ Route planned before bomb attack
⇢ Route planned after bomb attack
━ Jack, Angus, and Anna's escape route

was ruffled, his face a little dirty, and his clothes creased and torn in places. But the face was unmistakable: Dr. Pendelshape.

Anna was breathing hard, but she was also smiling and had tears in her eyes. And this time they were tears of happiness. She pulled herself to her feet and rushed over to hug Pendelshape.

"We did it," she said.

Anna, of course, had no idea what horrors her friends, the assassins of Sarajevo, had unleashed. She only knew that some sort of justice had finally been done for the crimes against her family.

Pendelshape smiled. "So it would seem, my dear, but I'm afraid I arrived a little late for all the action." He looked across at the boys, who had gotten to their feet and were dusting themselves off. "Well, I am glad to see that you have all become acquainted. It was just as I hoped." He gestured to some crates in one corner of the storeroom. "There, take a seat. We will be safe in here for a short while, but not for long. The police will be here soon, I'm sure. But first things first." He removed his cloak and turned to Anna. "Now, my dear, I fear that the authorities will be quickly upon you and your friends. You must flee Sarajevo immediately. I will take care of the boys. Don't worry about us."

Anna opened her mouth to speak, but Pendelshape put up his hand to silence her.

"There is no time, my dear. Trust me, Anna: you are in great danger. Look here—I have brought you some money." He presented her with a leather wallet. "Please, take it. You will need to start a new life away from all of this. I'm sorry this is so sudden, but it is the only way. You must go. Now."

Anna looked at the wallet and then at Pendelshape, not knowing what to do.

Pendelshape chided her. "Please, Anna, you must go. You are in danger. They will be searching all the cafés and houses. You have done what you came here to do."

She nodded and reluctantly took the wallet. "I understand. Thank you." She smiled, turned, and without looking back slipped through the door into the dust and heat of Sarajevo. Anna was gone.

"How did you get here?" Jack asked.

"Probably like you. With difficulty," Dr. Pendelshape replied.

"We didn't stop the assassination, like you wanted." Angus said.

"I know. It was, perhaps, too much to expect. I'm afraid I arrived too late from Vienna to help." Pendelshape reached into his jacket, pulled out his time phone, and flipped the device open. "The good news is that we have a time signal. Now we can finally travel back to your father's base, get you safely away from VIGIL, and then think about how we can complete our objective. We will be coming back to 1914 as soon as we have dealt with VIGIL once and for all."

Jack felt numb. He could hear Pendelshape's words, but they did not register. He could only think about the murder he had just witnessed. The wild look in Princip's eyes before he turned his gun on the archduke, the flashes from the muzzle of the pistol, the muffled cracks as the shots rang out, Sophie slumping forward, and the blood from the archduke's neck. . . . The sequence repeated itself again and again in his head.

Pendelshape had no idea what they had been through these last few days—the deaths that they had seen on their journey: the professor, Dani, Zadok, and now, finally, the archduke and his wife. It was too much. Jack glanced over at Angus. He sat on a dusty crate, just staring into the gloom of the musty storeroom. He looked pale and drawn. This wasn't like playing some sort of super-bonus round of Point-of-Departure, where you had to get three gold stars on every level. This was real.

Pendelshape sensed Jack's unease. "Look, I understand. I know you have endured a lot. We all have." Jack stared back at him blankly. Pendelshape sighed. "In truth we don't have much time, but it might help if I tell you our side of the story. Perhaps then you might understand a little better."

Jack shrugged.

"I was always on your father's side. Taurus gives us the chance to change the world for the better. We must be careful, but used with precision, we now have the tools to do infinite good. But Inchquin and the Rector poisoned the rest of the team against your father.

Day of the Assassins

They thought that it was wrong to meddle in history, even though our computer technology is highly effective at modeling the consequences of interventions. They still thought it was too risky. So as soon as we knew that the Taurus at the school worked, they closed the whole thing down. Put in place rules, protocols, all codified in the VIGIL Imperative. But they still remained suspicious of your father—they knew he wouldn't come over to their point of view. He remained a risk. So eventually . . . " He paused.

"Eventually, what?" Angus asked.

"They tried to get rid of him for good."

"What—kill Dad?" Jack said.

"Yes, Jack. And they nearly succeeded. So he disappeared when you were just eight and became a fugitive. I remained at the school. I pretended to side with VIGIL, but I was secretly loyal to him. That is why your father had to leave you and your mom, Jack. I'm afraid that's why you have had to grow up without him. It's not what he wanted. Not at all."

"In exile, it took your father a long time to re-create the Taurus . . . the machine that sent first Angus back to rescue you and then me, in that wretched tank. I took risks to help your father by channeling information to him. The work took many years. But from our earlier research we had already pinpointed a moment in time where we knew we could make a massive beneficial change in the course of world history."

"Sarajevo, June 28, 1914," Jack said. "Today."

"Exactly. The twentieth century was mankind's bloodiest, and that date—today's date—was the trigger. It needn't have happened. We conducted three short expeditions using the Taurus at the school during the testing phase, just before your father left. That's how I infiltrated the Black Hand and the assassins, met Anna and Dani, and set up the second cell, led by Zadok. We were going to return, having laid the groundwork, and then disrupt the assassination to prevent the war. Of course, we had also created many detailed computer simulations of the various interventions in time that we might make and how they might affect the future."

"Timeline Simulations."

"Yes. I remember when we cracked it—"

"Don't tell me—Simulation 0107. The wall chart that was missing from Dad's workshop at Cairnfield?"

"Yes. This was the scenario that optimized the future most effectively. It started with stopping the Sarajevo assassination."

"Then your plan failed because Dad had to escape from VIGIL."

"But when your father told me that he had perfected his own Taurus, he asked me to bring you to him so you would be safe. There was little time. So I decided to use the school Taurus once more to hide us in history—in 1914, in fact. The school Taurus was already configured for that period from the earlier tests."

"You knew you had to take me with you because if VIGIL had me captive, they could threaten Dad."

"Yes. But we would escape from the school and you would be safe. Before leaving, I would invoke a program that would wipe all the Taurus's control discs clean after we'd gone—remove all the software, design documentation, and wipe out all the backup devices. Without the software or documentation, Taurus is just a useless lump of metal. At that point your father and I would have the only working Taurus and VIGIL would be impotent. I had passed our time phone codes to your father so once we had escaped he would be able to track us and pick us up with his Taurus. Nothing could stop us then. We had it all worked out."

"But then the Rector found out. He intercepted Dad's message."

"In our excitement, we made a stupid mistake. Once they knew that your father had built his own time machine, they were very concerned. They had thought he had disappeared. Over the years VIGIL had ceased to be worried about him—and they certainly never suspected me."

"So they moved in just as you were about to tell us your plan in the Taurus control room at school."

"But you escaped, not surprisingly, scared to death by the Rector and the VIGIL thugs, and we were in a completely new situation. It was unplanned."

"Then you and Angus were rescued by Dad."

"Your father knew we might need backup. Over the years he has recruited a few very loyal supporters." Pendelshape nodded proudly at Angus. "And Angus kindly agreed to rescue you from the castle."

Angus looked down sheepishly, not sure whether to be proud of his actions or not.

"Why did you send Angus alone?" Jack asked.

"We didn't! Angus was included because we knew you would trust him. He wanted to come. But the signal failed as we were sending the rest of the team. The time phone signals are intermittent. It has always been a problem. The next signal was at Schönbrunn, and when we got a fix on Angus's time phone, we had a second chance."

"The tank?"

Pendelshape smiled. "A German Tiger tank from the Second World War. Your father has got a little collection of historical artifacts. And it did the job—or at least it diverted VIGIL sufficiently for you to escape." For a moment doubt flashed across his face. He leaned over so the boys could see the top of his bald head. "Nearly burned off the rest of my hair, though."

Pendelshape chortled. He seemed to think that it was quite funny—but Jack didn't. "I don't think you understand. There are people we have met here . . . who helped us, who were good to us. Real people."

"Right, sir, and three of them are dead now," Angus added bluntly.

Pendelshape replied dismissively, "Yes, yes. I am not saying any of this is easy."

This was too much for Jack. He felt anger welling up inside him. "You can't just say that. The professor—he was our friend. He saved my life." Jack shivered at the memory of the professor's death. "Don't you get it?" Jack was finding it difficult to control himself. "And Anna . . . she rescued us from Inchquin. Her brother was murdered . . . right before our eyes."

"With a lance," Angus added.

"And Zadok—who blindly trusted you—if he hadn't been there, the bullet that killed him would have hit me!"

Pendelshape snapped back, waving his time phone. "I'm afraid this time signal won't wait for us to complete this philosophical debate." Angus and Jack glared at him, and Pendelshape sighed impatiently. "Look, I understand that you have witnessed some bad things. . . . I'm sorry. And I know your father is as well. This is not how either of us had intended the mission to work out. But there is so much more at stake than one or two deaths." Pendelshape turned to Jack. "I can see that this is difficult for you, but your father wants you to follow him. Our desire is that you join us willingly. You can help us achieve a great deal. You can help us change the world." The boys continued to look unimpressed. Pendelshape rubbed his chin. "Maybe I need to show you how much is at stake here." He was mulling something over in his head. "Indeed. To convince you, perhaps I need to show you the consequences of today's events—give you a real history lesson, if you will."

He peered into the time phone and started to tap away.

"What are you doing?"

"Well, Angus, it is quite simple: we need to return to Jack's father's base. We can't stay here, but we can make a little detour." He paused. "Yes, I know exactly where we should go," Pendelshape murmured to himself. "I believe there was a large field hospital at that point behind the Allied front line. Now, if I can just code the right space-time fix . . . "

Jack and Angus exchanged nervous glances as Pendelshape busied himself with the time phone.

"Sir, are you planning what I think you're planning? Because if you are, I don't think that's a good idea at all. In fact, I think—"

Suddenly, the door of the storeroom flew from its rusty hinges in a storm of splintering wood. A young Austrian army officer stood in the doorway brandishing a pistol.

Pendelshape looked up from the time phone and spoke quietly. "Well, boys, I am afraid that whatever you think, it looks like we have little choice."

"Good afternoon, officer." Pendelshape said. The officer seemed a little taken aback by Pendelshape's confident English voice and eyed them suspiciously. "Come on, boys. Close in. Hands on the time phone," Pendelshape whispered out of the corner of his mouth.

The boys did what they were told, but alarmed by the sudden movement, the officer shouted an order and raised his pistol to shoot.

Mud and Guts

The shock wave from an air burst lifted Jack up and threw him backward twenty feet, his body twisting in midair as he flew. But where there should have been churned-up mud to cushion his landing, there was nothing. Instead, he fell into a huge empty space in the ground. With a crunching thud, his face, and then the rest of his body, hit the sloping inner wall of a large hole. As he slid down, mud filled his ears, nostrils, and mouth. He came to rest in a large puddle in the bottom of the hole.

Pendelshape's plan to give Jack and Angus an impromptu lesson on the horror of war was looking like a very bad idea indeed. Though it had sounded like he was aiming for some field hospital way behind the Allied lines, because of the intrusion of the Austrian officer, it appeared that things had not gone according to plan. The time-travel technology had placed them in the middle of no-man's-land during a major British offensive.

Just as they arrived, there had been an ear-splitting explosion and Jack had become airborne. He didn't even know if Angus and Pendelshape had survived the blast. And now here he was at the bottom of some putrid hole in the ground.

Suddenly, on the other side of the puddle, Jack noticed two eyes staring back at him from a mud-freckled face. The figure opposite was lying against the side of the crater, caked in dirt. From his uniform and helmet, Jack knew immediately that he was German. But judging by the fear on his face it, he was more a boy than a man. Jack could make out a large dark patch above his knee. The boy soldier was wounded. At that point Jack realized with dismay that within his white, fragile, boy-fingers, the soldier held a large black pistol. It was pointing at Jack.

He felt panic start to build from the pit of his stomach. The boy looked as terrified as Jack felt, but nevertheless Jack could see his index finger slowly squeezing the trigger of the pistol. There was a yellow flash and a loud crack as the gun fired. Jack braced himself— but the impact from the bullet didn't come. Instead, it had buried itself in the wall of earth to his left. The boy held the pistol up again, this time with both index fingers wrapped around the trigger, and squeezed a second time. . . . There was a click. The gun was empty.

At that moment a second German soldier appeared from behind the lip of the crater. Even at a distance, Jack could see that he was stockier than the boy opposite. The soldier surveyed the scene and quickly descended into the crater, moving with speed and confidence. Reaching the bottom of the hole, he bypassed his young comrade and marched directly through the puddle to where Jack lay. The soldier reached down to the bayonet hanging on his belt and fastened it to the end of his rifle, which he now lifted up and pinned under Jack's chin. Jack was helpless. This was it.

Suddenly, out of the corner of his eye, Jack detected a large, fast-moving blur descend from his side of the crater. The German soldier half turned, momentarily distracted. The blur moved with uncanny speed. Jack recognized the figure. Angus! The soldier had no time to react. Angus broadsided him with a crunching rugby tackle. Jack was first to his feet and grabbed the soldier's rifle.

The soldier stared back defiantly from his prostrate position on the crater floor. Then he reached to grab something from his back.

Jack raised his rifle and thrust the bayonet forward—instinctively copying the soldier's action from a few seconds before. But Jack misjudged, and the serrated steel edge of the seven-inch blade made contact with the lobe of the soldier's right ear, slicing right through it. The soldier whimpered in fear. Jack recoiled, alarmed at the ease with which the injury had been inflicted. Angus was now up on his feet. The soldier stared, pleadingly, first at Jack and then at Angus, standing next to him. A moment before, he had seemed like an automaton—a killing machine. But now he was helpless and terrified. Contrary to what Jack had first thought, he could not have been that much older than either Jack or the boy soldier who still sat quivering on the opposite side of the crater. And there was something else about the soldier lying at their feet, something about the face . . . and now with the injured ear . . . Jack waved the rifle.

"Go! Go on, get out of here!"

For a moment, the soldier looked confused and stared back at them questioningly.

Jack raised his voice. "Go! Now! The British will be here soon."

Euphoria spread across the soldier's face—it was if he had been reborn and his humanity restored. He scrambled to his feet and staggered through the water to the other side of the crater. He stopped briefly to haul his young comrade to his feet. Then, supporting his friend, he clambered up the opposite side of the crater and disappeared.

Jack was shaking. "Er, thanks, Angus."

Angus was silent and stared at the opposite side of the crater.

"You OK? You look like you've seen a ghost."

"I think I might have."

"What?"

"That soldier . . . I'm sure—" Angus stopped in mid-sentence and rubbed his eyes. "Doesn't matter. Come on, we can't hang around. It's dangerous here."

"Where's Pendelshape—did he make it?"

Angus jerked his head to one side. "He's behind me. He's OK."

They looked around, and sure enough, Pendelshape's head loomed into view above them on the crater lip.

"Come on, boys—the bombardment has stopped. We need to get out of here."

"Really? I thought we might hang around and maybe do a bit of shopping," Angus said to Jack as they dragged themselves back up to the top of the crater. The smoke was clearing, and a weak sun was starting to wink through the haze. They seemed to be on a slightly raised part of the battlefield.

Jack couldn't believe his eyes. They were in the middle of some sort of extraordinary, lifeless moonscape of craters and mud as far as the eye could see. There were no trees, no grass . . . nothing. On either side of them, in some places not more than a hundred yards apart, embankments of earth signifying the position of the two armies' front line trenches snaked toward the horizon. Barbed wire was strung out along each trench—in some places there were gaps where it had been cut or blown apart. As Jack gained his bearings, he began to notice that there were dead bodies strewn haphazardly about the landscape. In some cases only a discarded rifle or a helmet or a flapping piece of material remained. But they were there. And it was clear that some of them had been there for a long time. He'd been staring for ten seconds. But he'd already had enough.

"Look—they're retreating." Pendelshape gestured over to the German lines. In the distance they could make out the figures of hundreds of men picking their way from the German front line. "They're evacuating following the bombardment. Come on, we can take refuge in there."

They followed Pendelshape toward the German lines. First Pendelshape and then Jack tumbled over the side, landing on the fire step above the bottom of the badly waterlogged trench.

"It stinks in here," Angus said.

Pendelshape glanced left and then right. The trench was deserted apart from a single corpse that lay facedown in the water only yards from where they had landed.

"Quick—over there."

A small bunker had been dug from the earth on the opposite side of the trench, and they stepped inside gingerly. A makeshift bed had been set up in the subterranean room, and there was even a small table and chairs. There were papers strewn everywhere, and a chess set lay on the table with the pieces scattered.

"Should be safe here for a moment."

Jack sat down on one of the chairs. "I've had enough. Let's see the time phones . . . now!"

First Angus, then Pendelshape placed their time phones on the table. The yellow bar on each of them was burning fiercely.

"We still have the signal. We can get out of here. Now!"

Pendelshape seemed to hesitate. "Well, hold on . . . "

Jack was incredulous.

"You're not seriously suggesting that we hang around?"

"Well, now that we are here—"

Angus interrupted him. "Sorry, sir, you're crazy if you think we're staying."

"Yes, I think we've seen enough already," Jack added.

Pendelshape replied, "Good. As you have now observed that war is indeed horrific, we can travel back to your father."

Jack couldn't believe it. Pendelshape seemed to be almost . . . smiling. It was at that moment, seeing that smile, that Jack knew he couldn't go along with Pendelshape or, for that matter, his father.

Jack spoke calmly, but there was steel in his voice. "In the last week, we have been shot at, chased halfway around Europe, and seen three good people—friends—die. And now you've brought us here. You and Dad have taken terrible risks with our lives and those of many others . . . for your own ambition."

Pendelshape stood up. "But we have to change history. We have to change it so it's better, so it's good. . . . Don't you see? We must."

"You might think you have to. So might Dad. But I don't."

"What do you mean?"

Jack's heart was pounding. "We don't want anything to do with this. We've got our own lives to lead. We belong in our own time, and we should stay there." Jack tried to steady his voice. "Look, I think what you and Dad have done is"—he shook his head—"incredible. Really. Creating the Taurus. All that. But it's too much. Just one example—Angus and I worked out that if we had done what you and Dad planned, he wouldn't even exist."

Pendelshape waved his hand dismissively. "We can fix that. It would just be another variant of Simulation 0107."

"The point is, we belong in the present. I know that puts me at the mercy of the Rector and Inchquin and VIGIL."

Pendelshape was incredulous. "What? But they might kill you!"

"No, they won't. They would only threaten that if you and Dad were to use your Taurus. If you don't, they won't touch a hair on my head. So it's simple, really. If you and Dad promise not to use your Taurus, then we will be safe. We'll be left alone."

Pendelshape stared back at him wide-eyed. "So, you're going to make yourself a willing hostage to VIGIL? And stop us from fulfilling our life's work?"

"It's got nothing to do with you or your life's work. It's got to do with us. I'm doing it because in the last few days we've already seen too much death—more than enough to last a lifetime. I don't want any more. The past should stay where it belongs—in the past."

Jack knew he was right.

"So, you set your time phone to go back to Dad's base. We don't ever need to know where it is. VIGIL will never know and you'll be safe. I know you've also got the codes for the other Taurus at school. So you set Angus's time phone so Angus and I can travel back to school. Simple."

"But . . . "

"And do it now before we lose the time signal again," Angus said.

"I can't. Your father. . . . He will never forgive me."

But seeing the expression on the boys' faces, Pendelshape knew his cause was finally lost. He leaned over the time phones and started to tap.

"Good. Hurry up."

From outside the bunker they heard a distant whistle.

"What's that?"

"The British are going over the top. They'll be here in a minute."

Angus breathed into Pendelshape's ear, "Well, you'd better get on with it!"

"I'm—going—as—fast—as—I—can."

Jack jerked his head at Angus to move away from Pendelshape.

Suddenly there was an explosion farther along the trench.

"What was that?"

"A shell?"

"Or a grenade?"

"The Brits must be here already."

Angus turned back to Pendelshape. "How long?"

"A minute . . . at most." Pendelshape was sweating.

"Go faster!"

"You're not helping."

There was a sudden commotion from outside the trench.

A British voice shouted, "Check that end, Corporal!"

"They're clearing the trench," Jack said. "Hurry—they won't take any chances. They'll just assume we're the enemy."

At last Pendelshape lifted his head and slid Angus's time phone across the table, keeping the other for himself.

He had a sad look in his eyes. "It's recoded. You can go home."

"No funny business, right?" Angus said.

Pendelshape looked resigned and shrugged. "No. I am disappointed, and your father will be too, Jack. We may not see each other again. Certainly not for history class."

Jack flipped open the time phone. The bar was still shining bright yellow.

The British voices were now very close.

"In there, Corporal! I heard someone!"

"Any grenades left, Jim?" There was a pause. "Good—just chuck it in!"

The door to the bunker flew open, and a grenade rolled menacingly across the floor toward them.

Angus moved close to Jack so that they were both touching the time phone. Jack put an arm around his friend's shoulders and stabbed the time phone with his thumb. There was a flash as the grenade exploded.

Rising Son

Jack looked up at a massive dinosaur. Two eye sockets, way above, leered down at him from a large white skull. If the creature had still been in possession of its prehistoric eyes, maybe it would have winked at him knowingly. Instead the vast skull and the huge skeleton, to which it was attached, hung there lifelessly—a monument to past glory. Normally, Jack liked this place. Particularly the dinosaur exhibit. The Royal Museum in Edinburgh. He liked its open spaces and polished floors and the hushed voices that echoed through the exhibition halls. You could happily wander around for hours, lost to the world. But not today.

"So why did we end up here?" Angus asked for about the fifth time.

"I told you—no idea. Just be grateful that the grenade didn't get us before we escaped and we at least got back to approximately the right time and location."

"Close one. Do you think Pendelshape made it?"

"I think so. He pressed the button at the same time as us."

"Wonder if we'll see him again," Angus said ruefully.

Jack sniffed. "Wonder if I'll ever see my dad again."

"Sorry, Jack. You know what I mean."

"Sure. It's OK."

The clock at the end of the large entrance hall struck seven. In thirty minutes the museum would close for the evening.

"Where are they? They should be here by now."

The Taurus had dumped Jack and Angus in the restroom of the Royal Museum in Edinburgh—thoughtfully, the men's room, not the ladies'. It took them a little while to figure out where, and when, they were. Finally they made it to the large marble-floored reception area. The calendar indicated October 14. Only one day after Jack had made his fateful decision to use the Taurus to escape the Rector back at the school.

The receptionist did not quite know what to think of the two mud-caked teenagers, but she allowed them to use the phone. Jack called his mom. He could tell that she was immensely relieved to hear from him, and now she and VIGIL were on their way. Jack and Angus waited impatiently in the hall, trying, with difficulty, to look inconspicuous.

Jack spotted his mom first. She was running toward him, arms outstretched. In a moment, he was in her arms. Close behind followed the Rector, who was smiling broadly, and then his two old friends, Tony and Gordon, who stood back at a respectful distance. Thankfully, they were in their janitor uniforms and unarmed—assault rifles must not be generally permitted inside the Royal Museum.

Soon they were aboard the school minibus, speeding back home. It seemed a rather modest form of transport, compared to what they had become used to. And now their lives would be one long secret in order to keep the mystery of the school, the extraordinary technology within it, and the powerful people entrusted with its control carefully hidden from the rest of the world.

In the backseat, Jack and Angus were wedged between the large frames of Tony and Gordon. Angus had dropped off to sleep. As they sped along, Tony punched Jack in the upper arm, with, Jack thought, rather more force than was necessary. In fact, it hurt. He looked up at Tony, and his glare was returned with a wide, yellow-toothed grin.

"Gotta tell you, son," Tony said.

"What's that, Mr. Smith?" Jack replied.

"You were the best mission we ever 'ad."

Jack smiled, reluctantly. "I guess that's a compliment?"

Gordon chimed in from his left. "Yeah, kid." He put out his hand in a high five. "It is. *Semper fi,* lad, as the Marines say— always faithful."

Jack was surprised how quickly life got back to the usual routine. The powers that be went out of their way to try to make everything as normal as possible for them. After all, VIGIL was indebted to Jack and Angus. Tony and Gordon resumed their janitorial duties, and a new history teacher replaced Pendelshape as if nothing had happened. She didn't quite have Pendelshape's passion for the subject and seemed to be sticking closely to the curriculum. But, on reflection, that was probably a good thing. It was said that Pendelshape had been taken quite ill and had moved to Switzerland for treatment.

Once or twice, as autumn wore on and the last of the brown-and-orange leaves melted away, Jack found himself lying on the green lawn at Cairnfield, staring up at the sky, thinking about all the things he had seen and the people he and Angus had met on their adventure. They had all been wrapped up in their own lives, ambitions, and troubles. He couldn't stop thinking that, even though it had been nearly a hundred years ago, in a funny way these people were the same as, well . . . the same as him. Two arms and two legs, two eyes, same size of brain. They were just as smart as him, if not more so, and felt the same sort of emotions. The only real difference was that they had less history to look back on. It was only now, having seen it and smelled it, not just read it in a book, that he could kind of see Pendelshape's and Dad's point of view. These people were real. The deaths of the professor and Dani had made that agonizingly clear. In unguarded moments like these, Jack felt . . . well, responsible. He could understand his father's drive—to go back and, as Pendelshape had put it, "make things better." But Jack knew it was a temptation he must resist.

One day late that fall, Jack and his mom were sitting at the dinner table. His mom seemed much happier these days.

She started to clear the table and noticed a small plastic bag on the side.

"Sorry, Jack—I forgot—that's your new inhaler—from the pharmacist." She nodded at the plastic bag absentmindedly.

Jack smiled. "Thanks, Mom. But I don't think I'll need it."

"Oh?"

"I think I'm cured. I think they call it shock treatment. No more inhalers for me."

His mom smiled. "Good. That's good, Jack."

He shrugged.

There was a knock at the back door, and as usual, Angus did not wait for it to be answered but let himself in and came down the hall to find them in the kitchen.

"It's arrived!" He waved a thin package above his head, then suddenly remembered his manners. "Oh, sorry, Mrs. C."

"What's arrived?"

"The next Point-of-Departure, of course!"

In an instant both of them had left the kitchen and tumbled down to the basement. The hole in the wall had been repaired. It was now a door to an empty room.

"Hey, Jack, something else!"

"What?"

"Look at this." Angus passed Jack an old black-and-white photograph. It was frayed at the edges. Jack peered at the image.

"Remember?"

For a moment, Jack didn't know what Angus meant. From the photo stared a broad-shouldered man in a dress uniform. A German dress uniform. Jack studied the image closely. There was something odd about the man's face. Then he noticed it — one of his ears had no ear lobe.

Jack understood. "Ludwig . . . "

"The very same. My great-grandfather. Think about it, Jack. If your bayonet had been a few inches farther to the right . . . "

"You wouldn't be here."

"But I am."

"And the rest, as they say, is history."

A Word from the Author

A few years ago my dad showed me some medals that his father (my grandfather) had received during the First World War. He explained that my grandfather had been injured in the war and had later lost part of his leg. Though I never knew him, I was told that he was reluctant to speak about how he got the injuries or why he won the medals. I only know that what he did was brave—because I have a citation at home signed by the minister of war, Winston Churchill.

Anyway, unlike millions of others, my grandfather survived the war and went on to have children and live to a ripe old age, which got me thinking. He made important choices in his life: he chose to fight in the war. He chose to do something brave, and later he chose to have a family. If he had made different choices, of course, I would not be here and you would not have picked up this book.

The war he fought in was also caused by people making choices. Lots of choices over many years—some important, some seemingly trivial. The war was horrific and led to many other tragic events in the twentieth century. I wonder if the people who made those choices would have chosen differently had they known what would happen.

So I suppose this book is about choices. Some of the events described really happened, and some of the people really existed. Other people are made up. But they've all had to make choices.

You're probably going to make some choices today as well. Some will seem important and some not—although sometimes you don't really know which are the important ones until afterward, perhaps a long time afterward. Nevertheless, you need to try to choose well—because whatever you do, it could change the future.

Five members of the Black Hand in court following the assassination of Archduke Ferdinand. Princip is seated in the center.

BACKGROUND INFORMATION

What was the Austro-Hungarian Empire?

The Austro-Hungarian Empire, also known as Austria-Hungary, was a large, powerful state in central and southeast Europe that was broken up at the end of World War I. It was the second-largest state in Europe, after the Russian Empire.

What was the alliance system?

By 1914, the great powers of Europe were interconnected by a system of alliances. The Dual Alliance between Germany and Austria-Hungary was created in 1879, and Italy later joined them in the Triple Alliance. Otto von Bismarck, the architect of the German Empire, created the alliances as a defensive system. The defense was largely against France, which he regarded as the main enemy following France's defeat in the Franco-Prussian War in 1871 and its loss of the territories of Alsace and Lorraine to the newly created Germany.

In 1891, for a variety of reasons, Russia cooled relations with Germany and formed the Dual Entente with France. In the early twentieth century, Britain moved closer to her traditional enemies (France and Russia), partly fearing Germany's rapid buildup of an ocean-going navy that might challenge Britain's naval supremacy. In 1904, Britain settled her differences with France in Africa, establishing the Entente Cordiale, and in 1907, following defeat by Japan, Russia was eager to settle her differences with Britain in Persia and Afghanistan. This led to the Triple Entente between Britain, France, and Russia.

German military strategists were required to devise a plan (which became known as the Schlieffen Plan) to deal with a war on two fronts—Russia to their east and France to their west. This strategy aimed to defeat France rapidly, before Russia had mobilized her large army.

Although this alliance system was defensive in nature, when coupled with the military problem that Germany potentially faced war on two fronts, it became an important reason that a conflict, essentially between Austria-Hungary and Russia over their spheres of influence in the Balkans (or southeastern Europe), turned into a European war and then, with the entry of the United States in 1917, a world war.

What was the general mood within the Austro-Hungarian Empire in the lead-up to the assassination?

A key problem for the Austro-Hungarian Empire was that it was composed largely of minorities—Slovaks, Romanians, Croats, Czechs, Poles, Ruthenes, Slovenes, Serbs, and others.

The administration of neighboring country Bosnia and Herzegovina was placed under Austrian control following the Treaty of Berlin in 1878. In response, the Balkan state of Serbia created a liberation movement for Bosnian Serbs with a terrorist wing called the Black Hand. With Russian encouragement, Serbia also created a Balkan league with Greece, Bulgaria, and Montenegro, which aimed to exclude Turks from southeastern Europe. Two Balkan wars were fought in 1912 and 1913, and as a result, Serbia's territory and population doubled and its leaders became more ambitious. This generated fear in Austria and also gave encouragement to the Serbs living within the Austro-Hungarian Empire. Tension finally boiled over on June 28, 1914, when Archduke Franz Ferdinand (heir to the Habsburg throne) was assassinated in Sarajevo, the capital of Bosnia and Herzegovina, by Gavrilo Princip, a Bosnian Serb trained and armed by the Black Hand.

Why did the assassination of Archduke Franz Ferdinand lead to full-scale war?

Following the assassination, determined to crush Serbia for good, Austria issued an ultimatum to Serbia that would effectively have made Serbia into a client state of Austria-Hungary. Serbia rejected the ultimatum, and Austria declared war on Serbia on July 28, 1914. On July 30, the Russians started mobilizing their armed forces. The next day, Germany (Austria's ally) issued an ultimatum to the Russians to stop mobilization, and when they failed to do so, Germany declared war upon them.

On August 1, the French began to mobilize, and by August 3, Germany had declared war upon them and advanced into Belgium—following the logic of the Schlieffen Plan. This violation of Belgian neutrality caused England to declare war on Germany on August 4. Austria declared war on Russia on August 6.

What had started as a conflict between Austria and Serbia in the Balkans rapidly escalated into a war that involved all the great European powers. Germany and Austria-Hungary were joined by the Ottoman Empire and Bulgaria to complete the Central Powers.

Countries such as Australia, India, and South Africa were involved in the Allied forces as part of their allegiance to the British Empire. In 1915, Italy also joined the Allies, and in 1917, the United States entered the war on the Allied side.

Who was really involved in the assassination of Archduke Franz Ferdinand?

There were many people who assisted the assassins, but in Sarajevo on the day of the assasination were Gavrilo Princip (who fired the shots to assassinate Archduke Ferdinand and his wife), Nedjelko Čabrinović, Vaso Čubrilović, Trifun Grabež, Mehmed Mehmedbašić, Cvijetko Popović, and Danilo Ilić. A key architect of the plot was the Chief of Serbian Military Intelligence, Dragutin Dimitrijević (known as Apis, "the Bee"). Dani and Anna Matronovic and Zadok are fictional characters.

Is the Schönbrunn Palace real?

Yes. Schönbrunn Palace in Vienna is one of the most important cultural monuments in Austria and is a major tourist attraction. *Schönbrunn* means "beautiful well." The palace and gardens were home to successive Habsburg monarchs. At the age of six, Mozart performed in the Hall of Mirrors before Maria Theresa and her court. Marie Antoinette grew up there, Napoleon lived there, and Kennedy and Khrushchev met there in 1961. The "Schönbrunn raid" is fictional.

What is CERN?

The European Organization for Nuclear Research, known as CERN, is the world's largest particle physics laboratory and is situated near Geneva, on the border between France and Switzerland. Nearly 8,000 scientists and engineers (including around half of the world's particle physics community) work on experiments conducted at CERN, using CERN's particle accelerators. CERN also has a large computer center containing very powerful data-processing facilities.

Was HMS *Dreadnought* real?
Launched in 1906, HMS *Dreadnought* was the first British Royal Navy "all big gun" battleship, and it revolutionized battleship design. It was built at Portsmouth in only fourteen months. It was also fast—adopting revolutionary steam-turbine engines that had undergone little testing at the time. *Dreadnought* gave its name to a class of battleships that made warships built before this time virtually obsolete. Germany started to build *Dreadnought*-type battleships following Britain's example, and there ensued a naval race between Britain and Germany, in which both spent significant resources trying to out-build each other. At the outbreak of war, Britain had twenty-two *Dreadnought*-type battleships and Germany had fifteen—the later models were even bigger and more powerful than the original. HMS *Dreadnought* saw little action in the First World War and was decommissioned shortly afterward.

What is a *Schwarzgelb*?
To be a true supporter of the Austro-Hungarian regime was to be called a *Schwarzgelb*—reflecting the colors of the Habsburgs: black and yellow. It is also a term used to refer to policies in favor of the regime.

What happened to the assassins?

Gavrilo Princip was jailed after the assassination. He was technically too young to be executed under law. He died from tuberculosis in April 1918 in a prison hospital. In Serbia, he became a national hero. Moritz Schiller's delicatessen is now the Princip Museum, and two footprints on the pavement outside mark where Princip stood to fire the shots.

Nedjelko Čabrinović was sentenced to twenty years in prison. He died in January 1916, also of tuberculosis.

Vaso Čubrilović received a sixteen-year prison sentence. Released in 1918, he became minister of forests for Yugoslavia.

Trifun Grabež was sentenced to twenty years. He died in February 1916 of tuberculosis.

Mehmed Mehmedbašić was implicated in a new assassination plot. He was imprisoned, then pardoned in 1919. He returned to Sarajevo to work as a gardener and carpenter.

Cvjetko Popović received a thirteen-year sentence. He later became curator at the Sarajevo Museum.

Danilo Ilić was arrested by Sarajevo police a few days after the assassination. In the hope of avoiding the death penalty, he gave the police the names of everyone involved in the plot. In 1915, he was hanged.

Dragutin Dimitrijević (Apis) was arrested in 1917 and was sentenced to death for treason. He was executed in 1917.

How did the war end?

World War I came to an end on November 11, 1918, when Germany agreed to a ceasefire. The Treaty of Versailles was signed the following year. This treaty required Germany to accept responsibility for causing the war, as well as to disarm, make substantial territorial concessions, and pay reparations to certain Allied countries.

Archduke Franz Ferdinand, heir to the throne of the Austro-Hungaria Empire, is assassinated by Gavrilo Princip, a Bosnian Serb who opposed Austro-Hungarian rule.

1914

Austria-Hungary blames Serbia for the assassination. At this time, Europe is linked by a series of diplomatic alliances: the "Triple Alliance," consisting of the Central Powers (Austria-Hungary and Germany) plus Italy, standing against the "Triple Entente" or "Allied Forces" of Britain, France, and Russia. In effect, the assassination triggers events that lead to full-scale war.

∞

JULY 28
Austria-Hungary declares war on Serbia.

AUGUST 4
Britain declares war on Germany following the German invasion of Belgium.

AUGUST 6
Austria-Hungary declares war on Russia.

AUGUST 12
Britain declares war on Austria-Hungary.

AUGUST 23
British and French forces are successful in slowing the German advance at the Battle of Mons.

SEPTEMBER 6–10
The Allied Forces halt German progression in France as the First Battle of the Marne ends.

1915

A "race to the sea" leads to huge trench systems being established from the Swiss border through all of northern France. Events on a wider scale mean that the conflict truly becomes a world war. Japan joins the Allied Forces, and the Ottoman Empire aligns with the Central Powers.

∞

FEBRUARY 18
Germany begins to blockade Britain with the use of its U-boats (submarines).

APRIL 25
French and British forces attempt to open a new front in Turkey at Gallipoli.

MAY 7
A German U-boat sinks a luxury passenger liner called the Lusitania *traveling from America to Ireland, prompting U.S. President Wilson to urge Germany not to attack civilians.*

MAY 23
Italy declares war on Austria-Hungary and becomes part of the Allied Forces.

MAY 31
German Zeppelin airships bomb London.

1916

Many had thought that the wa would last just six months, bu at this stage, it shows further signs of stalemate. The war is sustained because people on both sides are willing to accep military losses and economic hardship. In this year, two of history's largest battles take place — the Battles of Verdun and the Somme on the Wester Front. These battles last for months and claim hundreds of thousands of lives.

∞

JANUARY 24
The British introduce conscript for men between the ages of eighteen and forty-one to build their army.

FEBRUARY 21
The Germans proceed with a m offensive at the Battle of Verdu The battle is fought between th German and French armies ar ends with a French victory. Th are more than 750,000 casualt

JUNE 4
Russia launches the Brusilov Offensive on the Eastern Fron This is a fatal blow for the Tri Alliance army and helps relie pressure on the French at Verdu

JULY 1
The Allied Forces begin the Battle of the Somme. This battle is fought between t German and British armies a aims to further relieve pressu at Verdun. There are more tha 1.5 million casualties.

TIMELINE OF WORLD WAR I

1917

Following German successes in the east, Tsar Nicholas II of Russia is forced to step down from power and a new Bolshevik regime is established under Lenin. Russia steps out of the war after an armistice in December 1917.

As German forces concentrate their energies on the Western Front, help is on its way for the Allied Forces as the United States enters the war.

APRIL 6
The United States declares war on Germany.

APRIL 9–MAY 16
Allied Forces launch their attack at the Battle of Arras.

JUNE 25
American troops start to arrive in France.

JULY 31–NOVEMBER 6
Allied Forces attack at the Battle of Passchendaele. During this offensive, the Allies move forward just five miles but gain the high ground that dominates the Ypres area. The cost of this advance is more than 140,000 lives.

NOVEMBER 20–DECEMBER 3
The Allied Forces use tanks "en masse" at the Battle of Cambrai.

1918

After Russia withdraws from the war, the Germans launch a final desperate offensive on the Western Front designed to defeat the French and British. By this stage, Germany is starting to suffer economic exhaustion, which is further exacerbated by a British naval blockade. On the other side, the Allied Forces, bolstered by the arrival of the U.S., have superior supplies of men and material. The Allied counteroffensive proves successful, and Germany signs the Armistice.

MARCH 3
Russia signs the punitive Treaty of Brest-Litovsk.

MARCH 21
Germany launches the first of three final offensives on the Western Front.

AUGUST 8
The Allies counterattack at Amiens, pushing the Germans back and freeing much of occupied Belgium and France.

NOVEMBER 3
The Austro-Hungarian Empire collapses.

NOVEMBER 11
Germany signs the Armistice, marking the end of World War I. Canadian soldier George Lawrence Price is traditionally regarded as the last casualty in the war. He is shot by a German sniper and dies at 10:58 a.m. — two minutes before the Armistice is signed.

1919

While the Armistice, signed on November 11, 1918, ends the fighting, it takes six months of negotiations at the Paris Peace Conference to settle the peace treaty — the Treaty of Versailles — between Germany and the Allies. This treaty requires Germany and its allies to accept responsibility for causing the war, as well as to disarm, make substantial territorial concessions, and pay reparations. The treaty causes bitter resentment and political unrest among the people of Germany.

JUNE 28
*Germany signs the Treaty of Versailles.
This moment comes exactly five years after the assassination of Archduke Franz Ferdinand.*

THE AFTERMATH

The First World War was one of the world's first global conflicts. Around ten million people gave their lives and many more were injured. Ultimately, the defeat of Germany and its punishment in the Treaty of Versailles set the wheels in motion for the Second World War.

CASUALTIES — IN MILLIONS (APPROX.)

TRIPLE ALLIANCE	TRIPLE ENTENTE
Austria-Hungary —1.2	France—1.36
Germany — 1.77	Britain—0.74
Turkey — 0.32	British Empire —0.17
Bulgaria — 0.09	Russia—1.70
	Italy—0.46
	U.S.—0.12

Look for Jack and Angus's next adventure!

The year: **1587**

The place: **London**

The mission: **To save Queen Elizabeth the First—the key to England's future**

978-0-7636-5075-9

www.candlewick.com